The Possibilities

The Possibilities

Kaui Hart Hemmings

Jonathan Cape
London

Published by Jonathan Cape 2015

2 4 6 8 10 9 7 5 3 1

First published in Great Britain in 2015 by
Jonathan Cape
Random House, 20 Vauxhall Bridge Road,
London SW1V 2SA

www.vintage-books.co.uk

Addresses for companies within The Random House Group Limited can be found at:
www.randomhouse.co.uk/offices.htm

The Random House Group Limited Reg. No. 954009

A CIP catalogue record for this book is
available from the British Library

ISBN 9780224102230

The Random House Group Limited supports the Forest Stewardship
Council® (FSC®), the leading international forest-certification
organisation. Our books carrying the FSC label are printed on FSC®-
certified paper. FSC is the only forest-certification scheme supported
by the leading environmental organisations, including Greenpeace.
Our paper procurement policy can be found at:
www.randomhouse.co.uk/environment

Printed and bound in Great Britain by CPI Group (UK) Ltd, Croydon, CR0 4YY

For my mother, Suzy Hemmings,
and my grandmother, Eleanor Pence

Part
One

Part
One

I pretend that I'm not from here. I'm a woman from Idaho, on vacation with friends. I'm a newlywed from Indiana. An unremarkable guest at the Village Hotel, exploring Breckenridge, Colorado, waiting for a valet to bring her rented car around. A drop of water falls on my head. I look up at the green awning and move so that I'm fully covered. A black Escalade blasting music enters the roundabout. The car is huge, and I expect someone huge to go with it, but out come three young boys—the driver, short, passengers, tall—and the valet, also a young boy, wordlessly takes the driver's keys, hands him a ticket, and nods his head.

My son, Cully, who used to work here as a valet just three months ago, told me that he hated to park cars for people his age, and I can see why. Growing up I'd feel the same thing, an embarrassment to work in front of friends and peers. The worst job I had was fitting ski boots for girls who came here on spring break from places like Florida and Texas. They were always saying, "It hurts," and I would say that it's supposed to, making the boots tighter.

I was also a waitress at Briar Rose, where kids from school came in with their parents and they'd place their orders and I'd take their orders as if we didn't know each other. I remember Leslie Day sucking the antler of her lobster and thought, *Only rich people could get away with that, or even know to do that in the first place.* We weren't poor by any means, but compared to a lot of newcomers whose fathers came to town to retire at forty, it sometimes seemed that way.

The valet uniforms are black slacks and a black fleece, something Cully was embarrassed to wear. Some of them wear black change purses around their waists. Cully would rather lose money. I envision him running and opening car doors, taking tips, not looking at the amount until they were gone. You pretend not to care.

I look at these boys all around the same age as my son, these boys with mothers and fathers, hopes and problems, and an embarrassing urge comes over me to hold them. To swoop them up in my arms, something Cully as a child always wanted me to do and I'd often get annoyed. *You're a big boy. You can walk.* At times he was such jarring cargo, especially when he was first born and I was only twenty-one. He felt like a school project, the egg I was supposed to carry around and not ever leave or break.

I should go. I have ten more minutes before I need to get to work. While I've been in this week doing preinterviews, today will be my first day back on camera after a three-month absence. I don't move. I look at one of the valets—the tall one with black hair, smooth like a helmet; I look at him like he's a kind of god. *Please, give me strength. Strength to return, to get back to life.* My plan is to move in seamlessly, drawing as little attention to myself as possible. I will reemerge wearing a figurative cap, similar to the one my twenty-two-year-old son wore, what the kids wear—a cap to hide their eyes, their face, a cap that says *I'm here but I'm not here.*

Cully is dead. He died. That's why I left work. Good reason, though I don't really have a good one for coming back, for emerging from hibernation. I guess I feel that I've reached that unspoken, societal deadline that suggests you reach for your bootstraps and pull. I feel like it's time to start working on getting somewhere else, some other periphery or vantage point. I don't need to move up, but maybe sideways.

The valet sees me looking at him and I look at my watch. I'm actually wearing one and don't just look at my phone anymore. Cully gave it to me for Christmas when he was still in high school, and

I came across it in my jewelry drawer recently, grabbing the dinky gold thing as though I had been looking for it forever. He must have taken his time, selecting it, probably thinking it was fancy. I'm wearing the idea of him shopping, his younger idea of me. I'm wearing the look on his face when I opened it, as if I had given something to him.

Six more minutes. I glance back at the valet. He was better-looking from a distance. Up close, he has very porous skin, a runny nose, and what looks like dandruff in his eyebrows. So that's it then. One life can just disappear, and one can keep going, one nose can keep running. It shames me, the amount of time I spent being angry at him. The high chair battles—*use your spoon, not your fingers. Cully! Use your spoon.* Who cares if he used his fingers! Who cares! The mistakes do bring a smile to my face though. *I* cared.

Another car pulls in and a different boy runs to the driver's side. This kid is thin, average height, though strong-looking. He opens the door for a man my age wearing a tight white turtleneck that sparkles in the light. People get out of their cars differently when the door is opened for them. The man emerges, shielding his eyes from the sun as if it's the paparazzi even though he's wearing sunglasses with lenses like mercury. He asks the boy if he knows how to drive this kind of car, a red Porsche.

The kid takes a brief glance into the car. "Yes, sir," he says. "I'm familiar with automatics."

I smirk. The man looks doubtful, hesitant to leave. When he finally walks toward the lobby entrance, patting his pocket for the keys he left in the ignition, the valet pantomimes kicking him in the ass. Then he catches sight of me. I smile, in on the joke. Cully would have done the same thing, I bet. He would be like this guy. This is the better valet.

He looks at me, smiles. I smile back, trying to communicate that I heard what he said to that guy. I got it. I know you. I am a different sort of adult. I had a kid just like you.

"You have your ticket?" he asks, in the same cold, dismissive voice he used with the man. I pat my pockets. "I . . . I think I'll walk."

I hurry away, as if caught doing something perverse. I look back to see him, worried he's kicking his foot toward my ass, but he's opening a door for a woman. A real guest. She is perfect, this woman. Beautiful, poised, groomed. Sometimes another woman's polished nails are enough to make you feel like a failure. Sometimes the lack of recognition—the valet was supposed to see me, understand me—is enough to break your heart.

The woman doesn't look at him as she gets out of the white car and adjusts her long, light-green coat. *I would have looked at you,* I want to tell him.

Chapter 2

I adjust myself on the uncomfortable and unsteady chair placed on a slight incline between ticket sales and the Peak 9 lift. Murky clouds begin to move in from opposite sides of the sky. I look at their slow crawl, the sky buttoning itself into an old gray coat. Everything has taken on a different hue, as it should. What good is change if nothing has changed?

"What should we do now?" Katie asks. She's my cohost, or I am hers. Katie Starkweather, once the weather girl on the six o'clock KRON 5 news. She can be effusive and loud, socially aggressive like a hairstylist, but she's organized and diligent. Our cameraman, Mike, doesn't believe Starkweather is her real last name. He thinks she made it up in meteorology school. We are the hosts of *Fresh Tracks*, a show that's pumped into hotel rooms. We tell you where to eat, what to buy, what to wear, what adventures to schedule, and what to experience here in Breckenridge.

"What do you mean?" I look at her, then soften my expression. It's as though I'm still surprised when people talk to me. I guess I expect people to not address me directly, like I'm a freak or a queen.

"How should we fill time?" Katie asks.

"The same way as always, I guess? As before." *It's a beautiful morning. Buy something.* That's all we ever say. Katie looks unsatisfied. I remember she always gets jittery before we begin even though we're not live. I guess I did too. I had that feeling of importance, like what you're doing matters.

"We hardly have a thing," Katie says. "I'm wondering how we can bulk it up since—"

I uncross my legs, gather up my jacket under my neck, the hot cold sunshine making me constantly adjust. "The largest gold nugget ever found in North America was discovered here," I say. "On July third, 1887, by a man named Tom Groves. It weighed one hundred and fifty-one ounces. They called it 'Tom's Baby' because Tom carried it everywhere like a newborn. It was about the size of a six-month-old." I look at Katie. "We could say that."

"You love town trivia," she says.

"I do!" I say. "I don't know why."

She relaxes, slightly.

"Seriously though," I say. "If we run out of things to say, I don't mind. Tourists like it." I like it—talking about town myths and facts. Things that happened yesterday that has made today today. It reminds me—and those who visit—of the lives here before us and the lives of the permanent residents. I've lived here my entire life, minus the 3.6 years that I lived in Denver for college. My father has lived here for most of his life. We can trace our roots back to 1860, when his great-grandfather came to work a hydraulic mine responsible for devastating the hillsides and water supplies. The same year the town supposedly named itself after the nation's vice president in the hopes of securing a post office. Breckinridge. The i was changed to e when they got their post office and decided the nation's VP was an ass.

I look around at today: the bouquets of condos, the sounds of the Spring Fling concert. Despite the town's development and additions—One Ski Hill, Shock Mountain, trendier restaurants with one-word names—it is still my same hometown. Yet I feel like one of these tourists clopping about in a place that belongs to everyone and no one, a blank slate I won't leave any impression upon. I feel like I'm passing through.

"Benefits," Katie mumbles, her right leg jiggling. I want to still it with my hand. She has furiously been studying the bullet-pointed notes Holly wrote down for us. "Safety. We'll just go through this list then? The value and benefits?"

Katie is wearing a tight, yellow sweater. She's pulled together and even though I felt like I was too when I left the house, next to her I feel wild. I have squally, dark-blond hair. Katie has good TV hair—it's light blond and it hugs her face like a pelt. Her lips are usually thin, but while I've been gone that has changed. Now they're artificially plumped, like she's sucking a thick milkshake through a thin straw. She's younger than I am by about five years, but she seems even younger because she doesn't have kids. She's now on her fourth boyfriend in one year, an accountant who is always blurting out odd facts about himself, like, "I never swear," and "Soft cheeses give me hives."

"Do you want to go over them?" she asks, holding up the notes.

"I'm okay," I say.

She holds back from making any kind of facial or verbal reaction. Death is a checkmate. Death is embarrassing. I want to tell her to not let me win that way. Mike tests the view of us, which always seems to make him uncomfortable. He needs to look at us but prefers to do it only through the lens.

"I guess you'll be shooting lots of cover?" Katie says to him. "We don't have much to work with."

"I'll handle it." He sighs as if getting alternate footage is some kind of task the world's depending on. I liked Mike, but it took him about twelve years to like me back, so I canceled my feelings. He has that very angry and jealous kind of short-man personality and simple, pull-my-finger humor.

Katie still has that nervous gleam in her eye, like we're about to interview a terrorist.

"It will be all right," I say.

"Oh, I know, I just . . ." She lets the sentence go and studies the notes, jiggles her leg. Left one this time.

Once upon a time I would have been very stressed out if the

person we were supposed to interview decided not to show up. I understand the nervousness, and maybe it will hit me once we start, but if we fail, if it doesn't work, then we just toss it and it's okay. We can do it all over again, we have another chance. The thought makes me wistful. I know a sense of consequence is essential to any job, but the conviction in the weight of my work, the search for import—it's downright elusive.

Yesterday a man named Gary Duran beat his pregnant wife in their home in Dillon. She and her unborn child took the Flight for Life helicopter to Denver. Everyone's waiting to see if she and her baby make it, but we don't report on things like that. Maybe if we did, I'd be okay. Maybe if we reported on the lack of low-income housing for people who work here but are forced to live elsewhere, then maybe I could muster some motivation, or if we focused on tragedies that made me more aware of the world beyond this. But instead we talk about lift tickets, then share tips from Keepin' It Real Estate and Savvy Skiing with Steve-o.

Mike hoists the camera onto his shoulder as if he's a soldier going off to war. He shoots the lift ticket kiosk, the main face of the mountain, the white groomed paths like pleats in a billowing skirt. I look at the ski instructors in their red vests, children trailing them like a whip; the chair lifts coursing the hills like veins, the huddles of skiers moving up and moving down—everything working faithfully like a heart. Everything here will be all right.

Our producer, Holly Bell, walks toward us from the ticket office with a brochure.

"Here's a good visual," she says, carefully. I've noticed that everyone is talking to me as if I'm deaf or slightly stupid. "The new price in print."

I take the brochure. "Thank you."

"You can hold it up at some point," she says. "And stand up, move around. Stay positive. There are so many benefits . . ." She walks away—she's always in motion. Mike thinks she also made up her name, and in this case, I agree. She was a pageant girl, then hosted a show like this in Sacramento. She still dresses like she's hosting the show, kind of like an understudy waiting for Katie or me to keel over. Katie worked alone while I was gone. This makes me slightly nervous, jealous even. She did just fine on her own, so I'm feeling a bit like a garnish.

I tap my hands against my legs. It takes so long for us to do so little. I want to go home and meet Suzanne, who has agreed to help me finish Cully's room. I think of the clothes and boxes, the stuff of life I need to organize. It's come to me suddenly—this need to cleanse. I guess I want my dad to have the downstairs to himself, and our getaway this weekend seems to be functioning as a kind of deadline. My dad, Suzanne, and I are going to Cully's alma mater, where they're putting on a kind of tribute to him at the Broadmoor Hotel. Suzanne's daughter, Morgan, has organized it, and I'm not even sure what it is exactly. She's a current student at CC (she basically followed him there), and is trying to take his legacy into her own hands. Morgan and Cully grew up together, and Morgan has always created a kind of myth of their friendship, which has become even more beguiling now that he has died. It's true they were close, especially before high school, but she treasured him more than he treasured her. The idea of a tribute to him is nice, but knowing Morgan, I can't help but think it's more about her need to claim him.

I shouldn't be cynical, and the truth is I'm looking forward to it. Not the event itself, but the way it marks time. It will be my first time out of town since he died. Maybe going away will help me reenter. I don't know. I make it up as I go.

Now Katie is drumming her fingers against her chest. I copy her to see what that does, and if it works.

"Are you okay?" I ask. I relate to the way emotions can manifest themselves physically.

I put my hand on her leg, briefly. "You're really good at this," I say. "You always come through."

"It would be easier if he just answered some questions," she says. "This is so last-minute. Don't you *know* him or something?"

"Yes, I know him," I say, disappointed she didn't appreciate my appreciation. "I know that he won't do it if he says he won't."

Our interviewee, Dickie Fowler, is the head of Breckenridge Resorts and he's also a friend. Suzanne is his wife. They are in the process of getting a divorce. His call. I notice in divorces, when doling out the friends, the women get paired with the women—that's just how it goes, though I honestly get along wonderfully with Dickie. We laugh and joke a lot, and we can be quiet together. He was supposed to be here to explain the increase in the price of lift tickets but decided the segment would be better without him. He's smart. He knows that sometimes the way he comes across and the way he looks—his expression is coy and smug, like the rehabilitated men in erectile dysfunction ads—can make him unsympathetic. People are more respected when they say less, I've noticed, and he doesn't say a whole lot in public.

"You don't want to just try and call him?" Katie asks.

Her jacket is so white, her teeth too. The sun is bouncing right off the bright snow, making her clothes and veneers even whiter. I think to myself, *It hurts me to look at you.*

"We'll wing it," I say. "I don't really think people are looking to our show for a major analysis." I tag on a laugh to soften things, but the laugh was a bit sharp.

Lisa, Mike's assistant (who has a passion for makeup), walks up to Katie, powder brush in hand, along with her black change purse full of beauty tackle.

"Seven dollars," Katie says with her eyes closed, rehearsing. Lisa moves the brush in upward circles over Katie's face. "Ninety-eight to one-hundred and five—"

"Jesus, that's a lot," I say. "And there's no snow."

"No kidding," Lisa says.

"It's not that big a difference considering the value," Katie continues to recite. "For example . . ."

We are half salespeople, half cruise directors. We need to "squeeze a chuckle" out of the disenchanted, to "heat things up" if they're not sold on the cold. We need to sell the idea of freedom—exclusive, outdoor, extreme freedom. Get Outside! Be Extremely Free! It makes my job and my dad's old one quite similar.

My dad, Lyle, was VP of operations. After Breckenridge was bought by Vail in '97 he helped the resort lengthen its grip—into gas stations, real estate, restaurants, hotels, retail, this show—so that all the profit went upstream, through the fingers, and back into the palm. I think of my seventy-three-year-old dad at my house now, most likely working on things that no longer involve him. The horse put out to pasture who has no interest in munching on grass.

"The benefits," Katie says again, now to me and not herself. "We'll show them that a greater expense results in a better experience, and even a better life."

"That's quite an equation," I say.

I can tell she isn't sure if I'm being sarcastic or sincere, which must be hard for her. At work, I have typically been the happy sort, but this week during preinterviews a caustic side is crossing over, infiltrating my professional life. I've become stormy and difficult, mean and sad. If I was confronted with someone like myself I'd feel so sorry for them. Then I'd get bored by them, and then I'd hate them for their sad, sad story. Each day I start out wanting to do better, to be kinder. Each day I fail.

Lisa, done with Katie, approaches like I'm a horse, letting me see her powder brush, a warning she's going to touch me. I love when she fixes my makeup. I like being touched without being touched.

"You look different," Lisa says. She moves the cool brush over my cheekbones.

"I'm not supposed to," I say. "That's the deal."

"What are you doing? Not as much eyeliner, it looks like."

"I'm simplifying." I laugh, but she doesn't look like she heard me. She's like real hair and makeup people in that they never seem to hear the answers to their questions—or maybe they don't respond to insincere answers. But it is an honest answer. My beauty regimen for the past months:

I don't use primer or my eyelash curler, and I don't wear lipstick.

No moonbeams, sunbeams, emulsifiers and exfoliants, or a hundred-dollar serum to make me sparkle and glow. Only now do I realize I've been shelling out cash for packaging and ad copy. It's all the same product, but one month a blush will be called Beach Babe Bronzer and the next month, Angel in the Sun.

I don't put on the self-tanner that makes my legs itch.

I don't shower or shave as often. My bush looks like a gremlin and I want to keep it that way.

I make lists in my head so I can
check
check
check things off.

"I've scaled back," I say. The brush sweeps my forehead then moves down to my jawline. *Smooth my eyebrows*, I think. I love it when she does that. I missed it while I was gone.

"You look good," Lisa says. Her face is close to mine. I can smell her watermelon gum. She places her fingers on my temples and checks my eye makeup. I look to the right. I can never look back into her eyes. She presses her thumbs to my eyebrows and runs them over the arch. I relax my shoulders. This is the best part of my day.

"Okay, let's do this," Holly says, and claps her hands together. I crack a smile. Everything is so silly to me.

Mike brings the camera to his shoulder.

Katie breathes out, then sits up straighter.

I'm ready. Ready for this thing, this job. I will try harder because it's not just me here.

"Okay, clap," Mike says.

Katie and I clap.

"And we're rolling," Mike says.

"What a gorgeous morning," I say to the camera. "Absolutely beautiful." And it is. It really is. I can still recognize this. I can still love feeling so close to the sun and peaks of mountains, still love life at this altitude—it makes me feel like every breath counts.

"Seriously," Katie says. "Seriously amazing, and every lift is up and running. I can't wait for all the snow that's supposed to come tonight!"

I try to smile and eventually get it up. Up and down. Smile reps. Exercising the muscle.

"It makes everything worth it," Katie says. "Even if you don't ski, the snow just gives you that warm cozy feeling. Makes me want to run out and condo shop! Now, Sarah, you're a big skier, right?"

"I try to get out there," I say, "but I haven't in a while."

"I've just heard from the COO of Breckenridge Resorts, Richard Fowler, that lift ticket prices have gone up seven dollars." Katie makes a pained expression. Then she shrugs her shoulders. On camera she always looks like she's playing a game of charades.

"But I guess that's not too bad," she says. "The new gondola goes right to the lots. Holds eight passengers and I've heard rumors of future heat and Wi-Fi. And the views of Cucumber Gulch are amazing."

She looks at me.

"They are amazing," I say.

"And once you're up there, the lifts are amazing too—the seats are so plush, I could sleep in 'em. Padded seats, fiberglass shields, lots of room, and safe—I know there's a responsive braking system and load-sensing devices. I could just ride that thing all day long! Best part of the lifts is they go to places like the Vista Haus, where you can have a beer, a glass of wine, some onion soup, or one of their famous mammoth burritos. I guess you get what you pay for! And that's a lot!"

I can't speak. How could I possibly speak? That was remarkable. That was preparation.

"What else do you get?" Katie asks. She puts on her thinking

face. "Hot guys on ski patrol." She laughs, then looks at me to continue.

Yes, hot guys on ski patrol.

The level-three trauma center where you'll wake from your Nor-
folk pine–induced concussion saying, "Dude, where's my spleen?"

Avalanche control equipment.

The rescue team that will find your son frozen in ice, fingers gripping his coat, body like an ancient artifact already in its glass case,
already stuffed with preservatives. You will wonder how it's possible
that your son, your baby, your friend, was here in December and now
he is not.

"You get moguls," I say, quickly trudging through an emotion
that feels like an injection of fear. "It costs money to make them, but
it's worth it because you've had a beer and you like the way you look
doing moguls." I exhale.

Katie laughs and shakes her head. "Too funny."

"And we'll do that again," Holly says. "Sarah, maybe comment
on the development, the evolution of this place. Yes, lift tickets are
high, but there are more lifts, more terrain, more bang for your buck."

"I know," I say. "Sorry. Getting into the swing of things."

I say something about evolution, but it comes off wrong. I say
this place used to be pastures and farmland, very ovine. I have to
correct Katie when she says, "Bovine?"

"No," I say. "Not bovine, ovine for sheep. Baa." I actually bleat.
"Sorry," I say.

We do it again, and yet, it's so easy. We get to start over, no problem.

I say something about change and adaptation. Too vague.

I say, "More bang for your buck."

I say something about burritos. It flies.

"Oh my goodness," Katie says. Her post-laughter segue face.
"Okay. Well, let's head on over to the Twisted Pine, our premier
furrier—animal-friendly furrier, I should add."

The statement is so ridiculous. I look around. Really? Do we just let this go? I can't help myself. "Yes, Twisted only sells free-range mink. Nothing there has bitten its own foot off!"

I smile at the camera, then happen to glance at Holly, who's staring at me, horrified, as though I'm a non-free-range mink, gnawing into my little paw. Yes, this is the exchange. In return for a hard punch, in return for getting completely hijacked onto a sick, sick ride, I have been given a little bit of leeway. But I don't want the exchange. Even though I take liberties, even though I feel entitled to mess up, I am not having fun with it. I am not liking the way I am punishing people. It's revolting.

Holly looks at the two of us, waiting. "I'm sorry," I say. "That was . . ." I feel a heat in my chest, not panic, but a kind of exhilaration and confusion. While I don't like my feelings, I still feel them.

Holly gestures for me and I unclip my mic and walk to her behind the equipment. She wears a maroon caftan-like sweater over black leather pants. Her gold hoop earrings have blue gems in them like little eyes. She is determined to not look like a producer. Her hair is in a perfect ponytail. My head is itchy from the sun.

"Hon," she says, "if you want, Katie can get this. Easy day. Only takes one of you. I can always step in too, if need be."

"I'm fine," I say. "I'm already here."

Her hip juts out. I stare at the hip. It's like a personal assistant. I almost laugh when I imagine it speaking.

"You just seem a bit distracted," she says. "I mean you're doing great, so great. So great! I'm just saying everyone understands if you want a break. A longer one. Or if you want to reenter more slowly. Do more behind-the-scenes work? Preinterviews, editing . . . This all must be so hard. I don't know what I'd do . . . where I'd be if . . ."

I wait while she imagines her children dead. Sabina, Gunner, and Lola: kaput. Her eyes well up and she shakes off whatever inconceivable worst-case scenarios she conjured up. She holds her hands awkwardly in front of her like she's gripping an invisible bat. I cough into the crook of my elbow.

"Are you getting sick?" she asks.

"No," I say. "I just had to cough. Hairball," I joke, but based on her expression it didn't come off well. "I'm fine," I say. "I'd like to be here."

I want connection. I want to be in control of something. I want new ground.

"Okay," she says.

I go back and Mike hands me my mic. He watches to make sure I clip it on correctly. This part always makes him antsy, the fact that we have breasts.

"Should we try for a few alternative sound bites?" Holly asks.

"Aren't your boots from Twisted Pine?" Katie says. "Maybe I can point that out?"

I look down at my lace-up boots with the rubber soles, a fluff of fur in the lining. "These are from Nordstrom Rack," I say. "They're faux."

"Let's just mention some of their products," Holly says. Her gaze at me is full of dread.

"Rolling," Mike says.

Katie launches in: "Today's Fresh Visit will take us to the Twisted Pine, our premier luxury furrier—animal-friendly furrier, I should say—where you'll find all of your fur needs for a very reasonable price."

I did not consider the fact that people may have fur needs.

"They carry mink, sable, fox . . . "

"Lynx, sheared beaver," I say, then laugh a little, and then some more.

"Yes, yes," Katie says. "And mink." She laughs too, and then laughs hard, the good, barely audible kind, we both do, and for a moment I feel like I can bring something true to all of this, that I can be allowed in somehow. Our eyes are full of water.

"I guess we'll do that again?" I say, still laughing.

She can't respond, still laughing. "Okay," she says and lets out a sigh. "Okay. Just don't say beaver." We settle down while Mike waits. He looks like he wants to shoot us or maybe even something more hands-on.

Katie and I make eye contact, deciding on something. She takes a deep breath, repeats her lines. I add nothing this time, what we silently agreed upon. Really, there's no need for me to be here. I should be put out to pasture with my dad. I could wear my faux boots and eat pho and make foes. Fo' sure. God, what is wrong with me? I mean, I know what's wrong, but why can't it be expressed in some other, prettier way?

"—then after our shopping spree," Katie says, as her voice slows and deepens and she transitions to a concerned face, "Justin Calhoun and Liza Norfleet will be joining us to talk about Loud Deaf World and their work in international deaf communities. We'll show a clip from their documentary, an inspiring story of an impoverished dead girl, or deaf girl rather, in Guatemala. I'll say that last bit again."

"Clap," Mike says. Katie claps.

"A poor deaf girl from Guatemala," she says.

"Perfect." Holly whispers something to Mike, then looks up at Katie. "I think we have enough if you want to sum it up."

Katie brings things to an end. Take it away, Katie. I tune out for a while. Eventually I make it back, just in time to hear her question, one she's been asking me on camera for years: "What is the third most popular activity to do here in Breckenridge, Colorado?"

At the University of Denver I decided I wanted to be a reporter. I got a taste for it from the Broadcast Club and wanted to recite breaking news. I especially liked the bad news—there was a thrill to it, and a bigger thrill of being the one to relay it. You have the power of information and the power to be trusted. I liked watching and hearing foreign reporters, their accents making them even more glamorous to me, because that's what I was after, surely: style and a voice. *For the World this is Neige Lampur.* I wanted, one day, to have a sign-off like that: "For the World this is Sarah St. John."

That was a long time ago. I'm forty-three now, my son is dead. I don't have any desire or abilities to address the world, but I can recite our resort's third most popular activity. My sign-off is this:

"Tubing."

Chapter **3**

I drive down the seven-block stretch of Main Street, forcing myself to be patient. We're a small town, but with 686 hotels and inns. Our population is around four thousand but increases to about thirty-five thousand during the season. Each year we start all over, a new batch enters, then departs. Sometimes I feel like I'm the only one who doesn't feel lucky and blessed to live here. Three hundred days of sunshine, breath-sucking views, living in other people's vacation destination. You've got nothing to complain about. Until you do.

Most people who live here fought to stay or fought to come back and make it. I fought to get out and got stuck, though maybe I used Cully as a way to make it okay to come back, telling myself that if it hadn't been for him then I would have been somebody, but I had to return and make the best life I could for us. I think, at twenty-one, that was the story I wanted to emanate. It was cowardly. I think that after the shock, I was relieved by the pregnancy. It allowed me to whittle life down.

I found out at the end of the semester when I was busy with finals and applying for internships at various news stations. I had a paper due on Islamic art, of all things, and was so overwhelmed, so tired, and I thought, *I don't have to do any of this right now. This can be delayed.* It was as though I pressed a reset button, and all my choices, all these opportunities and struggles, they all disappeared.

"I'm pregnant," I told my roommate. "I'm going to have a baby."

"Are you kidding me? Why? With who?" Trini Sengupta, a highly promiscuous girl who hated her father. She looked at me like I was a germ.

"It's what I've decided to do. I'm excited. I'm going to move back home for a while, raise him on my own." I sold her my story, painting a picture of novelty.

I turn off of Main and find a pocket of peace from the crowds. The few blocks to my subdivision are pedestrian-free; the air is warm. Too warm. It's hard to believe snow is supposed to come tonight. The earth hates us. Yesterday I saw a butterfly.

I turn on Carter and am surprised by the black truck reversing out of the driveway. My internal idiot reacts: *a friend of Cully's!* In high school his friends always used to be at our house, probably because of the skate ramp. It felt like customs—everyone came through at some point declaring themselves and leaving things behind. Mainly boys, most absurdly good-looking with the exception of Kevin (his skin pale and freckled, tight on his bones like a lizard's) and Markus (body like a full Hefty bag, starting out small, widening, then tapering in again). Some girls: Shay, the beauty, and her sidekicks, Gina and Ri-anna (whom the boys would sometimes call Gonor and Rhea). They would watch snowboarding videos with the boys, pretending to like it. They would politely smile when I entered the room, pretending to like me as well.

After college when he moved back in, he didn't have anyone over, most likely embarrassed to be living at home. Or just practical. Why come here when everyone you know rents their own place?

The truck reverses, and I pull up alongside it. The driver looks small in the seat. She's around Cully's age, I suspect. Dark hair, round, rosy face, shaky smile. Pretty green eyes, like gems. She looks startled.

"Hi," I say. "Can I help you with something?"

A voice on the radio booms. "I'm just saying"—the DJ laughs—"people don't know how to drive in snow." We are listening to the same station and realize this at the same time, both reaching to turn it down.

"Are you lost?" I ask.

She makes to speak but doesn't.

"Just watch," the DJ says. "After this storm tourists are going to be sliding all over the place."

"We're supposed to get a lot of snow tonight," she says. "Ten inches."

I smile sympathetically.

"I'm going around the neighborhood seeing if people want me to come by tomorrow. To shovel. I was just . . . I'll be going now."

"Great," I say, feeling sorry for her and maybe a little eager to have a young person around. I miss them, the kids—they disappeared when Cully died, stood me up. Pretty much all of the social things I did in life stemmed from him, from having a child. He was like a ticket. When he went off to college I still socialized, but mainly with people who had kids his age, or just Suzanne. Now what? I wonder. No one will ask me to do anything. Everyone will feel bad and awkward. Kids I used to know will come back here and feel sorry for me, bashful about their success, their jobs, their marriages, their children. I'm like the family with three or more children. You don't invite them over because they're too hard to feed.

"I could use someone," I say. I reach for my wallet even though this could all be a ruse and she could take the money and run.

"You don't need to do that," she says, when I bring my bag to my lap. "I'm not really serious—"

"Believe me, things are crazy." I rummage through my impractical bag that always brings me a frantic frustration. Energy bar, coin purse, receipts, crumbs. "If I don't pay you now, then . . . oh perfect, I don't have any cash. I can get some inside."

We stare at each other and it's only mildly uncomfortable.

She looks hungry. I could give her the energy bar. I could throw it through her window, but what if it hit her in the face? It's a nice face—full lips, high round cheekbones, some sort of ethnicity perhaps. Or not. Beautiful girls are different now. They have reservoirs. I think of myself, blondes, as dead ends.

"So," I say, "come back tomorrow? I can pay you then?"

She hesitates. Did she change her mind and want me to prepay? "Okay," she says.

Funny, Cully used to do the same thing. Take up his shovel during snowstorms, make an extra buck. I open the garage door with the clicker, comforted that my dad's not in there gassing himself to death. Not that he would, but I don't know anything about anything anymore. The girl still hasn't reversed.

"Okay, see you soon!" I say.

She looks like she has something else to add. I buy her some time. "Come by whenever. If I'm not home I'll leave the money up on the deck. Oh, and I don't know if you've been to that house yet?" I point to the one on the left. She shakes her head. "Good. I'd bypass that one. German fellow. Intense. Screams at his kids. Curse words—the whole bit. He hammers nails into things, I think as meditation."

She smiles, slightly. She doesn't seem like the other kids who move here. There are the arrogant, slacker types who don't make eye contact and then the chipper types who could just as well be working as entertainers on a Disney cruise. She seems to be neither. Someone with something thoughtful and purposeful behind her eyes.

"Sarah?" she says. "I mean, Mrs. St. John?"

I turn down the stereo further down. "How did you know my name?"

"TV," she says.

"Right." I'm surprised she has seen my show.

"I could start now if you want." She lowers her gaze and I look out my window at the ground.

"There's not really a lot to do right now," I say, sorry to say it.

"Right," she says.

I hesitate, not knowing how to send her off, and look up at the house.

"Actually, the deck is pretty icy," I say, happy I found a reason to keep her. "Maybe you could start there."

Chapter 4

When I come in my father is sitting on his spot on the sofa. Sometimes it seems he's been sewn there. He moved in almost a year ago after he sold his house and I wanted him to take the time to find a perfect place. At first, real estate consumed us. We had fun looking at staged apartments and condos, collecting brochures. Then, there was less urgency. He was finding a routine with us. He and Cully went grocery shopping together. They'd snowboard on weekdays and play pool every night that Cully was home. They'd watch movies and their shows: sports, the Discovery Channel, and *Wheel of Fortune*. Neither of them had ever had another male in the house before and each other's company seemed to complete something for both of them.

Before he moved in Cully would often go over to my dad's on Ridge Street, but it was different having him actually live with us. From my bed I could hear them downstairs playing pool or laughing at a skit on *Saturday Night Live*. There was a safety in the clink of pool balls, a sound that I very much miss. I didn't know how much I loved it until now.

After Cully's death there were no attempts to find somewhere for him to live, and now I'm not sure if there will ever be.

I look at the television and sure enough he has it on channel two. He can't seem to get enough of the QVC. Two women are on the television talking about a television.

"It comes into the room," one of them says. She has tight curls and a large forehead. "It becomes a part of you."

It's like watching a revival—the other woman throws her arms up in the air. I remember her from yesterday, shaking her head to demonstrate the power of a scientifically advanced hair product.

I hang up my coat but keep my boots on. I look outside at the girl on the deck. I've armed her with a shovel and she's looking at it like she's never seen one before. She is not fit for this kind of chore.

"They are so damn passionate," my dad says.

I look back at the television. "And animated," I say. "It's kind of astounding."

"That's what I'm talking about," he says. "And they can keep going. They just keep at it—the same product, their glee unwavering!"

Their passion evidently inspires him so much that he has purchased many items including face-lift tape. After listening to seven testimonials my dad was convinced that not only would he look better, he would feel better. It would, as Cynthia the life coach testified, "Waken you, enliven you, and restore you to the person you really are."

After placing the order he realized he had just bought masking tape for three installments of $29.50. When it arrived he tried it, of course. He latched one end of the tape to his brow, the other to his hairline. When I walked in he had only completed one side, and it had a Jekyll and Hyde effect. One side, gloomy. The other, well, a bit gay. One side, knowing. The other, full of wonder. He had never done this before retirement, and after Cully's death his purchases doubled.

"How did it go today?" he asks.

"Okay," I say, looking at the women, how they're reminding me of me, what I do. "Actually, it went horribly." I recall my attitude toward everyone, my irritability. I felt like a character out of a children's book. A dragon who's nice on the inside but ugly on the outside so no one wants to play with her.

"We had to talk about the new price for lift tickets. Dickie didn't show up, but we—Katie—handled it."

"What are they up to now?"

"One oh five."

"Balls, that's harsh. That's wild."

"I know."

I walk into the kitchen. He has left dishes in the sink and I load them into the dishwasher.

"But alas," he says, "no one should nor can complain. Balls, said the queen, if I had them I'd be king."

Here's where he will launch into something that will leave me bemused, yet interested.

"Complain about what, Dad?" I ask, paving the way.

"The increase in the price of lift tickets," he says. "If they want prices to be like they were in the old days, tell 'em to hang on to a piece of twine and be towed like a roped calf. They can have my wood hickory skis with the bear trap bindings and my boots that were made out of seal skins. Ha! Can you imagine all the asswads in their, in their uh, black tights and their Atomic boots—can you imagine them wearing my seals?"

"No, I can't imagine. Hey, so a girl is outside—"

"Tell your viewers—" He looks back at me from the couch to make sure I'm still listening. "Tell them ticket prices go up because this is the way people wanted it." He is yelling, but there's a glimmer of joy in his eyes. He loves this sort of thing. "Gentrification: creating a gentry— asserting upper-class credentials through ostentation and glut."

I lean into the counter. "Glut?" I say.

"Ticket prices are high because people want life here to be unaf- fordable," he says. "The best is only the best when others can't buy it. And you can," he says, speaking to the imagined public, "because you're blessed. Because you've worked hard. You want to top your friend's vacation to Lake Como. You want to buy a mountain home in Shock Hill. Donate it for a week at your kid's silent auction. And it's your right. Life, liberty, and the pursuit of second homes. Tell 'em that."

"Wow, Dad, okay. Great points." I smile, then resume my tasks, open the fridge. "Did you happen to go to the store? I didn't go."

"And don't forget to emphasize Breckenridge's motivation," he says, "which is always sourced in environmental, social, or cultural concerns. A Philip Morris tactic, right? Make cigarettes while creating a foundation—for the kids!—that helps people quit smoking."

"They got sued," I say, "and you're getting too worked up now. The fun is over."

"Breckenridge can do the same thing—convince people they're cutting down the forest and raising prices and this will somehow benefit our ecosystem, sick kids, and the arts. Anyway, you should say something like that."

"Watch the next show," I say. "Instead I'll be talking about fur needs."

"Create a formula," he continues.

"Take your pulse," I say.

"People feel safer when things cost more. They will elect a higher price because it speaks to their high standards. There are so many ways to suggest what one should desire."

"Okay," I say. "I suggest you desire going outside." I walk out of the kitchen, glance out the window, then walk closer to him because I suspect he may be wearing the face-lift tape, but I don't detect any. He just looks well rested. I sit down beside him. Though I have my complaints I don't know what I would have done without my dad right there in my face every day following Cully's death. He may feel the same way and I think our need degrades us a bit. We pretend it doesn't exist through annoyance with one another's habits, but without words we have forced each other to eat, get dressed, sweep the floor. There's a decorum to our lives, some amount of decency. We eat meals versus cereal with a bottle of wine and some popcorn. We don't pick our teeth and eat what we've picked. We don't spend all day in our underwear. We put the garbage out. When I'm with him, watching *The Biggest Loser* doesn't make me feel like one. I could be in Betty Ford without him. I like my wine. For now it brings me a little contentment, or something on the ladder toward it. Sometimes I think the abstemious need more help than the indulgent.

"Hey, do you like those?" he asks.

I look at the television, where a woman cuffed in silver bracelets insists she can't tell the difference between the David Yurman jewelry and its cheaper imitation, Yavid Durman.

"No," I say. "Tell me you didn't order them."

"I didn't order them," he says.

"And you haven't ordered anything lately, right?"

He doesn't answer, which means he has. I stand and the world around me twinkles with black stars. My insides feel soggy and mashed like canned chutney and I'm almost jealous of my dad. He is always nicely dressed in jeans and his favorite hooded sweatshirt, or sometimes a collared shirt. He's clean-shaven, clean-smelling, roughly handsome, somehow debonair, but I guess this is perfectly attainable for a man. By looking at him you'd never know he was a bit off, a bit down, unless you knew that most days he woke up and groomed himself only to sit at home alone.

"I hired a snow shoveler," I say.

"Why would you pay someone to do what I can do?" my dad asks.

"I thought you could give her a hand." I walk to the window.

"Her?"

"Yes. I felt sorry for her. Let her do it a few times. A lot of snow is coming tonight. She's kind of here now."

"What?"

"Come see." I watch her jabbing the shovel into the stairs. I really should stop her, tell her to rest. "She's scraping the stairs. Or trying to."

He walks up behind me. "Jesus, Sarah. Tell her to go home. Your fat friend is here. Suzanne."

"Don't say that."

"Just kidding around," he says.

"She's here? I didn't see her car."

"Well, she's downstairs. Look at her sweater over there." He tilts his head toward the kitchen. "The one smothering that bar stool."

I look over at her salmon-colored sweater. "What about it?"

"It's the size BW. Know what BW stands for? It's in cursive on the tag: Bountiful Woman."

"Why would you look at the size of her sweater? God, Dad, that's like looking at the underside of someone's china."

"Just wanted to know what I was dealing with."

I know he's trying to make me laugh and annoy me at the same time. "I'm going to go down so we can clean up, make some room for you. Why don't you go help this girl."

I look to the stairs, but now she's up here on the deck. "Oh," I laugh, embarrassed, but then I realize she can't see me.

My dad walks toward the door. "I'm going to tell her we don't need her."

"Don't!" I say and duck down for some reason, then look out again. She looks so serious, like she's the bearer of bad news.

"What if she's on OxyContin?" my dad says. "The kids do that now. And cutting. And sexting. They lure in the pervs. What if she's an axe murderer? A shovel murderer? She's small, but so are ferrets, quick and sharp. Remember that roofer at my old place? Stole my sled and weed whacker though I guess I don't do much sledding or whacking. That didn't sound right," he mumbles. "What do I care anyway? Steal my life."

"Don't be weird with her," I say.

My dad opens the door, shields his eyes, and stands on the deck. "Hi there," he says.

I walk up behind him.

"Hi," the girl says.

"I'm Lyle," he says, extending his hand. They shake. "I'm Kit," she says.

I edge in next to my dad. "Kit here is going to help deice our steps and deck and—" I try to loosen some ice with the toe of my boot, as if helping.

"I can see gravel," my dad says. "I don't think we need any shoveling today. Besides, shouldn't you be doing something else? You're too attractive for manual labor. Go ahead and pay your taxes so people can do this stuff for you."

I elbow him in the gut. Kit just smiles and takes a step back. She carries a black book.

"Actually there's a lot of ice here," I say. "You've been wanting to chip away at it. Kit could help you."

Kit. Interesting name, one I don't think I've ever heard before, except in books, perhaps, or that doll: Kit, the American Girl. Or Kit Carson. But he was a man.

They look at each other, then at the steps. It's as though I've suggested something they both don't want to do. I don't feel ready to leave them alone.

"Can I get you any water?" I ask.

"No, thank you," she says.

"How about a beer?" my dad asks.

I look over at him, but he just widens his eyes at me, then looks away.

"No, thanks," she says.

"I always offer," he says. "It's a little test I give to day laborers. If they say yes and take a few sips and finish it over the course of their work, then they were raised well and have a strong work ethic. If they sit on their ass and drink the whole thing, then they're lazy and taking advantage of you."

"What does it mean if they say no?" she asks.

"It means they're a woman," my dad says.

I'm afraid this is the second sexist thing he has said within one minute.

"Sorry," I say. "He's a bit . . . nuts," but she doesn't seem to be thrown at all. She holds up her hand, showing us her palm.

"A callus," she says. "From twisting caps off bottles of beer."

Good girl, I think.

"Ever heard of a bottle opener?" my dad asks.

She puts her hand back down by her side. "It's gotten to the point where I want to maintain it," she says.

My dad laughs and so do I. We both look at her carefully as if she is somebody new.

"The test continues," my dad says, and I relax. "I see if they leave the can, ask for the trash, or ask for recycling. Nothing pisses me off more than you kids who don't recycle. We are a virus and this earth is one sick body and we will kill our planet. It's a sure thing. People need to stop breeding."

She emits a sudden, hard cough.

"Would you prefer to work on your own?" I ask.

"I'm fine," she says. "I could use some direction." She smiles at my dad in a way that seems genuine and I can tell that he is won over. "I could use some muscle too," she says. Sold.

And so I leave them to it, going back in with the feeling of sneaking away as if leaving my child with a new babysitter. When I get back inside I look out the window at the two of them. I'm comforted and maybe just a bit perplexed.

Chapter 5

I walk downstairs and into Cully's room. It's a fluid, rehearsed move—I don't think about it. I don't break down upon entering. I don't even flinch. It's a room that needs to be cleaned, that's all.

"Hi, there," I say to Suzanne. She looks great as always, boot-cut slacks and a cream shirt with leather patches on the elbows. Her short brown hair looks like it's just been done, her bangs expertly sloping over the side of her face. "Hello, dear," she says. "You look great."

She has put on one of his CDs. The rapper says, "Life's a bitch and then you die." I walk to the stereo and lower the volume, then change my mind and turn it back up. Life *is* a bitch and then you die. It's the truest thing I've heard all day.

"Hope it's okay that I got started," she says.

"Of course," I say. "Thank you. God, *you* look great." I touch the ends of her hair. "I like it."

"Thanks. Just highlights. Upkeep." She takes a shirt off the bed and holds it over her torso. "Love this," she says. "Hog's Breath Saloon." She looks down at the hairy, globular hog on her chest. I look around to see what she's done but don't notice anything except for the clothes on the bed. I go to the chest of drawers to get more shirts. When Cully was young he thought they were called Chester drawers. I get a handful that don't look clean. Cully would just stuff his clothes back in. They're faded and soft and I bring one up to my face.

"It took me a while just to go through his wallet," I say. "This really helps."

"It hasn't been that long," Suzanne says. "You don't necessarily need to do this now."

"I want to," I say. "I feel good about it. Cully never liked *stuff*, you know?" I take a look around while we refold the shirts. It's a childhood room vacated, then returned to as a resting stop. A bed, two side tables, his desk and computer, a stack of books from college, mainly geology texts. In his walk-in closet are the things I kept for him—old report cards and art projects, painted handprints, pictures of us, his life curated by me.

"Did you notice I parked half a block away?" Suzanne says. "Part of my fitness routine."

Suzanne is seven years older than me, and while we never really knew each other growing up, our shared experiences make it feel like we've grown up together. We went to the same school, we both lived near the post office, our dads had similar jobs, and yet we yielded different results. She was popular in high school, went to college in New York, moved to Vail when her new husband was recruited there, and then moved here when she was pregnant with Morgan. We never would have been friends if it weren't for our kids, but that seems to be how your social life is constructed post-children. You can't imagine that girl with the red Land Cruiser who smokes cigarettes and ties her T-shirts in knots below her breasts will one day be your closest friend.

I go to the drawers for his shorts and pants and take a glance at her BW body. My dad's right. Suzanne has always been pretty "well-rounded," but she's gained much more weight in these past six months or so. I don't know what to do about her, my very best friend. Sometimes she's the person I imagine myself growing old with. She can make light of tragedy, expelling despair with a monologue, a joke, a few sound words—she sends it flying like a dead fish. She's fun to talk with, see movies with, drink wine with, but lately I find myself feeling annoyed every time she opens her mouth or puts something in it.

I've been narrowing in to things—the way she eats her vanilla low-fat yogurt, licking the foil top, her hand lotion that smells like deodorized feminine napkins, the way she stands too close. She's a personal space invader and sometimes one of her breasts will graze my arm, making me feel like I'm being hit with a warm bag of porridge. The list of annoyances, once minute, has become noteworthy, and now her daughter has joined my queue. I think she feels the same way about me, tallying up my quirks and trying her best to ignore them. Sometimes friends are so unfriendly to each other.

I put the boxers straight into the trash bag by the door, which gives me a feeling of guilt but also accomplishment.

"This shirt smells like . . . girl," Suzanne says, pressing one of the shirts to her nose. "Perfume. Smell." She holds the shirt near my face. I get a brief whiff of strawberries, or a makeup manufacturer's interpretation of strawberries. It's the smell of childhood and boredom and it takes me to junior high, to the bench by Keystone Hall where the popular girls would sit, where she would sit.

Maybe it was a girl, her head against Cully's chest, leaving her scent like a business card. Her perfume outlived him. It could outlive all of us. I imagine Shay, all cleavage and lipstick. She'd saunter around the house, her lips parted. It was like watching a beer commercial, and I'm sure she engaged in all of the things beer commercials subliminally promise. Maybe it's her. But not Gonorrhea—they weren't his type. Cecilia—I hope not. She wore ninety-dollar T-shirts and called cigarettes "fags." She once told me that she thought Marc Jacobs clothes looked pulled from the children's section of thrift stores. She and Cully would watch these movies that were supposedly highly acclaimed. Mostly the films were about people sitting around and saying witty things or about robbers saying witty things. They were unbearable and I know she thought she was really deep for watching them, and that I was an idiot for not getting it, for not understanding the symbolism.

"He didn't have a girlfriend," Suzanne says. "Morgan would have known."

Morgan would have wanted that role for herself, I think. "She didn't know everything, I'm sure." I try to say this lightly. "And I'd know if he had a girlfriend. He didn't, though I'm sure there were girls." Phone always ringing, activity always encircling, Cully calm in the middle, the eye of a hurricane. I go to the closet to carry out my dad's books.

"You sure you're not smelling yourself?" I ask, and we both smile. Suzanne is always in a cloud of heavy perfume and she has a different scented lotion for every part of her body. They're nice, though—her lotions and makeup that often make their way to me. She is the most generous person I know, and when I think back, the generosity to myself and others is always free of stipulations and expectations.

I didn't really notice before, but her scents always give me immediate comfort. It's something familiar, soothing, and maternal, and I wonder if our friendship fulfills that mother role I never thought I missed or needed. I look at her hands, going through the books— books and movies about dead boys—and I'm mildly embarrassed by the recognition, the idea that this may be true. We even argue like mother and daughter, and maybe that's why despite my annoyance with her, it's supposed to be this way.

"What is all this?" she asks.

"Just books," I say. "I don't know where half of them came from."

My dad has begun to amass all this depressing literature, secretly storing them like nuts for some future hunger. I want them out, which is okay with him. He says they didn't help, which makes me feel bad for him and his thinking that they ever could.

I place the box on the bed and mumble, "I can't believe how many of these there are, all on the same subject." I pick one out: *Boy, Interrupted*. Then another: *The Son Rises*. Good God. "And they're all about boys," I say.

Are they more interesting than dead girls? The thought leaves me chilled, and so does the thought of people across America going to a store or shopping online driven by their need for these books.

It makes me want to cry, for both the need and the courage to look for help.

The books seem to be making her uncomfortable. She busies herself with the clothes again.

"In the books girls seem to be murdered," I say. "Boys are killed when they're being adventurous. Sailing the rough seas or slaying an Arab or shooting a lion." Or outrunning an avalanche, I don't say.

I believe my theory is sound. The boys are conquering nature: a wave, a mountain, a volcano, an animal, a storm of some sort, all of which are a stand-in for some vague ideal. What is the ideal? What are they trying to do? What does that lion mean? Can't boys just observe the lion from a distance? How about a game of chess? It doesn't pain me as much to think of them this way—a vague everyboy, a character.

"We'd better be more adventurous so we can avoid being murdered," Suzanne says.

"That makes no sense," I say.

"I know, I—" She picks up a book called *Understanding Your Grieving Soul after an Adult Child's Death.* Such a long, exclusive title. Makes me think of those movies on Lifetime I find my dad watching: *She Met Him in November. Claire's Too Young to Be a Mother.* So specific.

"These can be really helpful, you know," Suzanne says. "They've helped me a lot with Dickie. The anger, the sadness, the letting go. We all go through these stages. Divorce is a kind of death, and—"

Okay, blow me.

"—there are stages of grief. I find it comforting that we're not alone. Big tragedies, small ones—"

So we're all predictable. Our DNA is practically identical to an orangutan's. That's just not comforting at all, nor is the thought of Suzanne and me going through similar stages. Divorce and the death of a child? I should at least be assigned different steps. But I know she's just trying to be helpful.

She groups together a pair of white socks with gray toes. Then she folds his ski pants—the black ones patched with duct tape. I remember the sound they'd make when he walked. It was probably the most familiar sound in the world, the hiss of his snow clothes, or in the summers, the rolling sound of his skateboard on the ramp outside my bedroom window, the ramp I had removed. Suzanne pulls something out of the pants' pocket, looks at it, then puts it in the garbage bag next to her.

"What was that?"

"A ticket stub," she says. "For a movie."

"What movie?" I walk around the boxes and fish it out of the trash, stopping myself from looking at everything in there, like my father used to do in our kitchen trash. *This tissue paper can be saved for Christmas presents! These bones can be used for soup!* I learned his frugality was sourced in his love of shopping. We saved the bones and bought a pizza oven.

"I asked you to put everything on the bed," I say.

"I didn't know you meant things like that," Suzanne says.

"It's exactly the kind of thing I meant." I hold the ticket. *The Other One.* Cully once saw a movie called *The Other One.* He was at Storyteller Cinema, watching a movie. He put the ticket in his pocket. He wore his ski pants to a movie. How funny. How odd. How wonderful. "This is significant," I say. "This is interesting to me."

"Sorry," Suzanne says. She is folding clothes rapidly as if in a factory line. If they were Morgan's clothes she'd take the time to look at each item, relating the back story.

"I should know better," she says. "I've been doing the same thing with all of Dickie's stuff."

"Not the same," I mumble.

"But I'm realizing that a ticket stub is a ticket stub, a tie is a tie, not an embodiment of Dickie, right? If we weren't getting a divorce, I wouldn't give a rip about any of the crap he owns."

Here we go.

"You'd think a man in his position would throw away his boxers when they got holes in them, but no—he just lets it all hang out. He may as well be wearing a skirt."

I'm a bad friend and I tune out. I listen to the music instead, which is oddly comforting, as if the rapper and I are in on something. *That's why we puff lye 'cause you never know when you're going to go.* What is "lye"? The street name for crack? For ice? Are those the same thing? Or is he saying, *That's why we puff live?* Why the hell can't these kids enunciate?

I slide the box of books with my foot to the door, where a filled bag sits like a bouncer.

Suzanne waves a receipt. "Mi Casa," she says.

I nod and she tosses. I consider retrieving it when she isn't looking, but I won't because that would be stupid. Stupid, stupid, dumb. I suppose I wouldn't obsess over the little things if there were more of them. His room has so few clues. One poster on the wall—Never Summer Snowboards—not too many clothes in the closet, CDs, one motocross magazine, desk debris. I didn't notice the sparseness when he was here, but now all I see is what little is left.

I notice the smells of detergent and Cully's deodorant. I run my hand down his hanging clothes. I find the navy-blue jacket I can't bring myself to get rid of.

"I'll keep this for my dad," I say.

"That's nice," Suzanne says. She unfolds the Hog's Breath shirt. "Can I give this to Morgan? She'd love it. Unless you—"

"Go ahead," I say, looking at the shirt, regretting it. I can't believe how quickly this is going.

"The other night she called," Suzanne says. "It was really late. She was walking home from some party. She was so upset."

"About Cully or the divorce?" I ask, feeling cold that I'm struggling to care.

"Both," Suzanne says. "But it's weird because I enjoyed it. I was happy that she was sad."

"That's normal," I say. "You felt needed and happy you could be there for her."

"But it's so rare," Suzanne says. "You know Morgan—so mature, always capable. For the most part she's coping. She's thriving as always."

Or more so, I think. Sometimes I think Cully's death has made her feel more important, but I understand what Suzanne's problem really is because I share it. She wants company down here. Her daughter has bypassed those initial stages of grief or did a crash course in them and now she's soaring in her stage of acceptance. She is now the daughter of divorce. She is a girl who will remember her dead friend. She is Morgan!

I was five when my mother died of lung cancer. I know what it's like to be young and to move on. For the first time I wonder how my dad felt—to see his child mourn the loss of her mother, then the next day want to play with her friends.

I wonder how he's doing up there. I'm sure he's enjoying Kit's company too much. I'm positive he's already asked where she's from, what her parents do, how old she is, why she's in Breckenridge, where she went or goes to college, what she wants to do with her life, and if she put ten percent of her earnings into savings. Hopefully he hasn't asked if she's on oxy whatever or if she's a cutter.

I place the folded clothes into shopping bags for the Salvation Army. They are just clothes, just objects.

"What is it, exactly?" I ask. "The party at the Broadmoor."

"It's just that," Suzanne says. "A party."

"So, no speeches or—"

"All I know is that Morgan has been working very hard," she says.

"Okay," I say, detecting defensiveness and responding as such. "I just wanted to be a little prepared, let my dad know what to expect."

"It will be like a cocktail reception," she says, suddenly assured. "A party. Just a little something where the college can recognize one of their own. In fact I think Morgan is setting a precedent. It's never been done before."

For other dead kids, I can't help but think. *For dead alums.* It's
strange the new ways I'm meant to feel good or honored.

"I bought this for you the other day," Suzanne says. She walks to her
purse on the dresser. I can tell she has read my thoughts, maybe wants
to corroborate, but that would mean taking something away from her
daughter. She hands me a red bottle. "Love this stuff," she says. "It's
some miracle skin cream made by monks in their rice paddy fields."

"Thanks," I say. "Is it expensive?"

"Of course."

"Does it work?" I ask.

"I don't know, does it?" She angles her face toward me.

I look at her eyes, her forehead and smooth cheeks. She looks
the same as she did last week, last month, last year. "You have such
nice skin," I say.

I remember the pot I found and walk over to his bedside table
and open the drawer. "Here. I have something for you too. Made by
farmers in their marijuana fields."

I hand her the three baggies.

"Oh wow," she says.

I have never seen anyone smoke so much pot besides Billy, Cully's dad, but he was a kid then. Suzanne is almost fifty and this pot
stuff is a new thing she's taken up since the trouble with Dickie
began, that and the eating, and she's gotten very good at both.

"And I have no idea what this is," I say, handing her something
with a cord and plug.

"That's a vaporizer," she says.

"What's that?" In my day I have smoked from a hookah, an apple,
a glass pipe, a Pepsi can, and a bong named "the reverend" but have
never heard of a vaporizer.

"It's to breathe vapor and not smoke," she says. "So it's clean.
Pure." Then she adds, "And so parents can't smell it."

We both raise our eyebrows at the same time and I smile even
though there's a tug—an irritation and shame that he kept a secret

from me, but of course he did stuff like that. The shame comes from having Suzanne witness it. I keep moving, filling the bags, then moving them to the hall.

"Well, go ahead and have it all," I say. "Smoke it or vaporize it, or whatever."

"I don't know," I hear her say behind me. "I feel like I shouldn't. It's something of his and—"

"For Christ's sake, it's drugs. If it was Xanax, I'd take it. I'm not going to frame it. He'd be grounded if I had found this before . . . "

"Sorry, I was just trying to be respectful."

"I guess I wouldn't ground a twenty-two-year-old," I say. "I'd just yell at him. I was always pestering him, nagging him." My eyes water. I keep moving, willing away emotion.

"He would have moved out soon," she says. "He would have gotten it together."

I walk back in and over to the stereo and put in a different CD— an old one by someone called Common Sense. I like it. It's rap, but not so angry this time. There's a happy beat. He has a charming lisp. *They say become a doctor but I don't have the patience.* That's good. Clever. I take a deep breath, the emotion waning.

Suzanne goes into the closet. I take another box of books to the door, scanning the titles on the spines: *Death of a Grown Grandson: A Survival Guide*, *Lullabies for Bereaved Grandparents*, and *Chicken Soup for the Bereaved Soul*.

I have not read a single one of them. The only thing I read was an article I found on the internet the very day of his death. It was an article called "The Golden Hour": the sixty-minute window a victim has after an accident to get help. It's an hour of hope and promise, better outcomes and statistics. I was so desperate, so foolish, and I can't believe I did that kind of research at that time. The day of his death. I must have been so lost.

We were far beyond the golden hour. Even though I had already seen him on the pass, my dad and I had to go to the hospital to confirm his death with Dr. Braun, whose hair was a fortresslike hedge of frizz. She wore cargo pants, a turtleneck beneath her white coat, and heeled Crocs, which made her untrustworthy. I wanted an old doctor, a white male alcoholic one, the kind I grew up with. Doctors like that could unfreeze him somehow.

Dr. Braun had said, "The parents of the other boys are on level three if you'd like to see them."

My immediate thought was, *What other boys?* No one else existed for me then.

I realize this is still my problem. I'm not happy about it. I don't want to be this way. It isn't that I value myself more than others. Maybe I just want to protect others from the likes of me, save them from having to draw from their deck of learned expressions and emotions.

"Good job," Suzanne says.

"Yes," I say. "We're doing good."

We've been working efficiently and I wonder if this has something to do with the tension in the room, if she even notices it. I take a look around, the bags of folded large T-shirts, the thirty-four-inch-waist jeans, the one snowboard poster, a remnant of his teenaged self. This is a room that belonged to someone who didn't intend to live here much longer.

"You want a glass of wine?" I ask.

"Of course," Suzanne says.

I GO UPSTAIRS and pour us a glass of chardonnay, the only kind of wine she likes. I think of it as the drink of old ladies. I'm about to go back downstairs, but the sight of my dad and this girl outside together makes me stop and watch. They are both chipping the ice off the front deck in what seems to be a chummy sort of silence. It looks like she's trying to chop down a tree with a butter knife, but she seems to enjoy it. I would—the repetitive choreography, late sun on my back, the lifting of big chunks of ice. It would be satisfying, like peeling paint or sunburned skin, or doing penance.

I put the wine down, get cash from the drawer in the kitchen, and walk to the deck door, sliding it open. "You guys okay?"

"We're doing well, aren't we, Miss Kit?"

My dad heaves his body into his shovel and grunts like he's bench-pressing. He does more in one dig than she does in five.

"I should get going soon," she says.

"Yes, you've got beers to twist open," my dad says.

"No," she says. "Just things to do."

I search my dad's face for disappointment. This is the most active I've seen him in a while. "You go sow your wild oats," he says. "Make a sweater."

"My wild oats have been sown," she says, and looks briefly at me. "I think I'll just go lie down."

"How much do we owe you?" I ask.

"I've got it," my dad says.

He takes his wallet from his back pocket and takes out more than the task warrants.

"It's okay," she says.

"What do you mean, it's okay?" my dad asks. "Are you doing community service or are you making beer money?"

He hands her the money and she takes it.

"Thank you," she says.

They look one another in the eye. I feel for him. He must miss having young company. He and Cully would snowboard together all the time. Cully had gotten him off his skis and onto a board years ago. Sometimes they'd take the shuttle and when they got off, walking with their boards tucked under their arms, beanies pulled down, from a distance, they'd look the same age. They'd look like friends. I wish I could see this again.

"Come back tomorrow," my dad says. "Then I'll really put you to work. Bring better gloves next time. Or hey, I have some for you." He looks at me, excited.

"We have all this stuff if you want it," my dad says. "Do you like rap? Or punk rock? New and old school. We've got tons of records, I mean CDs you can have. We've got gloves, hats—"

"They might be big—" I say, feeling a possessiveness.

"Books," he says. "*You* can have it all." He says this last line like a salesperson, then bats his hand in front of his face, swatting away his own joke.

She looks at me and seems to register something in my expression though I'm trying my best to remain blank.

"I should go," she says. She leans the shovel against the rail—a shoveler who borrowed our shovel. Our street is so quiet I feel as though we're on a stage. A soft spray of snow is beginning to fall.

"Really," my dad says, less enthused this time. "We really do have a lot of things you could use. You're welcome to come in and take a look."

I don't object. Something about her reassures me, an intelligence and sensitivity. My first inclination was to say, "It's mine," followed by the desire to hide, to not let her see who we are, what's happened to us. But my purpose is to clean out. So why not come in and shop his life? It would be nice to have her want something, to put his things to use. I imagine her with one of his books or one of his sweatshirts, something of his going on her adventures.

"You should," I say. "Come in. We're cleaning things out." I don't want to say the things belonged to my son who is dead, not yet. She'd feel like she was in a horror film. "My son has outgrown them," I say instead, and exchange looks with my dad.

"I need to go," she says.

"Snowboards, movies," my dad says. He is let down. "So much. A ski pass. I bet you could sell it. I guess that would be illegal. Clothes, but they're boys' clothes. You don't want boys' clothes."

"Dad," I say. I touch his shoulder. "Next time." We need to let her go now.

"Oh," Kit says. She looks confused, alert. "I thought you were husband and wife."

We both laugh and she looks at us, concerned. My dad revels in her mistake, but I watch her carefully. Something has shifted. She is not at all amused by the innocent mistake. I don't know what I should say or that I need to say anything. I don't think I'm capable of dealing with anyone more unusual than myself.

"Nope," I say. "This is my dad."

"Thank you, though," he says. "You made my day."

She looks like she has more to ask but is holding back.

"It was nice meeting you both," she says, rushing now toward the steps. "Thank you for letting me . . . do this."

"Thanks for your help," I say. "Be careful." I look at the top of the ice-covered stairs that they never got to. The ice has little dips in it like a golf ball.

"Your book," my dad says. She turns and looks at the black book on the railing.

"It's for you," she says. "It's a calendar."

"Okay," my dad says, and we watch her go. She walks fast as if we've said something that has offended her.

"That was different," I say. "You think she's Mormon?"

"Why would you think that?"

"I don't know. Don't they leave Bibles with you or something?"

"It's not a Bible," he says.

She gets into her truck and we watch her drive down the street. My dad waves, but she doesn't wave back.

"That was kind of odd," I say. "Did you guys talk much?"

"Sort of," my dad says.

"What did you talk about?"

He stares out onto the street, arms crossed in front of him, pondering something. My question finally reaches him.

"Uh, let's see," he says. "She loves the mountains. She just graduated from college. East Coast. She's from Bronxville, New York. She isn't ready to go to med school—her dad wants her to. She had a good cadaver physiology program at her high school. What else? Her name isn't short for Katherine. She's named after her grandfather, Christopher Lux. She was ready to go back home. She's lived here since July, but someone who lived here urged her to stay."

"Who?" I ask.

"I don't know."

"What else?"

"Hon, I wasn't taking minutes."

"Actually, it sounds like you were. You covered a lot."

"I like to talk," he says. "These kids all stalling. Figuring out what they want to be. It's nice to hear about their plans, or lack of."

Like Cully. I imagine this girl moving here and remember my longing to leave here, to forage for happiness, change, escape, re- newal, my own ground. At DU, I'd lug around my huge video camera and tripod. They became a shield in some way, a way to overcome shyness, a way to make my curiosity legitimate.

"Oh, and we talked about soups," my dad says. "Hearty soups. And I may have mentioned a few things about the ski business— coping with losses, new initiatives—"

"You must have bored her to death."

"No, I . . . she seemed interested. She held her own." He puts his hands on his hips. "We made a dent out here," he says. "That was good."

"Good," I say. I try to think of more work, more tasks, things to make him feel useful and strong.

My dad takes her calendar from the railing, flips to today's date. Blank.

I WALK BACK downstairs, stopping in the doorway. I wonder if my dad will move into this room, since it's larger than the one he's in, or if it would be too strange. Then again, he lived in the room he shared with my mom. There may be something comforting in the reuse. I walk in and put Suzanne's wine down on the desk.

"Much better," I say, my voice sounding different in the emptier room. "Where are you?" I hold my elbow with one hand, my glass of wine with the other.

She walks out of the closet, holding his newest ski jacket. "I think you should see this." Her voice hesitant, almost fearful.

I feel a swell of adrenaline. "See what?"

"Something of Cully's," she says.

I wait on edge, as if what Suzanne has found may be able to bring him back.

I look at the coat draped on her arm and in her hand, something small and black along with a wad of bills. Money in a coat pocket. I love finding money in a pocket—it's like a gift from yourself.

"Score," I say, and immediately feel guilty about it. Guilt, guilt, guilt. Can't go a day without it. After Cully died I felt guilty for singing in the car. That's when I was still counting. Counting the days since he died. I don't know what's worse—doing that, or having lost track, to have stopped counting, which I have. I've rounded up to months. Three. Guilt came for feeling hungry, for having that sensation. It came from yawning, from putting on makeup, dressing nicely. It came when I felt sexual desire. I remember the first time this happened—some scene in a movie set me off and I nearly wept, feeling so awful that I had a response, that I still felt anything at all. The body just keeps going. It doesn't care what you're up to. I remember how guilty I felt for not buying him the most expensive urn.

"This is a lot of money," Suzanne says. She spreads the money out like a fan.

"He was a valet. He always had a lot of bills everywhere." I keep my distance, looking at it, quickly.

"These are hundreds." She makes eye contact with me, but I can't hold it.

"Okay," I say. I take another sip, then point to the desk. "Your wine's right there."

"These are hundreds," she says again. "There's got to be about three grand here."

"Well, he was working at the hotel since, what, June? June until December, so—"

"So he parked a lot of cars?" she asks. "He was extra cute and polite and got tipped in hundreds? This isn't Vail."

"What are you getting at?" I look at the money in her hand, then away again as if it's something I'm not supposed to see.

"I'm not getting at anything." She waves the money, like a fan. The bills look damp and old. "But you don't think it's weird these are hundred-dollar bills? We tip with ones and fives—well, you do. I tip with a twenty, but—"

"He probably exchanged the ones."

"Why wouldn't he put it in the bank?" She gives me a patronizing look that I can't stand. I hate when her questions aren't really questions but her superior alternatives.

"I don't know!" I say. "What does it matter? Maybe he was going to buy something for himself. A car or a computer."

"Okay, this is a scale," she says, as if saving it if she couldn't get through to me the first time.

She extends the black scale toward me, making me walk up to it. It looks like a calculator. I take it, turn it on, and am tempted to weigh something. "You're like an attorney, springing evidence on me." I look at this object in my hands and give it back to her.

"I'm not trying to do that," she says.

"Then don't!" I turn away because my heart is beating so fast I feel I must look panicked. I walk to the stereo and start to rummage through CDs. My hands shake. Obie Trice, the Roots, NOFX, Rolling Stones. I flip through them all.

"Don't be defensive, Sarah. I'm trying to help. It's okay. I mean, you can put it together, I'm sure. The baggies of pot, now this. He obviously . . . had a second job."

"It can get busy at the Village," I say, still not facing her. "And people used the valets even when they weren't staying there. He did well. He worked hard. He worked all the time."

I turn around, keeping my hands in fists by my side.

"Sweetie, I know. Look, it was probably just pot—at least not the hard stuff."

"You don't know that! You don't know anything!" The room is too small. I have nowhere to go. I walk to the door. I need to leave this room, this friend, this life. I touch my throat.

"I know I don't know the specifics," Suzanne says. "But I mean"—she laughs—"you kind of gotta consider the—"

"You should consider putting a beeping mechanism on your ass in case you back up!"

The CD begins to skip, a sound I can't stand. I go back to the stereo, slam the button to make it stop, then look at Suzanne to see what I've done. Her eyebrows are raised in a way that says she is better than me and she will rise above my comment. She puts the cash on the bed, then raises her hands to indicate she tried, and now she's done. The room has an angry hush, like the silence after a lovers' quarrel.

"Whoops," I say.

"Yeah, whoops," she says. "I don't even know how to respond to that. Oh right, I can't! Because you're in mourning!"

My jaw tightens. I bite the inside of my lower lip and try to summon some control, some eloquence. "You can say whatever you want," I say. "So what if he didn't put his money in a bank. He was doing things his way. I know you didn't approve—you've never approved of him—"

"Stop," Suzanne says. "I loved him. I loved him so much. You know that. We all did."

My composure is a farce and I let it go. "I know." I sit on the bed, my hands shaking. There's too much adrenaline running through me for me to cry.

"Look," she says, "I know this must really suck."

I give a quick laugh of agreement. Her observation was apt. She walks over to me and places her hand on my shoulder. Gives it a quick squeeze. I feel like a kid being forgiven.

"I'm sorry," she says.

I can't believe I just told her to put a beeping mechanism on her ass like she's some kind of dump truck and she's the one saying sorry. I look up at her, the word *Mom* entering my head. She'd scoff if I told her that. Or maybe she wouldn't. Maybe this is something she feels herself. She's been a friend who's lasted through all the trends of friendships. I love her, I need her, and I don't have to tell her this. We don't have heart-to-hearts. In my life I have never had such an easy and unexpected relationship with another woman, not having to pander, not having to dress the part. It can be bliss to be so ugly.

I met Suzanne when Cully was almost two. I knew who she was but didn't think she knew who I was. We were going to the same playground by the rec center, our babies were eight months apart. She knew all the other moms there and seemed like the ringleader of the bunch. I remember always looking at everyone's wedding rings. Just like it is with the opposite sex, I felt immediately attracted to her. That happens sometimes: a recognition, or something about someone's face or mannerisms that make you suspect you'll get along. I could tell she noticed me too on those days at the playground.

"He's so big," she said one day about Cully, and then, "Actually, I don't know. I always say that to everyone."

I laughed. "Breaking-the-ice talk," I said.

"I know!" she said. "I hate it. What are the other mommy pickup lines—let's see. 'Do you like your stroller?' Or 'Is he eating solids?'"

"'I love your burp cloth,'" I said, at ease with my brand of humor.

We made plans for the following afternoon and I went home as if I had been asked out on a date. I told her immediately I was a single mom, something I never told other moms. It was always so awkward, and I didn't want to hear their responses because the responses usually made me think less of them and I didn't want that to happen. I wanted friends. But the single status seemed to cause other moms to back up, then back off. It's like when I was dating and would never consider guys who wore pleated pants or tie-dye. For them, my lack of husband was a deal breaker.

"Single?" Suzanne said when I told her. "Lucky."

I stand up now and drape my arm over her shoulder and turn us to face the window. "Fuck," I sigh.

"You can say that three times," she says. "At least it's pretty out."

Shavings of snow float by and the flakes swirl in currents toward the ground, giving them a mood of anger. I used to fold the laundry in this room, watching Cully play outside. Who would have thought back then that this would happen to that baby? That big baby. It looks so barren here. I see a thin skin of ice hardened over the small, slow-moving stream.

"What now?" I ask. We separate.

"Well, I was going to take you out to dinner," she says. "Now maybe he can take us out."

She gets her wine from the desk. "I guess you need to see the humor in it," she says.

"I don't see it yet," I say. "And I'm an imbecile. I don't deserve dinner."

"You're not an imbecile," she says. "It's not like there were clues screaming at you. It's not like it was something . . . I don't know, that *changed* him."

I trace back, seeing if she's right, if there was something that should have alerted me, but all I can think of is my bad job, my poor parenting. I backed off of him about not doing anything after graduating from college. At first I was a pain, trying to make him feel lazy and ungrateful; I was always recounting things other kids we knew were doing—building irrigation systems in Patagonia, teaching English in China, going to law/med/business school. Then I eased up, remembering all the people who took a pause in life. Billy, for example. His slower evolution, his two-year stint as a ski bum dishwasher.

I eventually warmed to Cully's temporary job, understanding that in order to stay in a resort town, you needed to take what you could get. He found the job that would allow him to stay and I needed to endure his pace. He had time, something I didn't have at his age. Time to want, to explore, time to be curious and to do nothing at all. I never thought Cully cut me off from what I wanted to do, he just redirected me. Reporting on the world's affairs, reporting on day spas: I pretended there was no real difference.

Now I realize how clueless I had been, that I took the wrong approach. I shouldn't have backed down. What mother is content that her son parks cars after graduating with a degree in geology and a minor in environmental science? What does parking cars have to do with these things?

Suzanne clinks my glass. "It's okay," she says. I'm embarrassed that she knows about all of this, about his and my failure. Morgan has always done everything right.

"He was young and free," she says.

"He wasn't though," I say, but I won't go on to defend him. I keep my thoughts to myself, knowing she'll pity me further. I thought that Cully was on the precipice of action. Every morning we'd read the paper together, on the couch, side by side, trading sections. He was always so serious when he read the paper, as if searching it for ideas on what he could do, who he could be. His dark brows would be furrowed, his jaw flexed, and I realize now that I had been given glimpses of him as a man.

"I want to work for the resort," he said one morning while reading the business section. "I'm ready."

"Yeah?" I said, putting down the arts section. "Doing what?"

He hesitated, and I related to the hesitation, reminded of the dread of telling adults what I wanted to do and feeling their slight condescendence.

"Anything at first," he said. "To get my foot in the door. Like Grandpa did."

"Sounds good," I said, trying to measure my next responses. "He started out running the ski school."

Cully laughed. "That would be classic. If I ran a ski school." He went back to the paper, but I could tell he wasn't focusing on it. "My degree helps, like—I think it's something they would want. I mean, it could apply to their business. And Gramps—he's a good reference, obviously."

He had put thought into this. I wanted to hug him but played it cool. He looked over his paper at me and played it cool as well.

That night he spoke to my dad at dinner, and again, I sat back, trying not to ask too much, to encourage or take away. I listened to him creep into the adult world, amused by his passion, which I hadn't seen before.

"The resort needs to be more green," he said. "I feel like they're just catching up. In Aspen they use biodiesel fuel in snowcats, they—"

"So do we," my dad said. "Have for some time—"

"They have efficient snowmaking equipment, low-energy snow guns."

"Move to Aspen then," my dad said. "Go find Hunter Thompson and trip out."

"He's dead," Cully said.

"Well, scratch that," my dad said.

I could tell Cully was going down some kind of checklist in his head and wanted to tell my dad to back off a bit, but maybe this was good, like an initiation.

"No, you're right," my dad said, "even though really the equipment only cuts a few million gallons of water. Say four million off of one hundred and sixty, a public-pleasing policy. Good, but it doesn't have much impact."

"That's what I mean," Cully said, his elbows on the table, his hands alive. "It's just a stamp to put on things. It's easy. But if you do more, it all accumulates and saves the resort money in the long run."

My dad nodded. "I agree. Absolutely. I'll leave it to you."

"Sounds like you're ready to work," I said.

"So, what else do you do all day?" Cully asked. "Or what did you do?"

"We found policy numbers and other things." My dad smiled. Cully was beginning to get impatient. He wanted details. He wanted to be taken seriously.

"Like what other things? Shit, it's like pulling teeth." His fork clanged against the plate, and I thought he was angry, but he said, "Whoops," and laughed.

"I did a lot of damage control," my dad said. "Read the news. Stayed on top of how the public felt about us, then responded. I also wrote propositions. Development ideas. Then I'd sort of try to sell the ideas, these dreams to the public without them thinking they were being sold anything. It's an honor to be here . . . We're doing you a favor by letting you spend money here . . . That's the message. What else, what else . . . "

"Dad, come on," I said, even though we were all having a good time.

"Were you proud of your work?" Cully asked.

My dad considered the question, and instead of giving a jokey answer, he sounded serious when he said, "Oftentimes. Yes. I was."

I had to look down at my lap to not give anything away. All my life he had wavered back and forth between loving and hating his job. Through all the resort's acquisitions and expansions he'd complain about the company clearing more acreage, appalled that the forest service would actually agree there was a need, only to come home from a day of skiing on that same acreage, declaring it beautiful, talking about the land as if he was a pioneer trying to sell off plots, and of course, everything that happened, he had approved it in the end. Only at home could he be the local.

"Great." Cully clapped his hands together. "Then I'm ready to go. Ready to sit around and think up ways to trick people."

"I didn't play tricks," my dad said, tilting his head up and scratching his cheek. He loved being asked questions. "I reinvented dreams, made the ridiculous seem perfectly reasonable."

"Dreams," Cully said. "Ridiculous!"

"I'm just kidding with you, sport," my dad said to him. "I made the resort money. That's what I did. And it was a great job. You feel like you're a part of this place. You're building your home, caring for it." I had never heard him speak this way about his job, and it articulated something for me as well, something that resonated with my own work. "And they need people like you who know it, who'll nurture it. Who will try to be good and try to be honest."

Cully looked down, proud, as if given an honorable task.

"I'll talk to Dickie," my dad said. "See where you'd fit. And then, as I said, I'll leave it to you. You kids up next will be great."

I enjoyed the conversation at the time, but not in the way I do now. I didn't think that it would be something I'd return to. You never know what moments will be significant until after they're gone. I return to this one because Cully was on the brink of something here. He was curious in his grandfather as a man, and he was excited about his own capabilities, his own future. I wonder if my dad thinks about this moment too.

I look at the cash on the bed, and it's as if everything has been negated. He wasn't on the brink of anything. He was selling dope.

"What was he doing?" I ask. "What the hell was he thinking?"

"I don't know," Suzanne says. "He was a kid."

She wouldn't think that if it had been Morgan.

"Thanks for helping with everything," I say. "I guess."

She shrugs. "After my mom died I found four bags of cremated pets in the back of her closet," she says. "You never know what you'll find. I'd rather score weed than dead Pomeranians."

And I love her again.

"I just want to know everything," I say. We walk toward the door.

There really is nothing else to do but know the things we want to know.

. . .

I LOOK OUTSIDE the living room window at my quiet street, the empty second homes. When I'm off Main Street, sometimes I feel like I live in a ghost town, especially with the warmth this year and lack of snow. We live off snow. Our economy could simply melt away, the mountains undress. I look down at the driveway, the thin layer of snow that has begun to settle. What were you doing, son? Was it just a phase? Did I not provide enough, nurture you enough? What was the point of school and college, the point of all those extracurricular activities, the point of playgrounds? Did I give you too much?

"You girls hungry?" my dad asks.

"We're going to go out," I say. "Just real quick."

"Not quick," Suzanne says. "We are heading out on the town. I'll have her back before dawn."

Suzanne takes her sweater off the stool and my dad looks at me and widens his eyes.

"I'll be home in a few hours," I say.

"You up for meeting Mirabelle first?" Suzanne asks. "She might head to Relish."

Mirabelle is a woman who hired a conductor to tutor her four-year-old when he picked up a stick and started waving it around. She and her husband are always offering their various homes to me: Maui, Park City, LA, making me feel like a Make-a-Wish kid. I've never taken them up on it knowing that these people collect people and soon enough I'd be trotted out at dinner parties as their "TV show friend," and then I'd be asked if I could feature a friend's new line of jewelry. I've learned my lesson. Just say no to these kinds of people. Not that I don't get along with many of them and have fun when Suzanne asks me to join them all for drinks, but there's a big difference between me and her other friends. I'm the only one with a job, something they find to be honorable.

We just discovered my son was a drug dealer. We just emptied his room. I don't want to meet Mirabelle and endure her head-to-toe catty scans.

"Come on," Suzanne says, seeing me hesitate. "It will be good to socialize."

"I've been out of the house all day, socializing. Maybe if we could just get a quick drink."

She is looking down at her phone. "Change of plan," she says. "She just texted. Says to stop by the rink. Something I have to see." She looks up. I haven't put on my coat.

"You know?" I say. "I'm kind of beat."

"Please," she says. "It's just the After-School All-Stars thing at the rink. Laurie's chairing and"—she looks in the mirror by the bar and puts on makeup—"we can just drop by."

This is so typical of her, to change plans and assume I'll follow. I'm putting my foot down. Even though my problems have outperformed hers for a while now, I will not go to a sporting event.

"You girls go have fun," my dad says.

"I'm just not feeling up to it right now," I say. I try to make eye contact so he can help me out, but he's looking at Suzanne with an intensity.

"Hey, Suze," he says, "those future plans—your husband's lawyers should probably stop saying there's no link between peak and base expansion. EPA knows otherwise. People will warm up to it anyway. The ones who'll complain will be the same ones who just bought their condos at One Ski Hill."

"I don't talk to Dickie," Suzanne says, finishing her glass. "He left me."

My dad says, "I hope not because of the weight gain? Now, that's not fair."

Oh my God. "Okay," I say. "Let's go." I put on my coat.

Chapter 6

We walk to her car, parked twenty calories up the street.

"Sorry, but will you drive?" She gets into the passenger seat before I can respond. I roll my eyes—my passive response—and get behind the wheel. I don't mind. If anything I'm a good driver. I love to parallel park and I merge and change lanes quickly. If I skid I know to pump lightly on the brakes and turn in the direction in which we slide. Suzanne will slam on the brakes, causing us to spin like Michelle Kwan. When merging she will check the middle mirror, then lean toward the side mirror, then look back over her shoulder, the window of time she could have used to merge usurped by a big rig or a Miata, either of which would make her gasp, overcorrect, and start the process all over again.

She flips down the mirror and puts on more lipstick. She's heavily madeup—her cheeks look like they've both been smacked, and her eyelashes are pointed like exclamation points. She has on her fur coat and stiletto boots that could be used to kill whatever animal her coat's made out of.

I'm instructed to drive to the rink by the Village. I do as I'm told, waiting for Suzanne to tell me what's going on, but she's quiet and on edge for the entire drive, which I assume is due to two back-to-back blows directed at her body mass index.

I pull into the parking lot. "What is this again?" I ask.

"After-School All-Stars," she says. "Raises money for their after school enrichment. Keeps them off drugs. I don't know. I'm sick of kids. We're always doing things for them, and they're fine. Perfectly content with a spoon and a pan. Like MacGyver. Give them a twig, give them a marble, they're all set. That's how Morgan was."

This isn't how I recall Morgan being at all. She had a playroom packed with gorgeous wooden toys, Barbie cars, kitchen sets, doll houses, then later, a playhouse, a playground set, an art room, a trampoline. Give her a twig and a marble and she'd pitch a fit.

I look for a parking spot. "And you want to see this game because . . ."

"I want to support the cause," she says.

"Don't you need a ticket?"

I drive alongside kids walking toward the ice and remember taking Cully to a few hockey games, buying him a huge foam finger and endless cups of hot chocolate.

"I wonder if Dickie's here?" Suzanne asks.

And now it becomes clear. "Please, Suzanne. He's obviously here. And that's why we're here." Why didn't this dawn on me before? I find a parking spot far away from the action, but I can see the rink and well-dressed people pretending to enjoy the game. "What happened?"

"Nothing," she says. "I got that text from Mirabelle. She said he was here and that he looked different. She used an emoticon that winked."

"Well then."

I have a feeling that we're not going to get out of the car for a while. She flips the visor down to look into the mirror again, turning her head to the side, then she snaps it shut.

"Can we move up so we can see?" she asks. She moves in her seat as if propelling the car forward.

I reverse out of the spot.

"I doubt there's parking up there."

"We don't have to park. I just want to see if he's even here. I don't want to get out."

I drive to the front, knowing I can't say anything. I had to come. I had to drive, and now I have to move. I owe her, not just for her help with Cully's room, but also for this period in my life. I've been in the spotlight for too long. Bad things happen to other people too—it's her time to shine.

I stop and turn off the engine and headlights, and hear a voice on the sound system saying, "He got it! Holzman did it again!" The outdoor speakers begin to play something I recognize but can't name. I watch a kid speed down the center of the rink with his stick in the air.

"This is nice," I say. "So the kids playing are the ones who benefit from the program?"

"Yeah," Suzanne says, scanning the people. She is clearly not interested. "It's not a full-length game. Just an example of where the money's going. After this they'll get shuttled to One Ski Hill for dinner."

A group of teenagers come out of the indoor rink, trying to see what's going on. "I feel so old," I say. "Look at these kids. None of them are wearing jackets. It's uncool now," I say, as if I know. "Warmth is uncool."

I think of Cully with his baggy pants and sullen caps. I loved his pants. How slack they were. For some reason they put me at ease. Morgan never felt like a Breckenridge kid. She hated skiing, hated the way goggles made her look. Hated the snow, the layers they demanded. When we all went out together we'd have to walk slowly to restaurants while she teetered on heels.

Suzanne starts to text someone. The kids are doing the same thing. Boys and girls, some with their arms draped over one another, the majority of them talking or texting or just staring at their phones. Do they ever talk person to person, or just when they're apart from one another? I should say to Suzanne, *Go away so I can talk to you.*

A girl with short brown hair, angled asymmetrically with ends like lightning bolts, walks in the other direction, pulling a backpack on what looks like all-terrain wheels. Suzanne lights a joint.

"Oh my God," I say. "Don't do that now." I look out the back window and duck a bit in my seat. "What if we got caught?" I imagine Katie reporting it on the news or the incident being written up in the *Summit Daily* police blotter, next to all the bike thefts.

Suzanne holds it in front of me. I automatically shake my head, but then think *Why not?* and take a prissy little drag, then one that's a bit meatier.

"That a girl," she says.

"Wait," I say. "Is this what I gave you?"

"No, it's my own. This is the good shit."

"Where do you get it anyway?" I ask, and hand it back, look around to make sure no one can see us. This is so bizarre.

"From my yard guy," she says.

"Pablo?"

"No, that's the yard yard guy. Leaf blowing and whatnot. I get this from Brian. He does more yard design. He's really into plants and soil. Like, he talks to the plants and shit."

She extinguishes the joint on the sole of her boot. "That's all. Just a refresher. Why, you want to buy some?"

"No, I don't want to buy any, I was just wondering how one even goes about buying this at our age and you know, with our lifestyle."

"You wouldn't believe how easy it is," she says. "It will be legal here real soon. Mark my words."

I flip my mirror down to make sure I look the same. My eyes seem smaller.

"And what do you mean 'this is the good shit'?" I ask. "What was Cully's?"

"I don't know," she says. "Kind of shwaggy-looking. Not something I'd buy."

"Why not?" I say, feeling absurdly defensive. I crack the window.

"It's green," she says. We look at one another, smiling a little. I feel like a young girl.

"No shit it's green," I say.

"I typically buy purple," she says. "At least lately. It's the strain that's going around. These things come in trends. Just like anything. Fashion, food, even countries to adopt children from . . . Remember when Romania had its heyday? Can you imagine adopting from Romania? You'd get some angry gymnast with fetal alcohol syndrome."

"What are you talking about?" I laugh. "Should we get out, or what?"

"No," Suzanne says. "I guess not. I just wanted . . . I don't know what I wanted. To see him." She looks out into the crowd. "To see him, maybe talk, I—oh, God. Oh my God. There he is. Do you see him? Right there! Oh. My. God."

"Where?" I search the crowd.

"Far right. By that heating lamp." She points and gestures, which isn't helping me.

"There are tons of heating lamps," I say.

"Right below it. Right there. Next to orange guy."

I scan the crowd for orange, seeing people dressed absurdly well to be out here, and then I land on him. He's pretty hard to miss. Dickie's an impeccably handsome man who exudes wealth and thorough showering. Black-silver hair, hard, square jaw, the lines on his forehead strong like cracks in ice. He always looks freshly pressed, smacked, and dry cleaned, and his expression is one of perpetual jocularity. He has his flaws—excessive teeth whitening, low attention span, the scent of a distillery looming about—yet he possesses a quality that makes everything he does seem right. He's kind of like my father, I realize, but effortful.

"He looks good," I say. I miss him. We were unlikely friends. Maybe because I was the only person who didn't want anything from him.

When we met I was working at the *Summit Daily*, where I wrote for the visitor's guide. Over dinner one night Suzanne told him about my old desire to be a reporter and Dickie told me to audition for *Fresh Tracks*, a new show the resort was going to air in the main hotels.

"You'd be perfect," he said. "A local girl giving visitors the inside scoop. I'll set it up. Give it a shot." I was buzzed on the good wine and the new friendship and connections. Suzanne looked across the table at me as though everything was already taken care of. I know he helped get me the job, but both he and Suzanne have never made me feel that way.

"What are you talking about?" Suzanne looks at me with watery, disbelieving eyes. God, I should never smoke pot. I've never been good at it. Some people are pros. The ends of my eyelashes seem to have acquired tiny weights and the word *fingerling* keeps running through my head.

"I'm sorry," I say. "I meant that he doesn't look different to me, like Mirabelle said."

"What?" she says again, and I realize something has happened. She hasn't even registered the comment. Either that or I've said "fingerling" aloud.

"He looks terrible," I say. "Like a potato."

"What do you mean? Look. Look at him." She shoves her hand, palm up, toward the crowd.

I scan for Dickie again, then see what she's shoving me toward. Shit. I see. He has acquired another mark of flair, and she is young and porn-bodied.

"She's . . . she's . . . she's black!" Suzanne says.

I put my hand on my mouth so I can be positive that what I'm thinking doesn't escape.

"What?" Suzanne says.

"I didn't say anything." I prop my leg up onto the seat.

"I'm not racist."

"Okay."

"I don't like poor people, I admit that. But I'm not racist."

I nod my acceptance.

"Where did he even find her?" She leans toward the windshield. It's like we're watching a movie at a drive-in. "I can't believe he's here in front of everyone. The Scovilles are here, Cindy Giacometti, Mirabelle—oh my God she must just be *loving* this. They're all gabbing about it, I'm sure, those sluts. This is unbearable."

For people I don't know well, I still know each one of her friends thoroughly from the soap operas they create, which are later broadcast to me.

"Who cares," I say. "Cindy Giacometti is miserable. You told me her husband says 'Fuckwad' to his reflection every morning. Ceri Scoville looks like that blond muppet from *The Muppet Show*. She's like a cartoon application of herself. Or something. Why do they all get that same fish-mouth face anyway? And Mirabelle? She's the biggest social climber I've ever met. God, someone rich comes to town and she swoops in for the attack!"

"Look at her," Suzanne says. "Look at that . . . that girl. What is she, a masseuse or something?"

I look. The woman—the girl—reaches into her purse. Dickie yells something and she laughs, but not too much, which probably means she's known him for a while. I feel so embarrassed for Suzanne, so sorry.

"He's the one that looks bad," I say. "No one is laughing at—"

"She looks like a TV host," Suzanne says.

I open my mouth, stare straight ahead. *Deal with it,* I tell myself. *Let it roll right over you.* What does that even mean? I watch the woman put on lip gloss. She's wearing knee-high boots with a mangy fur trim. Her breasts look powerful, like little generals. She looks trashy. I run my hand through my hair.

"I can see her lips from here," Suzanne says.

"She just glossed them," I say, feeling defensive of this girl.

"I had my lips done," Suzanne says. Her voice has become calm and spooky.

"I had my eyes done, my breasts. I took Paxil to kill my appetite. I've spent thousands on Pilates. I've taken stripper aerobics, for Christ's sake. Would have done crack whore toning." Her voice

breaks a little. "What was it for? What was the point of all that maintenance if I'm going to be traded in like a . . . like a frickin' leased
Honda?"

I remember when I went with her to Denver for her plastic sur-
gery, how every woman who walked out of the office looked the same
and reminded me of someone I vaguely knew. Do all wealthy men
like that carp with boobs look? Or do these women get together and
tell each other they look good so they can't see straight?

"A lot of clients make the same requests," her doctor said when
I mentioned it. "Pronounced, taut cheekbones, full lips, square jawline, eyes that look awake." I was glad Suzanne was just getting a little lift in the eyes. Her doctor's face was not a good advertisement for
his services. He looked like he was speeding down an eternal luge.

Dickie's girlfriend is thin yet plumped, something I feel can
never be attained again at my age, that thin, toned fullness. "You're
too good for him," I say.

"No, I'm not," Suzanne says. "That's the whole point. The whole
problem. It's so unfair. What happens to us."

Don't include me in this, I want to say. "We should go." I turn the key
so the radio comes on. "Okay? Let's get out of here. Let's just go home."

"Fine," she says. "Forget him, right? Let him have that happy
ending, then trade her in after a year. Or less, I bet! Let's go. Let's get
a drink somewhere. Hit up Cecilia's. Let's party." She punches the air
with her fists. "I don't want to go home yet. My lonely house. It's so
cavernous. I want to drink in a small space."

It's a familiar progression: sadness, anger, sarcasm, need for total
inebriation.

"I have wine," I say, thinking of my dad at home.

"No, I need to go out," she says. "I need action. And music. People! Poor Morgan. What am I going to tell her? I want to call her, but
she'll know something's wrong."

"My dad," I say. "I need to get home. The room, going back to
work—it was a big day."

"Of course," Suzanne says, and her mood shifts. "Big day for Sarah."

"What is that supposed to mean?"

She doesn't answer.

"Suzanne," I say. "Is there something you want to say? First you call me trashy—"

"What? I didn't call you—"

"You said that girl looked like a television host and—"

"I wasn't even thinking about you! I was thinking of those *Extra, E! News*, model girls. My God, don't flatter yourself."

There's a solid, single knock on my window and we both jump.

"Jesus!" Suzanne says.

The pale-faced girl with the all-terrain backpack stands outside. I turn the ignition on to put the window down. A song plays on the stereo—*Doncha wish your girlfriend was hot like me*—and the girl hands me a piece of paper. Her arm is noosed up to her elbow with rope bracelets. I read the flyer. It basically says that Suzanne's SUV is responsible for global warming, wars, and the massacre of thousands. I hand it to Suzanne.

"This car encourages the massacre of thousands?" she says.

"If not millions," the girl says.

A scene flashes in my head: Cully at nine, or somewhere around there. The two of us sitting down to dinner, Cully telling me about the hoses that are jammed down the throats of geese, pumping their stomachs with feed. He had a teacher at the time, Mrs. Lamb, who would fill their minds with her politics. We had to stop going to restaurants that served "that liver thing." Then came the dolphin and tuna problem. We absolutely could not have the stuff in our household even though I loved eating it right from the can. Now I wonder, Why didn't anyone fight for the tuna? Why do we only protect some creatures? Why not eat dolphins?

This young girl is staring at me and I wonder if she has asked me a question. I take in her beak nose and slightly protruding eyeballs and wonder if she'd hand out these flyers if she were any prettier.

That's what happened to Cully, I think. He became cool and stopped fighting. Or he just slipped into the next of many stages.

"Just something to think about," the girl says. "The earth your children will inherit."

"Oh you've got to be kidding me," Suzanne says. "This is just perfect. Listen, hippie—envy always comes to the ball dressed as self-righteousness and high moral standards."

"Did you just make that up?" I whisper.

"No," she says, her mouth unmoving like a ventriloquist's, then louder to the girl, "Do you know how much money I've raised for charities? For people with cancer, for hobos and kids and elephants. I can do more for this world in a day than you can do in a lifetime, so don't lecture me. Go do something with your life besides sticking slogans to your pitiful vehicle, a van, most likely, that probably can't even pass an emissions test. God, I hate when people tell me what to do. Do I ask you to brush your hair?"

"Earth Trust is just asking you to reconsider what you drive," the girl says.

"I won't reconsider," Suzanne says. "I do enough. I give, give, give. I could stab an endangered species if I wanted to. Everyone wants to save the earth at your age. Give it four years. You'll want an Escalade. Then blood diamonds. Then you'll want a coat that's made out of bunnies and eagles or some crap."

I begin to laugh but freeze when Suzanne says, "And her son has died. She has more important things to consider and reconsider, and doesn't need some chick in shit-colored corduroys talking about what our children will inherit. My daughter's inheriting a goddamn Bratz doll!"

The girl, a bit frightened, lowers her eyes, then walks toward a minivan and puts a flyer underneath the wiper.

"Minivans too?" Suzanne says. "No one's safe."

"You shouldn't have said that," I say. I'm gripping the steering wheel.

"Oh, she's fine."

"I meant, you shouldn't have said anything about him. You shouldn't use him to . . . to trump hippies."

I glare at her, hoping I'm communicating my anger because nothing seems to be getting through.

"I didn't mean anything by it," she says. "I'm obviously a little worked up and upset about other things." She gestures to the ice rink. Dickie stands with his arms crossed over his chest, a look of contentment not only on his face but rippling through his body.

"Can we please get out of here?" Suzanne says.

I make one of those juvenile scoffing sounds.

"What?" she says. "Let me have a moment, okay? One moment. Then we can go back to you."

"Oh, please," I say, but don't know how to follow up. I start the car.

"This is hard for me," Suzanne says. "I'm miserable, just so you know, and I need help too. I'm sorry, but I do. I'm going through this all alone. I can't talk to you. I can't talk to my other friends without them telling everyone they know. I can't talk to Morgan and show her how much I need her. I can't interrupt her life with my needs."

She begins to cry and I resent it. She has enviable problems, though I know that's unfair to think. I'm sure there are people out there who'd envy my problems, who'd call them "first world." I find that so hard to believe, but I know it's true.

I drive out of the parking lot, passing the girl, who's still putting flyers under people's windshields, reminding them of yet another thing they're doing wrong. What if I ran her over? What if some neurons snapped in my head and created this urge? Things happen in an instant. In five seconds the life that you know can be over. Five seconds, ten. The same amount of time it takes to shock green beans.

"Maybe we should skip the wine," I say. "Maybe the whole pot and drinking combination doesn't help."

"Don't be so quick to judge," she says.

I turn on the blinker, summoning a calm I hope shames her.

"Okay, that was rude," I say. "I meant it's not helping both of us. I wasn't directing it toward you."

"Your son sold pot, Sarah. And you had no clue. Don't judge me. Just let me mourn too. I know it's just a marriage, but let me."

The words seem rehearsed.

I drive. I grip the steering wheel and I drive. My son sold pot. That can't be the last word. There's more than that. There is supposed to be much, much more than that. When he turns thirty I'll be fifty-one. When he's fifty I'll be seventy-one. I've done the arithmetic, cringing at my age multiplying. Now I cringe at the cringing. How wonderful it would be to reach that age, to see him age with me, back behind yet parallel.

I drive through town as if in a trance, Suzanne crying silently beside me and the stupid stupid song playing, *Doncha wish your girlfriend was raw like me. Doncha.*

Chapter 7

After I drop myself off and Suzanne speeds away wordlessly, I make a meal with things on the verge of ruin. Green onions, sour cream, half a lime, steak. I make tacos without a taco. My father is on the couch watching a young star on television insist that she's just an average person. Why would anyone insist on being that?

I pour myself a glass of wine, then walk over with our dinners. I sit and curl my legs under me, then take a sip of wine and am ashamed by the relief it brings me. I'm a good drinker. I don't get mean or emotional. If I do become weepy it's because a shot of warmth and affection for humanity enters me unbidden. But now I think I could be entering shaky territory. I feel stupid and naive about Cully, and I hate getting into fights with Suzanne.

"I don't feel like eating this anymore," I say. "I want Cocoa Puffs."

"You on drugs?" my dad asks.

"What?" I say. "No."

"I can smell it."

I put my plate down and keep the wine. "I took a hit of pot. I forgot." I roll my head back and forth. "Then I fought with Suzanne. I've had a rough night."

"What did you fight about?" my dad asks.

"Nothing, really. I take up too much space."

"I think it's the other way around. Your weight is probably the same as one of her kneecaps."

"Dad, she's not even that big. We need to stop." As I say this I remember what I was thinking about in the car:

Her overdone foundation makes her look embalmed.

Her sapphire and diamond rings are giving her sausage fingers.

Her fur coat makes her look like she's being attacked by a Kodiak.

"I'm just having fun," he says. "Fat jokes are fun for everyone. Farts too. Always funny. In fact, I think she looks quite good."

"I know," I say. "She does. I should tell her that. I get so angry because she's so self-absorbed, but that's what makes me feel better at the same time. To have a friend who isn't tippy-toeing around me."

"This is good," he says, nodding and chewing. "You always know when to take the meat off the heat. And you know to let it sit. It's a good thing to know."

"You taught me well," I say, then lean over to reach my fork. I stab a piece of steak. "Good," I say.

He looks out toward the deck, pondering something in the distance, then resumes his dinner.

"I hope I did that for you," he says. "Teach you well. Been there for you. It must have been hard without a mother. I've tried . . ."

There are moments when his shoulders sort of sink a bit and I feel guilty for ever raising my voice at him, for being impatient, then further guilt for the guilt itself that stems from knowing a parent is going to die one day (when Cully is fifty-eight, I'll be seventy-nine and my dad will be gone). Guilt and having to remind yourself to wait it out gracefully, to cherish their existence, not everyone has their parents, and so on. Oh life. Oh death. Why haven't we all learned how to deal with it yet? The most basic thing in the world. Got to get life-trained. Death-certified.

"You did just fine," I say. I remember him always checking in with me, to the point where it got tiresome. I was okay, and his attention made me feel bad about this.

My dad looks at my glass of wine. "Got some cork in there."

I drink it.

On television a singer on a stage lit dark blue has his eyes rolled back, his body convulsing.

I get up to pour more wine. "Oh my God," I say.

"What's wrong, sport?"

"Nothing," I say. "Just got a little off balance." I hold the wine bottle upside down over my glass and give it a shake.

"Maybe ease up a little," he says.

I think of his past purchases: mops that can clean hard-to-reach places, a robotic vacuum, a fork/spoon/knife (all in one), an ab roller, ab stretcher, ab vibrator, knives that can cut through walls, all those books.

"You ease up," I say, "on buying crap."

I go back and sit down aggressively, making his plate bounce.

"Some things are clever," he says. "They'd be good gifts. Better than some of the things you put on your show. It's a sham you have to pay to be featured. Other places could use more help, seeing they're being charged up the ass for property tax—you know that it's more per square inch on Main than a shop on Fifth Avenue in New York City? I should go in and—"

"Dad, shut up about all that already. You don't work there anymore! No one cares!"

I don't dare look at him. Why is it that when a child feels sad or ashamed, they're mean to their parents? Do we do it from age two to their deaths? My tear ducts get to work. They never fail to work after I've been cruel to him.

The couch shifts as he gets up. I was perfectly situated and now it's ruined. I adapt and move to the right, sighing extra audibly. I hear him walk down the stairs to his room.

I get up and busy myself by sorting through the mail on the counter. Cully keeps getting random things—offers for free oil changes, catalogs from Motor Trend, requests from Easter Seals, and I never get around to making any of it stop. Maybe I won't. I remember we'd still get mom's catalogs in the mail, flyers and things that are easier to keep getting than to make them stop coming. I think we both liked it anyway. My hands are shaking as I pick up the mail, pretending to be busy, but just thinking of my dad alone in his little room, so much like Cully's room with its lack of expression. I give in, walk down.

He must think about my mom at times like these. He never shares his experience with death to help me, and I guess I'm grateful. He must know the need to feel alone and slighted, like no one has ever felt the same way before. I remember not running to my dad when my mom died. I was home from kindergarten. I heard him talking on the phone in the kitchen and knew what was happening, knew what he was being told. He called to me. I told him I was busy. I was watching an animated Japanese film. I continued to watch it. I remember refusing to stop. The memory I have of how I felt at the time is stilted, and maybe this isn't a memory but the way I actually felt at the time—the emotions pounded out flatly and loudly as if on a drum:

The movie was scary.

I had to watch it.

I had to be brave.

Everything was going to be different in good ways and bad.

My mom isn't sick anymore. She isn't alive.

She won't be there to read to me as I eat my cereal in the morning.

She won't drive me to ballet and give me the thumbs-up from the bench.

She won't kiss the top of my head and tell me that I smell so good or that I need a bath.

I won't have to mind her. I can be loud and careless.

The movie is scary; it's making me cry, the movie.

The cancer is dead, but it died with her, like a friend.

This was the thought that finally made me sob like the child

I was, and the sobs turned into wails at the sight of my dad, head down, coming to tell me what I already knew.

I STAND IN front of my dad's closed door and feel like an apology is due but am not sure whom the apology should be from. We all have so many problems. Sometimes you just have to fend for yourself.

"Dad?" I say before opening the door.

"Come in, champ."

His back is toward me. He adjusts a painting on the wall near his bed.

"I heard you stomping down the steps," he says. "You don't have to warn me. I'm not masturbating or anything."

I scan his room and it reminds me of Cully's. There's more me in here than him. "Putting up your pictures?"

"May as well."

The paintings used to hang in his office, images of the Old West and the old town. I feel that he too is a framed sepia photograph, something from old Breckenridge that the company put up because he looked good in their corner. A local kid with deep roots, rising up from ski patrol to VP of operations. I had no right to belittle him that way. The picture is an oil painting of an Indian crouched on his galloping horse, arrow poised to slay a boxy buffalo. Its title: *Circle of Life*. I laugh.

"What?" he says.

"That painting." I point to the shaggy buffalo sniffing the prairie land, the skinny Indian, ass in the air like a jockey at Churchill Downs. "It's a riot."

"You're a riot," he says.

"I was thinking," I say. I walk into the room and place my hand on the wall. "We could knock this down and connect to the other room. It could be a great space. It could be like a condo down here."

He looks at the wall separating his room from Cully's and squints. He's never been one for remodeling; everything is fine as it is, or can be.

"I see," he says. "That would really transform things."

I nod, eager, ready to pick up a club and start whaling. Then, once again, I feel guilty. Am I too eager to demolish and eradicate? No, I tell myself. You're adapting, you're surviving. Something like that. You're trying to get to that elusive other side.

He stands with his hands on his hips, maybe imagining the transformation. "I think it's a good idea. Whether I stay or go, it's a good idea, a good change. Here. I have something for you."

He walks to his shelf, then hands me a knife. It has a black rubber handle that's comfortable to hold. On the handle is a switch.

"Turn it on," he says.

I do as I'm told and a light turns red. "I've seen the infomercial for this," I say, remembering the man having a terrible time spreading peanut butter onto a slice of bread. He would slab it on with an ordinary knife, but the knife would stick and tear the bread apart. He made subsequent attempts, each time failing, while a sympathetic voice-over narrated his aggravation. His kids, grumpy and ugly, stood there waiting for him, exchanging bratty glances.

"It's got a special warming agent," my dad says. "It will soften your peanut butter so it can glide on easily. I thought you could use it since you make me all those sandwiches. I know it's a pain in the ass."

He sits down on the bed. The last shot in the infomercial shows the father using the new knife to slice into a stick of hard butter. He does so easily, then spreads it on the bread without ripping it apart. His children are proud, and when he drops them off at school with their sack lunches, mothers look at him lustily. "Thanks," I say.

He shrugs.

Next to his bed on the wall-sized storage shelf I see more boxes, most with pictures of the box's contents. There's an air ionizer, a five-speed back massager that looks like a small intestine, a Robotic Floor Vac with remote and wall mount, Christmas ornaments that change color at your touch, an embroidery machine. Next to the embroidery machine is an old pillowcase that I assume my father has tried, and failed, to embroider. He almost completed a letter: an S, perhaps, but gave up. The design looks shaky and manic, an art project by a person in some kind of recovery program. All the objects. It crosses my mind that I will inherit them one day. One of the saddest parts about a parent's death must be feeling burdened by a lot of things they left behind. The thought makes me want to get rid of all my bad underwear.

He follows my gaze, looks back at the shelf. "Yeah, yeah," he says. "I know."

"No, it's okay. We all need different things." I try to look at him like the children whose father finally made them a sandwich.

"I'm going to go try this out," I say, but I don't leave. I lean against the door frame, feeling the weight of fatigue. I'm down here to show that I'm sorry, but I also need him. This knowledge I have of Cully won't make sense until I share it with him. I hesitate, but then think that whenever my kids confided in me, I felt soothed and proud, necessary. "Dad?"

"Yeah, sport." He starts to unbutton his shirt.

"Cully was a drug dealer."

"Oh?" he says, his hands pausing on a button.

"Pot. He sold pot."

My dad nods and squints as if trying to make a decision.

"I didn't know this," I say. "And maybe there's more I don't know. Maybe he was out of control. I failed. I failed to keep him safe. I think that's what people think. Maybe everyone thought he was a bad kid and I didn't know this." I am gripping the knife; the red button comes on and I press it off.

"I'm so embarrassed," I say. "I just feel stupid." I want to slump down to the floor, but I hold myself up. I wait for his judgment.

My dad stays on his bed with his shirt partly undone. His torso is concave, the hair on his chest a gray black.

"Well," he says.

I wonder if he's just as ashamed and disappointed. He must be.

"It's too late." He scratches his jaw. "Nothing you can do about it now."

I look up at the painting over him, then back down. He's still pensive, trying to figure this out. I am rooting for him to solve it.

"Torture yourself if you want," he says. "But know that even if he were alive, even if he was doing something completely different, you'd still have those thoughts. I'd think all the time how I was messing you up. No mother, no siblings, and I didn't invest all my money in the resort like some of my friends. Then I'd see other families—they'd do everything right, and you know what? Most of their kids were still idiots. Cully loved you and he felt loved by you. He made both good and bad decisions. He was a happy boy. That's all. Besides."

He gets up and walks to his closet to hang up his shirt, turning his back to me. Sometimes I think he cries when I'm not looking. I've always imagined him doing it while hanging up his clothes or putting things away. It would be too indulgent to cry without accomplishing anything else.

"Besides what?" I ask.

"Besides, you don't know what you've done. He didn't have the chance to become himself, or to become a man. We're very different from the people we were in our twenties. At that age I was a very different person. So were you."

I think of that self, on the verge of becoming another self. Then having Cully at twenty-one, right when I wanted nothing to do with motherhood. It was a beautiful mistake. Would his mistakes have one day been beautiful?

"We've got a lot of lives in this lifetime," he says, and I'm almost certain he's thinking about his life with and without my mom.

His back is still to me and I know he'd be more comfortable if I left. That's the whole deal with being a parent—you have to give them an answer and you can't let them know you need them right back. You can't let them know you're in pain and that you work so hard so that everything will be okay without you. My mom never let me see her fear. She must have been so afraid to let us go.

"Remember your hair?" he asks. He glances back.

"What about it?" I ask.

"Your hair," he says, letting his hands hover over his head. Then he turns to me with a face that's recollecting something, pulling from the trenches of memory. "The way you wore it. In college."

I shake my head and grin with one side of my mouth, recalling my hair I'd insist on blowing out, then curling. It was an aggressive bounty of bleached blond tight curls and stiff bangs. I wanted to look like Tina Kilpatrick on the Denver news and unfortunately, I did.

The week before Cully died he had cut his hair, and it made him look so grown up and handsome.

I'm about to say good night, but then I notice Kit's black book on his shelf. "You're keeping the calendar?"

He looks at the shelf. "I wanted to look through all of it," he says. "Before I see her tomorrow."

He looks like he's questioning something in his head. "It's an odd thing to leave," he says.

"Ask her about it," I say.

"You think she'll really come back?" he asks.

"Why wouldn't she?"

He looks up at me and then the confused expression leaves his face.

"What?" I say.

"There was something she said. We were talking about things— her dad, nature, you know."

I pretend to know.

"I asked how her dad felt about her living here after college. She said something about him telling her that people in ski towns were prone to STDs. Wasn't the outdoor type. She said she loved Indian Princesses, but while the other dads would be pointing out edible plants and berries, hers would be telling her that people like Ralph Waldo Emerson were fiscally retarded and there was nothing remarkable about men who got their jollies from drinking water out of a hoofprint."

"Wow," I say. "Sounds like you guys had a lot to talk about."

"It's just funny because Cully once said the same thing—about Emerson, about the hoofprint. Isn't that strange?"

"Maybe it's from a movie," I say, but something in me flutters.

"Maybe," he says.

"Anyway," he says, "I'm off. Off to bed. Good huddle."

"Good night," I say. "Love you."

"Love you more," he says.

Chapter 8

I should have listened to Holly. Work was an incredible disaster. I had to interview a "terrain park specialist" named Bone, who, while in school with Cully, was known for taping pictures of gay pornography to the backs of tourists. After that we went on to visit B Beauty, where we had to test out and comment on the clever names of the lipstick colors—Shop Teal You Drop! *Ha ha!* I tried to do my job, make people want things they don't need, little luxuries that will break and peel by the time they return to sea level. They will want lipsticks they already own. They will want a lipstick holder and other lipstick accessories, something I didn't even know existed.

"Sarah, maybe more enthusiasm?" Holly said to me and pantomimed enthusiasm, which made her look like a crazed downhill ski racer. I rolled the lipsticks up and down, thinking that if this were a movie I wouldn't be here. I'd be at home, perhaps. There'd be a shot of me looking at a picture of my son, a slow song in the background doing the work for me. Maybe I'd be gearing up to take his ashes to some exotic place he always wanted to see.

A book would jump ahead and then meander its way back to one of the many beginnings. Cully as a child. Me giving birth. In print my thoughts would be beautiful, understandable, and fluid. There would be themes. It would be deep. I would not be so acerbic. I'd be a sympathetic character—warm and lovable, fragile. Neither the movie mother nor the book mother would clock in.

I park in the lot above Empire Burgers, wanting to take a little stroll before seeing Billy. I called him as soon as I woke up, not really knowing why. Maybe it's the same urgency that normal parents feel when they find their child has done something either good or bad. They want to confer and share so they don't experience it alone.

I walk down the steps to the sidewalk, past the boys eating burgers and drinking beer, aware that everyone loves to people-watch and right now I'm people. I watch them back, narrowing in on a tribe of kids in bright, toxic outerwear. I remember Cully called these neon kids with their skinny jeans "skittles."

I ate here once with him. He met me after a shoot. We noticed a lot of old people, then found out it was Senior Discount Tuesday. That's all I remember. And that it was a really good burger. Cully had such a hearty appetite. Maybe he was stoned.

I'm patient with the tourist family in front of me and don't bother to pass them. I look at their asses, all identically large and undefined like cumulus clouds. The father is studying the town map, holding his hands out wide, walking slowly.

"I'm telling you," his young son says, looking at his phone. "We went too far. We passed it. Dad. Dad. Dad."

"We passed it!" the daughter says. I'd say she's around six. "I want to go home!"

You are meant to be lost, I want to tell them. The walkways are designed to confuse; there are inlets and levels so you're always wanting to see what's up, down, through, or around the bend. There are alleys, some which connect, some which end in parking lots—all so that you feel like frontiersmen, like you've discovered something off the trail, off the map. Tourists will spend more this way. I know the backstories, the histories, the plan of this place. I imagine the settlers and the whores, the pastureland, the miners and dredgers, the few wives and women, the Ute Indians, my ancestors and Cully, all in perfect, silent geological layers.

The family stops in the middle of the sidewalk to gather around the phone. The little girl sees me and flutters her eyelashes and raises her hands above her head in a ballet first position. I don't smile. I will leave it to other people to tell her she's cute. My son was a shwaggy pot dealer and I'm off to tell his father.

At the crosswalk I go around the family. I pass Shirt and Ernie's, almost to my destination, when I see the owner of the shop, Lorraine Bartlett, making a beeline toward me. I pretend I haven't seen her and try to find my phone in my purse so I can do the Hi-I'm-on-the-phone walk-by, but she gets to me before I can get to it.

"Sarah!"

"Lorraine!" I say. "Hi there."

She approaches with that dreaded look of reverence.

"How are you?" she says, her voice syrupy. She looks around like we're on a stealth mission.

"I'm okay," I say. "You?" I take a step back.

"Hanging in there," she says. "Well, more than hanging. I'm doing well, actually. Pete got into law school. Danny found a new pet project—the garage, so we'll see how that . . ." And so on. One question launches a thousand ships.

I cross my arms over my chest and grin. I look around, as if for help. I feel like a trapped bird.

She too had a son who was killed in an avalanche years ago. Cully was in eighth grade when it happened and her son was a senior in high school. His body was never found. Lorraine came over a few days after Cully died and tried to recruit me into grieving the way she had grieved, which was by wearing pins stamped with her son's face and giving interviews to the local newspapers advertising her club, PAAD, Parents Against Avalanche Disaster, as if by not joining PAAD you were promoting avalanche disaster. While I seek common experience, at the same time I hate it, how it weakens my own pain, which I cherish. I cringed as Lorraine stood at my front door and said, "We need to stick together." She kept walking, into my house, into the kitchen, lured by the glint of picture frames perched upon the shelf behind the wet bar.

"Please help yourself," I said, before realizing it was the pictures serving as the magnetic field, and not the booze. I was disappointed, because for a moment I was thinking drinking might get us through. We could do shots, cry, laugh, in that order. I reluctantly went over to the bar, looked at the pictures, at Cully's lovely eyes. I touched the photographs, pressed my finger upon him. I said something—I forget what exactly, something false and poetic like, "Sometimes, I feel like he's just in the other room." I regretted it immediately, feeling the flashlight of the heartache police chastising me for doing heartbreak all wrong. I started to hate Lorraine Bartlett for making me feel I had to somehow prove my sorrow.

"Our boys," Lorraine said, looking at me, with a scary intensity. I forced myself not to look away, to furrow my brow and look at Lorraine's small, milky-blue eyes, her stub nose. None of her features really went together. It was like she was designed by committee.

"They loved the same things." She laughed quickly. "They probably would have wanted to go this way. Doing what they loved."

I didn't look away. I stared into Lorraine Bartlett's eyes as if they were an oncoming truck. *Come on, freak show*, I thought. *You gotta swerve after a comment like that*, but she didn't. *Doing what they loved?*

Cully was at A-Basin, off the trails, with friends from work. It's a place he'd go to all the time. Avalanches happen, yet he had the beacons, he had the poles, he had the experience and an ego that was intact. He was a mountain kid. He had outrun avalanches before. Lorraine's son didn't know shit about the back country. He took Basic Skills in fifth grade, which taught kids like him how to throw a ball. The point is, they were not alike.

I saw my son dead. The medic told me not to look just yet, to wait until they got him down, but I felt I owed it to him. It was the very least I could do—look at him.

It was like seeing an ancient artifact. He looked bloated, unnatural, some kind of special effect. The worst thing was that he looked afraid, and I couldn't see how this expression could ever be thawed. This was the last feeling he had in the world, and to this day I imagine him as eternally terrified. He was not happy or thrilled. He was most definitely not doing what he loved, and I should have said to her, *Look, loony. Imagine me strangling you with a Ski Breck! T-shirt, something you sell, something you apparently love. "Boy, she sure loved T-shirts. She would have wanted to die this way!" I mean, the fact that someone loves chicken doesn't mean they want to choke to death on a bucket of wings.* But I wouldn't have said that then. I wasn't angry then. I wouldn't say it now because I don't really feel that way—my thoughts just rumble and churn.

I remember that day Lorraine had looked as if she knew an important secret that I would soon learn. I couldn't escape her awful gaze because she was holding my hand between her own as if warming a waffle. I caught sight of the pin she was wearing advertising the death of Jackson, and couldn't imagine doing that with the image of Cully—wearing him as an accessory as if his twenty-two years of life had become no more than a cufflink. Jackson would have been a twenty-six-year-old, not a high school boy, and I imagined he'd be embarrassed by this pin if he were alive.

I thought to myself while looking at Lorraine, *You grieve horribly. I am a classier griever than you,* and then, *Cully, I wish you were here to see this,* a thought that still crosses my mind daily. I'm so used to storing things to tell him at the end of the day, collecting anecdotes to hand over. I was thrilled when I had something out of the ordinary. He was my sounding board. He was my sound.

"I just wanted to say how proud I am of you," Lorraine says to me now. She still has that look, I realize, as if she knows something that I'll soon enjoy—like a surprise party. Tourists flow by and I feel like we're a boulder in a stream. I wish I had a witness. I keep looking around for someone to side with me.

"I'm proud of you too," I say, lightly.

"Your show," she insists. "I saw you guys shooting this morning. I think it's wonderful that you're back at work. I know it really helped me. It takes a lot of courage, a lot of strength."

Is she complimenting me or herself? I hate the unearned kudos. People get shot in the head and are called brave when they recover. People lose a son in an avalanche and they're suddenly admirable. I've done nothing. I have no courage. Courage is only possible when you choose to do something. I didn't choose to lose him. And I'm working because I have a mortgage and pride and a father who eats out too much and shops from the couch. I'm here because I need to try to reassemble, to cross the bridge, outwit the trolls. God, Cully loved that book—*The Three Billy Goats Gruff.*

"Do you want to grab some coffee?" she asks. "Now? Or whenever. I know it takes a while to fully heal, not that you ever do, but I'd love to tell you more about PAAD. I'm still very involved, and I think you'd get so much from it. And with your access to TV we could—"

With death, if anything, comes freedom. I grab her shoulder and say, "Oh my God. I think I'm going to have diarrhea."

"Oh, God," she says. "You better . . . the bathroom in the visitor center is the closest. I have a Pepto if you need—"

"I'm fine," I say. "I gotta go!" And I run-walk back to my car.

"Yes, go!" she calls, rooting for me to not shit my pants.

It's not until I'm in the car that I realize: her son is dead and I just lied to her. I ran from her. And she needlessly admitted to having Pepto.

"Why?" I say out loud. I still don't know how to grieve correctly. I don't think I'll ever know how to express sorrow, or to show people that beneath all this is someone kind. I'm mistaking the good people for trolls—they are not who or what I have to conquer. I flip down the shade to check myself in the mirror.

"You again," I say to my reflection. I look like someone superior, inferior, repulsed, misled.

I can't take myself anywhere.

. . .

I PULL INTO the parking lot behind Eric's and see Billy parked, strad-
dling a chopper, which amuses me. He looks like a teenager. I pull up
beside him. He looks at me, then away, then back again, recognizing
me this time. His cheeks move toward his eyes. He takes off his helmet. I wish I looked a little better. I feel self-conscious all of a sudden
and about as sexy as a pioneer woman. I check my face in the mirror.
I suck in my stomach.

I get out of the car, then walk to his side.

"Hey, babe," he says.

I don't protest "babe."

"Interesting way to arrive," I say. I look at him carefully and see
Cully everywhere. The long legs, soft brown hair, the earlobes and
stance. Large mouth, sharp ridge of nose, lean, friendly muscles.
Those same dazzling blue eyes, that easy air and confidence that's
both alluring and intimidating. Billy's eyes twinkle. It's true—that's
what they're doing, what Cully's eyes used to do too.

He gives me a hug and I remember how much I loved being
hugged when he had on his hard leather jacket, the pockets pressing
into my ribs, belt buckle into my stomach. He's wearing what looks
like that same belt. I'd sit on his lap and he'd absentmindedly tap my
leg with the long end he always left wagging. It's as though he hasn't
changed clothes since I was twenty-one.

"How's Durango?" I ask.

"The same, but different," he says.

"Sophie?" I hope my voice sounds normal. I always ask about his
fourteen-year-old daughter but never really want to hear about her. I
don't even think of her as Cully's stepsister. I know Cully forgot most
of the time too. He never wrote her name on forms when asked if he
had a sibling.

"She's good," he says. "Going through this grumpy stage
though . . ." I can see him stop himself from saying more. I don't ask

about his ex-wife, Rachel. Even though marriage didn't work out for him, I was always jealous of the way there was no consequence for having a baby with me. He continued on his way, whereas my life was rerouted entirely.

"She's with her mom in San Diego, visiting Rachel's parents."

"Is that yours?" I ask, looking at the bike.

"No," he says. "I'm delivering it to some computer geek in Beaver Creek. He doesn't even care about me riding it in winter. Idiot, but it works out that you wanted to see me."

I walk over to the chopper. "It's not winter. Tomorrow's spring. This is really nice." I run my hand along the seat.

"Thanks. I finally got him to scratch his ideas, then made him believe my ideas were his all along. I can't see him riding this thing though. He's more of a . . . scooter type."

We stare at his work, heads down, as if in prayer.

Billy, like so many kids, came here after graduation to live and ski for the season. He stayed for almost two seasons, working as a dishwasher at Steak and Rib. I met him the summer after my junior year in college at a dive bar called Fajitas, which has since been replaced. He was nothing like the preppy boys I had dated. He was quietly wild and in no rush. He wanted to design motorcycles, something I thought quaint. At the end of the summer I was ready to go back to school for my senior year. We broke up as we knew we would. It took me until January to figure out I was pregnant. Five months along. I remember being in my dorm, hand on the telephone, in disbelief that I would forever be linked to this summer fling. Time and distance had made him embarrassing.

I imagined going to live with him in some small town we could afford, saying things like, "Bring them groceries inside," our kid begging to go to outlet malls and wearing his or her pants up to his or her navel. Billy would come home from the bike shop smelling like gasoline and I'd smell like mayonnaise-based salads. I'd later find I had him all wrong.

When I reached him he had moved back home to Durango. He said he was working with his father, who owned an automotive group that operated franchises for about fifteen auto and motorcycle companies. Car salesmen, I had thought.

I told him the news.

"That's unfortunate" was his first reaction.

"I don't expect anything from you," I said. "I just wanted to let you know. I'm going to keep it." I remember sitting on the bed in my apartment on campus, talking quietly so my roommate wouldn't hear. She and some other girls were laughing outside the door, getting ready to go out.

"I can do it on my own," I told Billy.

"I'll help you," he said.

In my head, I dismissed him. I told him I would be in touch. I just thought he should know.

The next day, he tracked down my father at his house, stood in the doorway, looked him in the eye, and told him he was the man who got his daughter pregnant.

"I'm Lyle," my dad had said. "And I didn't realize my daughter was pregnant."

"Fuck," Billy said. "That's unfortunate." My dad invited him in. They had a few beers and my dad made pulled pork sandwiches. They've been talking to each other ever since.

"You okay?" Billy asks me now.

"Of course not," I say.

"Want to get a bite?" He tilts his chin toward the shops at Riverwalk.

"A small one," I say.

AT THE CROWN, I sit at a front table, next to a couple playing chess. Billy orders the coffees. He's flirting with the barista, I think. He makes chopping motions with his hands trying to describe something. She looks nervous, like she's expecting a punch line she won't understand.

I decide I don't want a coffee. I've noticed that being depressed is like being pregnant. I have weird cravings and food aversions. I walk up to the counter and tell Billy that I've changed my mind.

"Could I get a cocoa instead, please?" I say to the girl. Her name tag says "Tammy, Michigan" and she's chewing gum with such vigor it looks like she's munching on cartilage.

"A cocoa?" she asks. "Like, a hot chocolate?" She has an earring in her eyebrow. I almost say, *Whoops. You've got an earring in your eyebrow.*

"Yes," I say. "Like a hot chocolate." Billy must have rolled his eyes or something because Tammy smiles, then turns to get my drink, making a show out of having to pour out the coffee.

"Wait!" I say. She stops pouring and looks back over her shoulder.

"I'll take it if you're just going to throw it out."

"Like, to buy?" Now she chews with her front teeth like she's nibbling an ear of corn.

"No, but if you're going to throw it out anyway—what's the difference?"

"I have to throw it out."

"That doesn't make any sense."

She winces her understanding. I notice her thin, muscular legs and her ass—it's so round, a perfect cap to those legs, like a cherry at the top of a sundae. Cully would have loved to have sex with this girl. I don't know why this thought doesn't make me uncomfortable, but I want it all of a sudden—for him to have lots of sex with Tammy from Michigan and with other girls like Tammy and I feel so bad that he can't, that he can't feel desire ever again or do these things other boys get to do.

Billy leaves a twenty on the counter. "I'm going to sit down," he says.

Tammy begins to talk to another employee, a boy with orange hair. They're laughing about something and I'm a bit pissed off that they're alive.

"Is the machine broken?" I ask.

"No," she says, and goes back to the machine. She holds the cup under the spout and presses the button. "Oh," she says. "Maybe it is broken. Oh my God," she says, making it sound like one word: *ahmagah.* "You're not doing a Fresh Visit, are you?"

"No," I say, surprised she knows who I am, considering she's given me such attitude. I hate being recognized and bothered, yet am somewhat insulted when it doesn't happen. It's rare that someone like her would recognize me though, since our show is mainly watched by people in the hotels. Though I suppose kids like her watch the show to see the places they know, or more realistically, to make fun of it.

"I'm just here as a regular person, though I could make a recommendation," I say.

"That would be so funny if we were on *Fresh Tracks*," she says to the boy.

"So rad," he replies.

Yes, the second reason, to make fun of it.

"Where's your name tag?" I ask the boy, attempting to ease up.

"What?" he says, and presses his chin to his chest.

"Like Tammy's."

"Oh," she says. "This is, like, vintage. It's ironic."

Tammy, or whatever her real name is, opens the lid of the machine and peers in, then reads the directions on the side of the device. She takes out a tub of powder. "I'm not sure how this works," she says.

"Just give me a cup of hot water," I say. She hesitates, then fills a cup with hot water. "Now put some of that powder into the water. Here. I'll do it." She gives me the cup; I put a scoop of powder into the water and feel absurdly satisfied.

I walk back to the small round table, take off my coat, and settle myself like a bird.

"Life is so difficult!" I say. I'm sweating.

Billy looks at my chest and I wait for him to look me in the eye.

"You look different," he says.

"For God's sake, I know what you're referring to. I'm wearing a push-up bra."

"You look amazing."

I scratch my neck. I don't know what to say to that. "I hate that word," I say. "Amazing."

"So how's the show?" he asks.

"Okay," I say. "Fine. My first week back." For the first time I understand that this is truly an accomplishment. I sip my hot water with powder, knowing Billy's trying to figure out why he's here. Without Cully we really have no reason to see each other again. The thought of this makes me sad: another person lost.

"Yesterday was my first day on camera," I say. "Earlier in the week, we just did some preinterviews."

"Good for you," he says. "For working."

"There's nothing good about it. It's my show and I need to work, obviously."

"Yeah, but you could take more time, right?"

"I don't know," I say. "Maybe. Sometimes I think I made a wrong choice. I hate being back already, everyone saying, 'I'm so sorry about your son!' like they're talking about a robbery or a . . . I don't know."

He nods slowly, repetitively, with a slight smile, something he always does during conversations. "I know," he says.

"I keep getting distracted."

I remember Katie laughing at the name of my lipstick when I presented it to the camera. "Love it," she sang. "I'm definitely going to get that one. You hear that? I'm giving it lip service! And guess what I . . . "

I watched her mouth open and shut, a tiny ball of spit shooting to the side like a spark. I looked at her lip liner and the line of her actual lip, the pink space between the lines like a whole other lip. I stared at this extra lip, zoned out.

"Sarah, you need to respond," Holly said.

I came back from wherever I had been. "I can't."

"What do you mean you can't?" Holly said.

"I wasn't listening, so I don't know what to say."

Mike looked amused.

"I'm not going to tell you how to respond," Holly said. "This is what I was trying to talk about with you earlier. If you don't want to be here, then go. I know this must seem trivial to you, but this is what you signed up for."

"Sorry," I said. "I really am." I didn't remember ever signing up for any of this.

"At least pretend you're here," she said.

I was a little thrilled and in awe of Holly's frank anger. Katie lowered her voice. "You're doing great. We'll edit this into a masterpiece. Say one of your town facts. I'll edit it all later. It will be perfect. Or not. Who cares?"

I listened to Katie and spoke: "Back when Breckenridge was evolving into a town," I said, "a man named Father Dryer set up a parish to stop all the drinking and partying. Every morning he'd ring his church bells, waking up all the hungover residents. He wouldn't stop even though everyone complained. One day some of the towns-people used dynamite mining caps to blow up his church steeple."

When I looked around, everyone in the room—Mike, Katie, Lisa, the lipstick lady—actually seemed interested, waiting for more.

"No more bell," I said.

Then Holly looked like she was going to go postal.

"Yeah," I say to Billy. "I'm not doing too well at work."

"What else is going on?" Billy asks.

I lower my eyes, shy to need him. We're sitting too close to one another, and these tables are so small, I can see the pores on his nose, the hairs in the middle of his eyebrows that need to be, but will never be, plucked. He holds his hands together and taps his pointer finger against a knuckle. Maybe I just needed to see him, to see a version of my son. I needed to see someone who knew me when I wasn't the person I am now.

I stall by taking a bite of his muffin and commenting on how good it is. "Yum," I say, my purpose under my tongue like a wad of gum. "What is that? Blueberry? Very good. Hydrated. With a nice crunch at the top."

"Hydrated?" he asks.

"I hate the word *moist*," I say.

He looks at his watch. I look at his wrist, the broken pinky finger, the scar on the middle knuckle. He and Cully have had so many injuries. It's funny how similar they are even though Cully never grew up with him.

When Cully was born, Billy would try to come to town as much as possible, but the five-hour drive and his work schedule made it difficult. What I had thought of as a car lot was actually a flourishing family company that Billy was helping run. Motorcycle design was a side passion, also something that ran in his family, and which in the end became lucrative for him. His grandfather was a designer and engineer for Ducati and in the fifties his father had worked with Fabio Taglioni in developing Ducati's desmodromic valve system, a fact I committed to memory because it impressed guys. Dickie practically had a stroke when I told him. It took me a long time to adjust to this image of Billy as a businessman, a boss, running a thriving company. Was this the same guy who fashioned a bong out of a pint of Häagen-Dazs?

When Cully was older, he'd go and stay with his dad sometimes, but when Billy married Rachel, the visits dwindled. When Sophie came along, visits were practically nonexistent. But it worked. We all got along, we all kept in touch. When anger strikes, I tend to really run with it, but it never struck. Not for me, not for Cully. We knew Billy was always available. It just happened that we ended up not needing him to be. But maybe I was wrong.

"I have his cell phone," I say, and watch Billy's expression, but it doesn't change. He looks relaxed, like he's getting a foot massage. He looks at the couple near us. "I used to love playing chess," he says.

"He called you a lot," I say.

He nods and thinks about this. "Well, yeah. He'd call every now and then. Check in."

"That's nice," I say. "I never knew that when he was alive." I've known about the calls since I found his phone but have never really thought about them until yesterday, after finding the pot. Now for some reason I feel cheated on.

"Was he okay? I mean, did he need help or—"

"He was fine. We talked. Is that all right?" His smile twitches.

"Of course. It's fine. It's great."

"Is that what this is about?" he asks.

"No." I sigh. "It's everything. I was just surprised, that's all. I'm cleaning out his room, that's why I wanted to talk to you. I thought if there was anything you wanted . . . you can look through it. I found marijuana in his drawer," I blurt. I'll test the waters.

"And you thought I'd want it?" He laughs.

"No, I'm just telling you I found some, with the seeds picked out. He put them on an ashtray. I would have been angry, but instead I was just impressed that he picked out the seeds. Because it affects your sperm count, right?"

"Yeah," Billy says. "But he probably picked 'em out because they taste like ass, not because he cared about his virility."

"Oh," I say.

"He sold pot," I say. "He did that too. He sold it."

He looks up, then nods as he looks away.

"Did you know that?"

"Of course I didn't know that," he says.

"How do you feel about it?" I feel like a shrink.

He takes a sip of his coffee, and I can see the irritation in his eyes. "I guess I'm disappointed, but what? What can you do? I don't think it's something that would have lasted. I don't know. What can I say?"

"I don't know," I say. "I didn't mean to spring it on you like that. I just . . . wanted to tell you. Just to say it out loud."

"I bet," he says. "That's crazy. That's too bad."

He leans back into his chair, though he doesn't look relaxed. "How do you know?" he asks.

"A scale," I say. "It was in his closet, plus baggies of pot and money. Lots of money." Billy flashes a quick smile, reminding me of the feeling I'd have when Cully was little and he'd do something I had to scold him for even though I found it to be funny.

"You must be finding all sorts of things," he says. His eyes move to the back of the shop, then back to me.

"Not too much, really," I say. "Boys. I mean if it were someone like Morgan, then I'd—"

I can't believe I just said that. I traded in Suzanne's daughter. I hypothesized her death.

"How is that Morgan?" he asks.

I take a sip of cocoa to avoid answering.

"Is she all set for this weekend?" he asks. "So, it's a memorial service? Or—"

I almost choke on my sip. I swallow and my tongue feels raw. "How do you know about that?"

"I'm his father," Billy says. "Don't you think I'd be included?"

"Yes, yes, of course," I say. "It's just that it's Morgan's thing, so I didn't know how you'd even hear about it. It's not like it's a real service or anything. It's a party or—I don't know what it is. When I ask Suzanne she gets irritated because I don't think she knows either. Sounds a bit silly."

"Is it because she organized it and not you?"

"No!"

"It was good of her to include me," he says.

I feel like he's implying that I didn't include him in mine—in its organization—and I look down.

I distanced Cully from Billy, for so many reasons that varied over the years. Inconvenience: the five-hour drive, longer in winter. Pride: I could do it on my own. He got in the way of our routines. Protection: I envisioned a bachelor pad filled with chicks and beer.

And then later, fear. I feared that Cully would want to live with him, his cool dad with his cars and motorcycles, bigger house, stable relationship with the stay-at-home wife.

"When did she even invite you?" I ask.

"At the service," he says.

"At the service? His service that I had four days after he died?"

The couple next to us looks at us and grins, as if we're all in on something fun together.

"Honestly, I didn't know what to say," Billy says. "She said she was planning her own service at CC, something more celebratory, and she'd be honored to have me there."

"That is so annoying." My leg is jiggling like Katie's.

"Why?" he smiles, knowing why.

"Why?" I ask. "Because she was thinking of this way back then. Because—"

Billy holds up his hands. "No, I know. I feel the same way. She's a bit much."

"And you're going to go?" I lean back, showing my ease, but I don't last long. I sit up and cross my arms, my fingers digging into my skin.

"It would be rude not to," he says. "Maybe we can drive together."

I shake my head. "That girl."

"She's sweet though," he says. "Her speech was nice. Sad."

At the small service in our back yard she spoke, so poised and articulate, even through tears. No one could bear it, seeing this girl, this childhood friend, holding forth, choking on her grief, yet delivering it without backing down.

"Cully was like my brother. He was everything to me," she said to all of us around her—my dad, me, Dickie and Suzanne, Billy, some of Cully's friends from high school, Billy's parents, and Billy's daughter, whom I swear I saw texting. At the moment, I was so relieved Sophie looked nothing like Billy and nothing like Cully.

"You are everything to me," Morgan said, looking up. Her voice was loud, trembling, but commanding. "You are supposed to be by my side and I will go through the rest of my life imagining you there. You will be there."

I walked to her, embraced her, and didn't let go.

It was touching; it made me lose myself, shake with sadness and relief. I appreciated the speech, until she said a similar thing that night at Suzanne's house to friends who came over to comfort her. I don't dare look at his Facebook page, which she manages.

"Well, then," I say. "So, we'll go together."

I want to call Suzanne, ask why she didn't tell me. I want to tell her how I feel, but what would I say? Your daughter's too inclusive? Your daughter is bathing in the glow of tragedy? Your daughter needs to grieve differently? Your daughter is faking it? Because I know none of this is true.

"That's all I really wanted to talk about," I say. "I'm glad that you guys spoke to each other so often. I am." I just wish I'd known.

Our hands on the table almost meet in the middle.

"I'm glad too," Billy says, his eyes watery. He sniffs and clears his throat.

"If you want any equipment or gear of his, let me know," I say. "Or a keepsake."

"It would be nice to have something of his," Billy says. "I'd like that. Maybe one of his snowboarding medals or . . . I don't know. The watch I gave him. A book he liked. Maybe that one about animals in space."

"You know about that book?"

"I gave it to him," he says. "When he was around ten, remember?"

"You did? God, he was obsessed with that book for a while there." I picture him on his bed, reading the book, how the house would be silent and I'd run around looking for him, thinking he was getting into trouble, and there he'd be, immersed. "All those Russian test monkeys," I say.

"The dog, Laika."

"The dog," I say. "I think Cully was upset by it sometimes."

"Probably, but some animals came home intact."

I take my purse off the chair and put my coat back on, but Billy makes no move to go.

"Maybe that's why he was so into it," he says. "To see who'd make it home. I'd like to have that book."

"Okay," I say.

Billy swishes coffee in his mouth. I hear "Daniel" by Elton John on the speakers; the woman next to me takes her turn and the man laughs and bounces his leg.

"And a jacket maybe," Billy says.

"A jacket?"

"Yeah, something of his I can use. I'll take something like that."

"I'll put some jackets aside," I say, knowing the blue one I was saving would be perfect.

"Thanks again for meeting me," I say. "It's hard to talk to people. It's hard to be with people. They really bother me now. People at work, friends, Miss Irony over there."

"I don't like people either," he says.

"You are people," I say in a way I hope conveys my appreciation of this. He shrugs and we sit in silence for a while, finishing our warm things. I always want warm things in the morning—eggs, coffee, oatmeal. Cully liked cold food, huge bowls of cereal.

"I should go," I say. "Lots to do. I guess we'll be in touch about tomorrow."

"Do you want any more of my moist muffin?" he asks.

"Eew, stop it," I say.

He finishes the rest of his coffee as though it's a shot of whiskey, then shuffles the crumbs of his muffin into a napkin. "Why don't I just come by in the morning?"

"Okay," I say. "That will work." He stands and helps me up. Cully had the same height, but it wasn't just his height that made him seem immense. Like Billy, everything was so large—his legs and chest, his arms. On the couch I'd look at our legs side by side, amazed that he was ever my baby.

"Look at you!" I'd say, and punch his hamstring. "How did this happen?"

Billy and I walk toward the door and I'm oddly proud to be walking with a man. I haven't been on a date in years. The town's too small, a little pool to choose from, and no one stays around long enough. The last date I went on was two years ago with Case Delaporte, a timid, nerdy kind of man who wore loafers and khaki pleated pants, those deal-breaking pants that I overlooked. He was like a banana plant in an evergreen forest, but I gave him a chance because he was employed, intelligent, and didn't talk incessantly about snow conditions.

His mother had just passed away at ninety-nine and I'd try so hard not to cringe at his overuse of the word *grieve*. It was like *nipple*, or *vagina*. *Grieve. I'm grieving.* Gave me the creeps. After a few dates I considered slipping my hand in his pants, accosting him, testing to see if he was really grieving or just using the word like some guys use roofies. But my mind projected: he was probably a horrible kisser. He most likely had a small penis, and I'd have to fake my enthusiasm for it, encouraging the thing like it was a clumsy Little Leaguer. There'd be slipping, losing, and searching, and how do you give a hand job to a baby carrot? Over.

Jeff was prior to him. We were together for a while. A cocky, athletic sort who had nothing on his bookshelf but *Men's Health* magazines. He was a resort exec who would always be on the phone and saying, "We'll talk. We'll see," while making a face at me indicating that they would not talk and they would not see. *Try harder*, I'd tell myself. *Give in.* I would get myself to think about Boo Boo magic. When Cully was little and got hurt, I'd rub Boo Boo magic onto his trouble spot. It was really just sunscreen, but he was lulled by it. Maybe a relationship with the Golden Boy could work this way. It would be Boo Boo magic on the wound. It wouldn't really work, but it would work anyway. But I couldn't get over our differences. He had a big truck that was hard to get into. He'd say "T Day" instead of "Thanks-giving." He never spoke of marriage. I've given up on that anyway.

I don't even know how I'll date again. Or have sex. I can't imag-ine showing anyone my body. I can't even imagine someone wanting it after knowing my loss. Death and dating don't mix, and I can't imagine explaining it to someone new, watching them go through apologies and condolences while I wave them away like a plate of bad hors d'oeuvres. Like crudités.

I look back at the girl known as Tammy, imagining her legs clasped tightly around Cully, her long hair against his bare chest, his face tense with expectation.

"You seeing anyone?" I ask.

Billy opens the door for me. "Nope. You?"

I laugh as my answer. We walk down the steps to Main Street and stroll toward the lot. I shield my eyes from the sun, then feel guilty about it, like I should be grateful for the sun, for all this beauty, for being alive.

We walk behind some slow movers.

"Crowded," Billy says. "Good, I guess."

He looks at the shops we pass, maybe feeling the same way I did earlier—like a visitor in a place you once knew well. It manages to change without you noticing—like not seeing your child age until you look at pictures.

"All these shops blend in with each other," he says. "They're like the same place over and over again."

"I know," I say, as we pass a T-shirt shop, a souvenir shop, a gal-lery, repeat.

We walk by a group of young guys coming out of Motherloaded. One pats his stomach.

"That hit the spot," he says. "That was so insane last night."

Billy and I look at one another and smile to ourselves, maybe to the guys too, as if telling them, *We used to be like you.* We all repeat ourselves. They won't know this for about a decade.

"That was crazy," Billy says, imitating that cool kid drawl. "That was insane."

The boys saunter down the street in front of us, one of them shouting out a "Wad up!" to friends across the street. With these transients there's an entitled sense of ownership, of community, and yet I like them, these temporary residents. I appreciate their sense of adventure, their willingness to be behind and a bit ridiculous. I wonder if Kit came to the house yet.

We cut through the alley to get to the lot. We slow our pace. "Always good seeing you," Billy says.

"You too," I say, trying to be light and peppy.

He grins. He has a nice set of teeth. He looks like one of those Brad Pitt types, pretty yet masculine, the kind that married women have affairs with because their husbands don't know romance from a bag of chicken feed. I look at his legs in his jeans.

"All right, then," he says, opening his arms. I walk into them. Tears well up but don't fall. They always come now when someone embraces me, my body's own grateful reaction.

He moves his hand to my lower back.

"What are you doing?" I push him away. "What the hell is wrong with you?" My chest moves up and down. "God, Billy."

"What?" He smiles. "It's not like I grabbed your ass or anything. You were the one getting all snuggly."

"I was not getting all snuggly," I say. "I was just—I don't know. I was just hugging you goodbye. Fuck." It felt good. I'm angry that it felt so good.

He ruffles my hair and I cringe. "I'll see you soon," he says. "Unless . . . should I not go? I don't need to go."

My breathing slows. "I'm a little messed up," I say. "I don't care if you go or not."

He puts his hand on my shoulder. "I know. I'm not . . . in your life or anything, but I'll always be here for you, okay? I can be."

For some reason all I can think at this moment is, *What is my purpose? What is my connection to the world now that Cully's gone?*

"Is that the same belt you've always had?" I ask.

He looks down. "No." He laughs. "Or, I don't know. Maybe."

He bangs his helmet against his leg and I finally ask him the question that's been in the back of my mind since talking to my dad last night:

"Did Cully ever mention a girlfriend?"

He looks hesitant, like he's unsure if what he knows will hurt me.

"He didn't mention anyone to you?" he asks.

"No," I say.

"He did tell me about a girl. Not from here. I don't know how serious it was."

"Must have been a little serious if he talked about her with you." I try not to look or sound upset. "What was her name?"

He scrunches his nose.

"It wasn't Kit or anything like that, was it?" I hold my breath.

"No," he says, unsure. "No, but something short like that. I think it started with an *L*."

I feel both a relief and a disappointment. I don't even know why it crossed my mind. Maybe just the way she seemed to know us, the way I seemed to know her. I liked her, and maybe that's it—as with Tammy, I'm trying to set Cully up.

"I'll see you tomorrow."

"And I am looking forward to it," he says.

He puts his helmet on, then fastens the straps. He gets on the bike, starts it up; the chopper's engine roars. I get into the car and watch him getting ready to leave, an inexplicable yearning for him to stay and come home with me, to eat at the table, to fix a broken appliance, I don't know. Then I call out, "Billy!" He doesn't hear. He drives away. *May as well stay the night*, I was going to yell. *We have a guest room now.*

Chapter 9

When I get home I am shaky from the day. I walk toward the kitchen, then two steps away, decide to rest. I put my purse on the table, leave my coat on and my shoes, then press my back against the wall and sink to the floor.

My dad finds me this way, legs in front of me, shoulders slumped. I'm like a cavewoman meditating.

"Sport," he says, and makes to sit next to me, but I say, "I'm fine, I'm fine," not wanting to feel more than I do. I think of the last time he found me on the floor; I was sobbing like a jilted girl at the prom. Ugly, desperate, aching tears. It was after Lorraine came to visit.

He sat down beside me, held me, then brought me onto his lap and rocked me like a baby. I don't recall his ever holding me like that before, and affection was something I had never really needed from him, but at that moment, I relented. I let him hold me. I let myself quake. After I settled down, I got off his lap, knowing this sort of comfort and release would never again be repeated unless one of us got shot and lay dying. Even then.

"When you got hurt," my dad said then, "as a kid, you used to run at me like a bull runs at a matador. I'd brace myself when I'd see you coming. You'd throw yourself at me and wail. I'd sit down with you on my lap. You'd cry, but then you'd get occupied with the hair on my arm. You'd start pulling on it and you'd forget what hurt. But I guess you reach a point where you can't sit on your parent's lap anymore."

He stands over me now. I want to pull his arm hair. "Tough day?" he asks.

"I'm okay," I say. "Just resting."

"Work okay?" He holds out his hand and I let him pull me up.

"No," I say. "That's the problem. I'm not good at it anymore and I'm making people feel bad. I'm not being a nice person. And I hate it here." I look around at my house, finding faults everywhere. The glass windows need to be cleaned. The fabric on the dining room chairs is faded. The hardwood floors need to be resealed. The dryer takes forever.

"You'll get there," he says, in a way that doesn't sound very convincing. He helps me out of my coat and hangs it up for me.

"I can't get there. I said on camera that one of the lipsticks looks like a dog penis. I want to get there, believe me," I say.

"Then do a good job," he says. "Maybe skip all the dick talk."

"Thanks, Dad. Good point."

I go to make myself a drink. I decide on an old-fashioned without the bitters and the other stuff. I guess that would just make it bourbon. I add the other stuff because it seems classier, something someone who is "getting there" would have.

"I'll have what you're having," my dad says, infuriating me that I've completed my task and now we'll get to the final destination at the same time. It's like zipping your car madly through the lanes only to have the slow idiot pull up alongside you at the light.

"Make one yourself," I say, then add, "Sorry, I got it."

I repeat the process and make the drink, then bring it to him nicely and lovingly. He stands at the far side of the kitchen island and seems to be contemplating the swirls in the granite. I place his drink down in front of him and clink his glass.

"So you saw Billy today?" he says.

"How did you know?"

"He called me. Told me he's coming to the Springs with us. I told him to come sleep here, but I guess he has a place in Beaver Creek for the night."

"How nice. He talks to you, talked to Cully. I didn't know you were all so bonded. I don't know anything."

"There's no secret," my dad says. "You know we still talk. You say it like it's a bad thing."

"It's not a bad thing, I don't know." I take a sip and sit on the barstool. "I really don't care. I just feel like I'm discovering a whole bunch of new things, that's all."

"Me too," he says.

"I bought Morgan a dress today," I say. "At Valleygirl. Hopefully she'll like the label. Want to see it?"

"No thanks," he says.

It's fitted, green, and reminded me a bit of the dress she wore when she took Cully to her junior prom when he was a senior. She was so proud by his side. Cully was a good sport, enduring the photos without looking like he was enduring something.

My dad stares at something, his eyes not focused, then he takes a sip and cringes.

"Dad? What's up?"

"Nothing, sport," he says in a way that reminds me of the way I spoke to Cully when I wanted to appear upbeat, not involve him in adult problems.

I take a sip of my drink and ask, "How was your day?" with an ice cube in my mouth.

"Complex," he says. He leans against the counter as if recovering from a run.

"What happened?" I crunch the ice.

"I'm not sure yet," he says, and finally looks at me.

"What is it?" I ask. "You're scaring me."

"I don't know yet," he says. "I'm still thinking about it."

"Thinking about what?"

He looks out toward the living room window and I follow his gaze. "Dad?" I say. "What are you thinking about?"

"Motives, life, days, months, people," he says. "The people who come into our lives. The little interruptions."

"What are you talking about?" I keep my hand around the glass. "You're being weird."

He gets something out of the grocery bag he uses as his purse and slides it toward me. It's the calendar.

I place my hand on top of it. "Did she come today?"

"No," he says.

"Wasn't she supposed to?"

"She didn't," he says.

"Maybe she forgot because it's on her calendar," I say. "Or maybe she only shovels when it doesn't snow."

My dad isn't amused, which worries me.

"I looked at it last night," he says. "Looked at it carefully."

"Yeah?" I say, making my voice even. "And what did you see?"

"Take a look." He nods his head toward it.

I open it up, not understanding what this calendar will explain. I swallow, flip the pages, scan the boxed days marked with different colored pens. It's not even a new calendar. It's like leaving someone with marked-up Post-its.

"Look at it," he says.

"I am." I turn to July, but it's blank. I turn to past months. I see "Hunting" on the twenty-first of April and I read some of the scribbles: *Ghost Town* playing at Ollie's at ten, 1/8 Ang, 1/8 Cecilia. 12–4, 6–close. 422-1313. Durango on the fifth. Springs on March 23, which is odd because that's tomorrow, the day we go to the Springs. I look up.

"She's going to the Springs tomorrow?"

"Keep looking," my dad says.

It's not until I land on May 18 that my father's message reaches me. MOM B-DAY, it says. May 18 is my birthday and now, finally, I recognize that this is Cully's handwriting. I take my hand away from the calendar as if it has just burned me.

"I don't understand."

I pick it up this time, hold it closer, flip through the pages, not really seeing anything. My mind flips too, not able to land, focus, retain, piece together.

"I don't understand," I say again. I never even knew Cully had one of these. I look for something, something to hold on to, like a rock climber searching for a foothold. What is "Hunting"? Hunting for what? I cannot imagine Cully hunting. I can only imagine him making fun of hunters or letting the animals come to him.

"What is happening?" I ask.

"She must have known him," my dad says.

"No shit, but what is this? Why did she leave this? Why did she go about it this way? Who is she?"

How do I not know this girl? How do I not know about this book he relied on to organize his days? I remember Cully's T-shirt that smelled of strawberries. Is Kit the girl on his shirt? I want to ground him. I want to lock him in his room. No, I want to look up at his face and shield my eyes from the sun.

"Maybe she was his girlfriend," my dad says.

"No," I say. "I've never seen her before." I realize this doesn't preclude her from being his girlfriend. It's just something to add to the list of things I didn't know.

"Or a friend," he says. "Obviously someone close enough to have something of his."

"Why didn't she just give this to us in the first place? Why the hell did she come over and do manual labor?"

"I don't know. Maybe she was afraid—"

"Afraid of what?" I yell, answering myself.

"Beats me," my dad says. "It's a conundrum."

"I feel violated!"

"That's pushing it," my dad says.

"It's not pushing it," I say. I go to the other side of the island, needing something to do. I turn on the water faucet—no reason—then turn it off. "She was snooping on us. She was lurking—I knew something was funny."

"Lurking with a day planner behind her back. Where is Neighborhood Watch—"

"You're upset by this too. Don't pretend you're above it. Life, people, the interruptions." I try to imitate his enigmatic speech.

"I'm not pretending," he says. "But I'm not upset. I'm contemplative. I'm . . . at a loss."

"I'm at a loss." I look around the living room as if something might present itself to me. "And I'm upset."

"Yes, that seems to be your thing lately."

"It's not my thing! Here. Hand me that." He slides the calendar across the island to me, but I don't open it.

"Maybe we should pretend we didn't discover anything," he says. "We could keep giving her chores."

I drum my fingers against it. "She's not coming back, I bet. She just left this, caused a stir, then off she goes. That hoodlum." I open to the first page.

"Okay," my dad says, "easy now." He picks at his lower lip. "Well, I'm off to bed."

I look up. "You're just going to go to bed after all this?"

"No use dwelling on it when nothing can be done this second."

"But you're just going to go to bed? It's—" I look at my watch because I have no idea what time it is. "It's seven."

He finishes his drink, then slides the glass toward me, expertly. I catch it.

"I'm going to go down to my bed to think about all of this," he says, walking toward the stairs. "Probably retrace the conversation I had with her. Then I'm going to read, maybe watch TV, do my night beauty regimen, then fall asleep. Is that okay?"

I try to think of something to keep him in the room. "You haven't eaten anything."

"I went to Fattie's with some of the guys. Then to Rasta Pasta. I had a craving."

He stops at the top of the stairs.

"You need to stop going out for dinner all the time. It adds up." I don't mean this. I love when he goes out and socializes.

"When you're my age you'll understand," he says. "I'm closer to death. I can spend money on Rastafarian penne. Now good night." He walks down the steps.

"Why can't you retrace your conversation with me?" I say.

"Because you're not a nice person," he yells.

"Good night then," I yell back.

"Love you!"

"Love you more," I mumble, knowing the reason he's disappearing. He doesn't like when he doesn't have the answers. He doesn't want his child to see him at a loss.

I GET READY to look at the book, holding off until I have everything I need. I get into my pajamas and my warm bedroom slippers. I make dinner—pasta and broccoli with shaved parmesan and a little olive oil and lemon. Not very rasta, but good. I drink some wine while I cook, a New Zealand sauvignon blanc, then I bring my dinner and wine back to the dining table. I put on music—Van Morrison—then wonder if that's too gloomy or if it carries too much heft. I let it play and decide the music is hopeful.

I sit down. I have a bite of dinner. I have a sip of wine. Then I open the calendar to the first page. No handwriting, just small blocks of the twelve months to come. The next page, a list of holidays. The next page, blank lines for contacts. And then, evidence of life.

January fourth, "Costco." Cully would go with my dad to Costco in Gypsum. They loved this excursion, though they pretended it was such a hassle. I smile to myself, imagining them pushing the cart, elbowing strangers for samples. They liked to brag they had a free lunch but would come back with so much stuff. They both loved to shop.

I keep browsing the calendar and now understand the need for it. His work schedule wasn't uniform. There was no consistency from one week to the next, and this book allowed him to lay it all out. I trace over his handwriting with my finger. I take my time with each page, even though it is essentially dull reading. "6–close," "12–4." Nothing to glean here. Nothing that stirs me or gives me insight into the boy I love. And yet I'm comforted. I like the feeling of going through something of his and feeling unremarkable. I am steady. All our birthdays are on his schedule, my father's and Billy's, which touches me.

I go to his last month, December. December 30.

He wrote "Basin" on the day he died. Basin. So casual. Just head to A-Basin, then head home. When you go out to have fun, you are supposed to come home. He didn't write "Die." That wasn't on his schedule.

There were two search-and-rescue Labradors, with little, sponge-like noses. I came to the pass that afternoon and there they were, the dogs, so happy, their triangular faces darting up and down one another's legs; their entire bodies wagging.

I was tricked by their happiness. I had already been told Cully had died, but when I saw the dogs, I felt such relief, like someone had moved a gun away from my temple. It lasted a second, this feeling; I was put back into place by absorbing the expressions of those near, by letting my knowledge surface—the dogs were being rewarded for finding what they had been trained to find. There were no voices on the radios, no buzz of snowmobiles; the rescue helicopter had stopped typing overhead. Everything was quiet, and the quiet had to be the loudest thing I had ever heard.

"Where are the others?" I had asked Paul, one of the men on the rescue team. We were standing near the road in about a foot of snow. "Denver?"

"No, Summit Medical Center," he said.

"Alive?" I asked.

"Yes," he said. His look seemed to ask, *Is that a problem?* "Minor injuries, so no need to transfer."

"Why?" I asked. I remember feeling like this was all something I could work out.

He bent his knees a bit to come down to my level. "Why?"

"What made them live?" I asked. "What made their injuries minor versus lethal?"

I scanned the mountains—the black craggy scars down the white face. They loomed over us.

"The snow they were under was light, fluffy. Your son was under about three feet of wet, heavy snow. It's like concrete. Ma'am," he added.

"But why?" I asked again. I thought I was being clear and strong. He must have thought I was out of my mind. I was insanely practical, a bit combative, trying to solve a meaningless mystery. "Why was his snow heavy and theirs light?" I persisted. Paul looked like he was testing out an answer in his head. I moved on. "What are the others in the hospital for?" I asked.

"Max has a broken rib cage and hypothermia," he said. "Cory, Ryland, Travis, and Ethan are all being observed and checked out, but they appear to be fine."

I may have scoffed. I hope I didn't.

Max, Cory, Ryland, Travis, and Ethan. *Where are they now?* I wonder. *Where have they gone?* They were boys I didn't know—two from Rochester, one from Laguna Beach, one from Denver, and one from somewhere that I can't remember or never knew. Cully's seasonal friends.

What went through his head before the lights went off, before his heart stopped pumping? Did he know that was it? That his life was going to end? Did he think about me or his grandfather, or Billy? Did he cry? Or did he think about something nice, resolved to depart peacefully. How did he say goodbye?

Maybe in the snow he closed his eyes and traced back through time, flipping imaginary pages. Maybe he didn't think at all, just fought for air, for his life, or maybe he just thought, No. Not like this. Maybe that's all he had time for, or it could have been even more succinct.

Maybe he just thought, Fu—

And then it was over.

Maybe he thought about her, Kit.

I turn the page.

After my birthday in May there is nothing.

I put the book down. It's a calendar, I know, but it feels like a book to me. I finish my wine and my dinner. I feel cheated that after all this ceremony nothing has changed.

I get up and test out the knife my dad gave to me while drinking more wine and glancing at the closed calendar. After cleaning the kitchen, I walk up the steps to my bedroom, feeling as if I've just run a long race. Here I go up the stairs and tomorrow I'll continue. I'll try again.

It's there at the midpoint of the stairs where a blaze of light comes through the front window, giving me a scare—how bright it makes the darkness, as if someone is searching for me. Search and Rescue. Flight for Life. They've come for me. I duck—an automatic reaction—and then I hear a crash.

Part
Two

I open the front door; the air is cutting. I will always love the mountains for this: the initial step outdoors, the decisive air, the bruised blue of night and swarm of stars, the chomp of snow, and the silence, all of it enlivening and heartbreaking. A chunk of snow drops off the branch of the spruce tree and onto the hood of the angry-looking truck. Motes sparkle in the air. I don't know how it is that I'm registering the air, the night, when here she is, Kit, this burden, this mystery. Maybe this is how it will be from now on? Nothing can be shocking. Nothing could be harder.

The snow has stopped falling but has accumulated on the driveway. She turns off the headlights. If she weren't a girl, I'd be frightened. I probably still should be, but I'm not. I've seen her use a shovel.

She has barely missed crashing into our mailbox, but she's tipped over the trash can—it looks like she's hit a black bear. I imagine my private life strewn all over the place: Breyer's Mint Chip, wine bottles, asparagus stems. Cully would have done something like this for kicks. Maybe he would have had a life full of stunts and scars. Or maybe he'd be an engineer. Maybe Kit could tell me.

The motion sensor above the entrance steps finally senses me and shines a path of light down the driveway. She opens the door to her truck, but it hits the mailbox, so she moves to the other side. Once there she hesitates, like she's deciding whether or not to go through with getting out, but looks up and sees me.

I walk down the steps in my nightgown and look at my pink bedroom slippers. Air runs through the feathers that sprout from the toes, making them stir wildly. I think of a bird doing a mating dance. I walk and affect sobriety until it becomes true: I am sober and highly capable and we are going to get down to business.

I walk down the snowy driveway, trying not to slip. "What are you doing?" I call out when I'm nearer to her.

She gets out of the truck and walks toward me, then slips and lands on her butt, making no effort to get up. She looks like she wants to stay there and sink into the ground. I stand before her.

She looks up at me, then down at my slippers. "Flamingos?"

"What? No." I am both surprised and at ease with the rhythm of this interaction. It's like I'm with someone I know well enough to argue with. "Are you okay? What is wrong with you?"

"I'm totally fine," she says.

"No, you're not," I say. She reminds me of myself earlier on the ground.

"Are you talking physically or . . . other?" She tries to get up.

"All of it. You just crashed into my garbage can. You're not even flustered." I extend my hand. We take each other's wrists—it feels like a secret handshake—and I pull her to standing. We are face to face, so close I can smell her hair, also beer and a smell that reminds me of a dive bar's sticky floor. She's not the girl on his shirt. Or at least not tonight. I take a step back.

"I had an accident," she says, and this sounds as if she just peed her pants. "I don't know what happened. The roads are super slick."

"Oh, please." I want to be angrier than I am, but her oddness and brazenness are appealing. I feel that we've bypassed politeness, gotten a lot out of the way.

"How many bottle caps did you twist open tonight?"

She looks at her callus as if it will provide the answer.

"It's freezing," I say. "It is so cold." I take a few steps and look up at the bright stars, which always seem to be more vivid and closer the colder it is. "Well?" I look back at her. "Come inside. What the hell are you doing? What is your deal? I read the calendar, you know."

"Yeah," she says, as if expecting as much. She sighs in preparation, steps up to me. I walk her toward my house, my hand on her back for a second, guiding her. By her walk I can tell that she's been drinking a lot more than I have. I want to tell her she's lucky that I'm such a mess, physically and other. Most people would demand more. They would call the cops. We reach the top of the stone steps and I open the front door. She drags her shoes on the outdoor mat and overdoes it, stalling, as if by crossing the threshold she's locked into something, which I suppose she is.

I flip on the third light by the door, which is the softest of the three, lighting up the edge of the living room.

"Come on in," I say. "Kit, the American girl who lies and drinks too much."

She walks in, looks around. I look at the back of her, hair stuffed into a black beanie, fitted jeans, a trim figure.

"Did you come to shovel?" I ask.

She doesn't answer. She looks like she's being scolded.

"I don't lie," she says.

I smile, shake my head. "I'll get you some water." I walk past her to the kitchen. "Or do you need coffee? Something to eat?"

"Maybe," she says. "Probably should."

I take in the sight of her in my home. A shiver moves through her face.

"Why don't you wash up a little?" I say.

"Probably should," she says.

I feel like I could tell her to drop and give me twenty and she'd do it. I point her to the bathroom and feel a sense of satisfaction from taking care of someone.

SHE COMES OUT of the small bathroom off the kitchen. We both look at each other, then look away.

I think about what I can say, what I can ask, but my thoughts get all jumbled. They stumble around like idiots.

"Beautiful home," she says.

She looks around and I become conscious of it, noticing things I normally wouldn't—furniture (heavy, brawny), lighting (friendly and low), smells (trees and leather, and the rose oil I have on the bookshelf). I become a bit proud of it all. I managed to make a home here and it holds its own next to the massive second homes it shares the street with. She looks at the bronze eagle statue on the shelf by the fireplace. "That belonged to the previous owners," I say. "Seems like every mountain home has one. I thought it was funny and kept it."

She wanders back toward me.

"So you haven't been here before?" I ask.

"No," she says, and clears her throat.

"Why are you here?" I fill a glass with water.

"I was just driving home. I had a few beers so I got off Main. And then since I was in the area, I was trying to see . . . I spun out somehow."

I look outside. "You found yourself on Sunbeam and then Carter?"

"Yes," she says.

"What were you trying to see?"

"Just the . . . real estate," she says. "I can go now. I don't really know what I'm doing. I'm sorry. I'm not myself."

"I can't let you go," I say. "You're drunk."

"That's right." She brings her fingers to her temple.

"I can't let you drive," I say. "Not on my Movado."

She looks at my wrists to see if I'm wearing a Movado watch. I look at her wrists. Tiny and bony. They should have little satin pillows to rest on.

"That was funny," she says.

"It's not my joke. This woman I work with, she says it all the time. I'm not very clever."

"Neither am I."

"Actually," I say, "I am. I can be."

"Me too," she says.

"Come have this water," I say, and push the glass toward the stools.

She takes off her coat and holds it primly. It's a nice, elegant coat.

"Clever," I say. "You're clever like a snow shoveler who doesn't bring a shovel."

I gesture to the barstools, feeling like a bartender. She sits. I lean against the counter opposite her. It's like a cross-examination.

"So what were you doing?" I ask. "Coming home from a party?"

"At some point there was a party," she says. "Then I left and went to a bar."

"Which one?" I ask. I'm amused by her concentration. She has lovely, soulful eyes, a mischievous mouth.

"Eric's, then Salt Creek," she says, and pulls the collar of her sweater away from her neck.

"Good God, I remember when I used to go there," I say. The Gold Pan, Napper Tandy's, the Brown. My feet haven't graced their floors in ages. Now I go to places like Ember, with things on the menu like veal roulade and kaffir lime purple rice pilaf. In my youth I would have scoffed—too yuppie, too fussy—but theses places weren't even around then. We just had restaurants with poppers and sloppy joes, onion rings, and fried things.

She finishes the water and rubs her nose. I should give her a drunk driving lecture. Not only could she have harmed herself, she could have hurt someone else. An elderly person, perhaps, or a ten-year-old. I think of a song Cully always listened to, about how it's dangerous to drink and drive because you just might spill your drink.

"You shouldn't have been driving," I say. "You should have called a friend."

"My friends are drunk," she says.

I smile, lenient since she's not my own.

"It was dumb," she says. "I've done some very stupid things."

I go to the cupboard and get a bowl. "Is that your truck?" I ask. I open the pantry door to get the box of Cocoa Puffs.

"No," she says. "My friend's. Jim Wick. He has a glass eye and two cars."

"Is he your boyfriend?" I'm not sure what I want her answer to be.

"No," she says. "God no."

I pour the cereal into the bowl. This is what she needs—a bowl of cereal, the childish kind that makes no claims of having any vitamins. No fiber, no riboflavin or antioxidants—these things we think we know about. She watches me as if I'm performing magic.

"What happened to his eye?" I ask.

"I don't know," she says. "I wouldn't believe the story anyway. He lies a lot. I don't know why."

"Maybe to go with his shifty gaze."

She smiles. "Looking at him can be tricky."

I push the bowl toward her. "Will this work?" I ask.

She takes off her black beanie and I'm surprised by her healthy locks of hair that fall past her shoulders. "Yes, thank you," she says.

I get the milk out of the fridge. When I turn around her hand, full of cereal, is pressed against her mouth.

I pause, then go on. "Cully does the same thing," I say. "He'd do the same thing—eat from the box. In a trance."

I put the milk down in front of her, wait for her to pour it, then put it away. I grab the plate with the peanut butter sandwich on it and place it before her.

"You happen to have a sandwich made?" she asks.

"I have four more," I say. "I was testing out a knife."

We seem to have reached a point of non sequitur acceptance. She sits there, not eating.

"Ah," I say. "Spoon."

I go to the fridge again, hand her a cold spoon, and prompted by
her look say, "I like cold spoons. I keep them chilled."

She takes the spoon. "Cold," she says. She begins to eat, and I
can tell she's trying to do it as soundlessly as possible. She tries to
suck the cereal, maybe to soften it up a bit, then chews again, carefully. I want to tell her, *Go ahead and crunch! Really, get into it!* but she
already looks like a cornered pigeon. She must be sobering up, her
bravery being replaced by manners.

I sigh. "Kit, Kit, Kit. Short for Christopher?"

She is momentarily surprised, then maybe remembers sharing
this with my dad. I pour myself a bowl of cereal too and chew cou-
rageously.

"I tell people it's short for Heather," she says, and smiles with her
mouth full.

I immediately think of my interview today with Bone Taylor.
When we were done I had asked him if he smoked pot. We were by
the railing and I was looking out at the people riding up the lift, the
different pairings: girls and boys, groups of boys, strangers, fathers
and sons.

"Um, I have," he said. "I mean . . . is it a problem for the interview or something?"

"No, it's not a problem. I just wanted to know. Did my son ever
sell it to you?"

Bone looked at me, his big eyes full of puppy sorrow. "No," he
said. "He didn't. I knew him in school, but he was younger than me,
so we didn't really hang out."

"When people die suddenly you kind of try to piece them together." I looked down at Bone's park. "I had the question. Thought
I'd ask it. This all kind of gives you an excuse to talk to people this
way." I looked at him to see if I was making any sense. I wanted to,
because it was making sense to me, that tragedy gives you an excuse, like you're exempt from real life, from manners. But of course

it doesn't. Everyone has a tragedy and you don't see the whole world sitting it out, excusing themselves from the table because they're full.

I could see him nodding his head, understanding, or at least offering that impression. I was relaxed by him and with him. "I need to call you something else," I said. "I can't call you Bone. What's your real name? I don't think I've ever known."

"It's Boner," he said, and we both burst out laughing.

"Sorry," he said, holding his hands up. "That was so inappropriate. You remind me of my mom, that's all. We joke like that. I'm kind of inappropriate."

My chest felt funny, and I realized it was from a true laugh, that and a warmth from imagining him and his mother joking around together.

He nudged me. "You're funny," he said.

I looked up at him and had to shield my eyes as I did with Cully. "Why?"

"Just the way you went about that." He imitated my question. "'Do you smoke pot?' You scared me."

"I'm scary," I said, and sighed. "I know your mom. She still doing real estate?"

"She is," he said. I thought back to how I met his mom and it was from interviewing her husband, who ran the Summit Stage bus company. It had nothing to do with kids, with Cully. Work has also been my ticket in to places, in to people. I needed to remember that.

"Tell her I say hello," I said.

"I will," he said. "Her maiden name is Keith. That's my real name." He laughed. "I should probably start going by it now that I'm getting old."

"You have time," I said.

I look at Kit eating her cereal and wish I could tell Cully about both Kit and Keith. These stories from today have nowhere to go.

"I like your name," I tell Kit. "Lately, all I hear is Isabelle."

"I used to babysit an Isabelle," Kit says.

"Mothers these days—they arm their kids with pukey cute gear and give them pompous British names."

"Mothers these days," she repeats.

I stir the milk with my spoon, nervous about bringing up the real topic, maybe reluctant to have whatever this is be concluded. "We need to talk about why you're here," I say.

She nods and furrows her dark, full brows.

We start to say something at the same time.

"Go ahead," I say.

"No, after you," she says.

"Don't you hate that?" I say. "It's like when you want to let a car go first, but they want you to go, and both of you go, then have to stop. You end up being angry with the person you were trying to be nice to."

"It is like that," she says. "But I'm not angry or anything."

Neither of us go.

"I was just going to say that it started to snow," she says.

I look toward the deck. Big fat flakes swirl as if caught in an undertow. It always startles me, the quiet way snow sneaks in and changes the landscape.

"That's all," she says. "No one here uses salt. It ruins the look of snow. People here like the look of snow."

I stare at her. "That's what you were going to say? How about explaining yourself?"

She looks up at the ceiling and scratches her nose. The firewood pops. I hadn't realized my dad had started a fire; now I see it simmering.

"Let's start with why you have Cully's calendar, or how you knew him in the first place. And by the way, salt ruins the paint on cars. That's why we don't use it."

"I'm sorry I went about things this way," she says. "Cully and I—"

"Were you his girlfriend or something?" My tone is sarcastic, insulting, as if the possibility of them is something laughable, if not horrific, though if he were alive I'd be happy to see her accompany him through the door. "Or I guess his girlfriend's name began with an *L*," I say.

"What?" she says, and looks like she might cry. "Did he say that?"

I feel bad, like I've told on him. "No," I say. "Not to me. Were you his partner?" I ask. "Partner in crime? Have you come for the money?"

"Money? What?" She genuinely looks confused by my questions, which comes off as a rather sweet expression. She tilts her head and flexes her jaw, and now I'm confused.

"How did you know him?" I ask.

"I was a waitress at the Pub," she says, but she looks like her mind hasn't caught up to where we are yet. "We crossed paths. I'd see him parking cars. He'd come in a lot. He liked sweet potato fries." She looks down.

"Were you a customer?" I ask. "Is that it?"

"A customer?"

"I know everything," I say. "About the pot. About his little business." I realize I'm using my spoon as a pointer. "You don't have to pretend."

"I'm not pretending," she says. "I didn't understand. But no, I wasn't a customer. I've never even bought pot before."

"Well, aren't you a good girl."

"It's not that," she says. "I just . . . never had to."

I stand up straighter to gain some height.

"Because you're a girl," I say, remembering how boys would buy everything. "Wait until you get old, then you'll have to buy from the help."

She looks so sadly confused, like she's been beamed into Siberia. She isn't eating anymore. I'm scaring her too much. I uncross my arms and place them gently on the counter.

"I was talking about my friend—she buys from her yardman— never mind." I sigh. "So who were they? Who would buy it? How would he do it? Go to all the restaurants, the schools? Was he known for this? Did everyone know that's what he did? Was he the town dealer?"

"I don't know," she says, and she genuinely looks unsure. "I don't think he was a known guy or anything. Some people . . . "

"What? Go on."

"Some people just go in on a big amount and sell it. It wasn't, like, his career or anything."

My eyes well up with tears. "Really?" I say. "So, he wasn't troubled or . . . he wasn't the weird dealer guy—"

"No," she says. "Nothing like that. He just . . . had it sometimes. It wasn't a big deal. I mean, sorry, I'm sure it's a big deal to you."

"No," I say. "I mean, it is, but I feel better."

Growing up here, it was Franklin, Sean, and Josh S., Sunny, and Skip. The dudes with the weed. Now one's a developer, one's a lawyer, Skip owns a restaurant here, and Sunny's an engineer. I have no idea what happened to Franklin.

"Tell me all you know," I say, calmer now. "Don't worry about me."

"He'd sell to people around work sometimes," she says. "Mainly at the restaurant, or people would come get their cars parked and leave money in the glove compartment while they went to the Pub or bars down the street. Cully would park, take the money, replace it with . . . it. Or they'd just pull up, get what they needed, and leave, drive-through style."

"Drive-through style," I say.

"It was smart," she says, shrugging.

"Smarter if he provided burgers and fries to go with it," I say.

She relaxes a bit.

"This was only once or twice though," Kit says. "I promise. I don't think it's that uncommon."

"Okay," I say, and part of me truly feels relief and I wonder if I'm allowed that. Kit looks at the sandwich, then at me. I can tell she really wants to take a bite.

"So you knew him from work," I say. "Why did you have his day planner?"

I see her swallow. "He left it at our friend's house and I was going to give it back to him at work. He . . . I wasn't able to do that." She looks down, tucks her hair behind her ear. "After he died I kept it. I didn't know what else to do with it. Then earlier this week I saw your show. I saw them make some announcement you were coming back and they mentioned Cully."

I saw the announcement on TV as well, Katie saying, "We'll be welcoming Sarah back to the show tomorrow. Her son, Cully, is in our thoughts and prayers." Katie shook her head, looked down, then back up at the camera, and solemnly announced the upcoming interview with a jewelry maker who specialized in turquoise.

"I didn't know you were his mother before that," Kit says. "I was about to leave for Denver, for this . . . thing I had to do, but instead I found myself coming here. I guess I just wanted to see you first, his family. To see if you were okay. I felt I should return his things. I got stuck in a bad plan. I just said a lot."

"So you didn't know I was his mother before?"

"No," she says. She sniffs and looks up.

"You didn't know him very well then."

"Well," she says, but hesitates.

"Well what?"

"The people I've met here . . ." She proceeds cautiously. "It's not like we really talk about one another's mothers. We barely ask about each other. You just hang out. You just . . . start."

I know exactly what she means. When Billy landed here I didn't think to ask about his roots and he didn't ask about mine. No one does, really. You get here and you're a blank slate. You just start.

"Did you know him well, then?" I ask.

"I think so," she says. "Maybe. Who really knows, you know?"

"What does that mean?" This line of conversation is soothing to me.

"I mean we all let people know us in different ways," she says. "We didn't know a lot about each other's backgrounds, but maybe that means more. I don't know what I mean. We were friends. I liked him a lot." She holds her head in her hands.

"So he brought his calendar to parties?" I ask.

She rights herself again, then slouches. "It was in his backpack. Here's his backpack." She gestures to the chair beside her. I hadn't noticed her bringing it in.

"So, what was it like?" I ask. I want to sit down but not next to her.

"What was what like?" she asks.

She begins to eat again and she chews louder now, which unreasonably makes me feel like a good host.

"The party," I say. "What was the party like?"

"It wasn't really a party, just a normal . . . gathering."

"What's normal?" I lean into the counter. I want to get comfortable. I want to hear a story. Parents, no matter how much they think they know, never really know their weekend children, their nighttime children. I once thought I was the exception, that I knew him better than most mothers know their sons.

"This is normal," she says. "We do this. We sit and eat. We drink beer instead of milk from cereal bowls. We watch TV instead of the snow." She looks behind her. "Or a fireplace."

"How old are you?" I ask.

"Twenty-two," she says, as if this has just dawned on her.

It's probably past midnight. I think, *Do you know where your child is? Where she's been? Where she's going?* She takes a bite of the sandwich, leaving a smile of bread.

"Cully would come home smelling just like you," I say. "Like beer."

"I'm sorry about all of this," she says.

"Me too," I say. My neurons are having a disco in my head. I can't believe we're here eating children's cereal. "I'm sorry for the inquisition. Sort of."

"I deserved it," she says. "And didn't mind it."

She taps her fist against her head. She sips some cold milk from the cold spoon.

"It's late," I say.

She sighs. "I know. I need to go."

I look outside at the snow unfurling gently yet plentifully. I will never tire of this kind of snowfall.

"You've had quite a night." I walk to her side of the counter. I look at the backpack on the bar stool beside her and place my hand on it.

"So I can drive home now?"

I take her bowl to the sink. "You can sleep in the room down-stairs," I say. "I just cleaned it today. Come. I'll show you."

I wait for her to stand up.

"I can't sleep here," she says, but she stands, and when I walk she follows me across the living room.

"Why can't you?" I ask. "You crashed into my garbage cans. This is much more polite."

"I don't want to intrude," she says.

"You already have," I say lightly. "Intrusion, check."

She follows me down the steps.

"There's more to this," she says.

I look back at her on the steps. "Oh, God," I say. "Your nose."

She wipes her nose, looks at the blood on the back of her hand.

"Did you hit yourself when you crashed?"

"No," she says, making her way down the steps like an Ambien zombie. "I'm always getting bloody noses even though I'm accli-mated. I don't belong here." She sniffs, then presses the shirt under her sweater to her nose.

"Don't do that. Let me get you tissue." I walk to the bathroom across from Cully's room. "Bathroom's right here if you need it," I say, then come back out with a box of tissues. She's sitting at the bottom of the steps, squeezing the meaty part of her nose and looking down.

"Look up," I say.

"You're not supposed to do that," she says. "Tilt your head back and you risk the chance of blood running down your esophagus and into your stomach."

"Oh," I say. "That's right. You might go to medical school?" I stand in front of her, feeling helpless, and also thinking of all the times I had given Cully the wrong advice, responsible for blood running down his esophagus.

"I might," she says. "My dad's a surgeon. He's pushing for it." She glances at me while keeping her head down. "He thinks my future looks malignant."

"You seem pretty sensible to me," I say. "Well, sometimes."

I try once again to pawn off the tissues. She takes the box and stands, then looks at the one she was squeezing her nose with. "All done," she says.

I gesture to the room, slightly panicked in the way I am when someone drops by and I've got personal things strewn about.

"Here you are," I say, looking at the room through new eyes. It's a formidable room, and does look a bit like a guest room now, which is pleasing. I refrain from doing anything B&B-host-like, offering a mint or turning down the bed, or pointing out the closet and drawers.

"Let me get you another shirt," I say.

She looks awkward in this space, like a customer in a dressing room, waiting for the saleslady to hang up her clothes and go. I move to the boxes lined neatly by the door and open one to look for a shirt, then consider that this wouldn't be right.

"This was Cully's room," I say, thinking she should know.

She nods as if she suspected this.

"The bedding is new," I say.

She nods again, smiles—I think, politely—and then she seems to wilt a bit. "Sorry, I'm so tired." She walks to the bed, slides off her boots, and gets right in under the covers before I can offer to lend her pajamas. I tell myself not to offer pajamas or ask if she's sure she doesn't want to change her shirt at least. I need to go.

"You shouldn't be cold," I say. "It's always warm down here."

The snow falls past the window in a graceful slant.

"Thank you," she says, and looks near tears. "I don't feel well."

"I know," I say.

She starts to take off her sweater, but she's struggling from her position so—I can't stop myself—I help her get it over her head, and I hold on to it, draping it over my arm, but my feeling of trying to be the gracious host slides into something else.

"Kit, you could have gotten hurt tonight," I say. "Think, okay? Think before you treat your life so lightly."

"I've been fine so far," she says, and it sounds like she's talking in her sleep.

It's a response that surprises me, for its quickness and its sassiness, but also maybe because of its intimacy; it's something you'd only say to someone you knew well. Her retort reminds me of being ten, skiing alone, riding the chairlifts, going fast down the blues, and then the black diamonds, falling a lot, sometimes hard; or at thirteen hitching rides from strangers to get home or to Vail or Loveland Pass to ski. The drivers were teenagers, worried mothers, men, lots of men. I remember a man named Eagle in a Camaro, who talked about war and would pat my leg after saying things that were meant to be funny.

At fourteen I started drinking with all my friends—wine coolers at bonfires—and we'd always ride in the backs of trucks driven by very stoned, very drunk boys. At sixteen a specific incident happened where I was hurt and at first too proud, too ashamed, to ask my father for help.

Everyone who's alive can say they've been fine so far.

I know she's trying to sleep, may even be there already, but I ask, "Did you tell Cully something about your dad and Emerson and a hoofprint?"

She doesn't open her eyes, but she smiles. "Yes," she says.

"You told it to my dad today. He had heard it before from Cully. He must have liked the line."

"That's sweet," she says, and I have a feeling that if she wasn't his girlfriend she may have wanted to be.

"Good night, then," I say.

I watch her for a moment. She grips the edge of the blanket that she's pulled up to her chin. Her mouth parts. She's sinking into sleep. I shake myself out of it. For a moment I was almost at peace.

Chapter 11

Billy arrives when my dad is on the phone. He circles the room as if in a museum—he looks at the furniture, gets close to the pictures, running his hand along the spines of books on the shelf by the fireplace. He was here for the service but probably didn't absorb a thing then. I watch him from the stove and tell him what happened last night.

"Was she drunk?" he asks.

"Yes," I say. "She said she found out who I was, then came to give it back to me, but got nervous. Here. Come look." I gesture to the calendar on the counter, and he picks it up then sits down next to my dad.

It's strange seeing them side by side. He flips through the calendar while my dad talks on the phone, a business call about things that are not his business.

"All in a twist over the boreal toad," my dad says on the phone. "The lynx I can understand, but a toad? I mean, come on. They've been around since the dinosaurs. Their time is up."

"He shouldn't have retired," I say to Billy.

"Ever consider the idea that he didn't want to?" Billy asks.

"He wanted to," I say. "They always want to, then never know what to do with themselves."

I walk over with his black coffee, place it down on a *Colorado Homes* magazine, which my dad has scribbled notes on. On the cover of the magazine is a loft in Keystone shaped like a mailbox. The heading: "First-Class Delivery." I imagine the writer striving for the perfect mail pun. Priority Living. First-Class Package. Stamp of Approval. It's sad imagining the writer settling on this particular one.

"Why did he move in?" Billy asks, quietly.

"He sold his house and wanted to move into a condo. I told him to move in with us until he found the right one. And now . . . we've gotten used to one another."

Billy takes a sip of the coffee and looks back down at the calendar. I sit down next to him to look over his shoulder.

"Your birthday's in there," I say.

"I saw that," Billy says. "Funny he has this."

"That's what I thought."

"I mean it's funny because I gave it to him," he says. "Just one of those free things I got somewhere. I didn't think he'd use it."

"When did you give it to him?"

"In November," he says, without hesitation, looking at me. "He came down for my birthday."

"Oh," I say.

I imagine him driving those five hours, window down, heater on, music blaring.

"What did you guys do?" I ask.

Billy turns the pages. "Um just, you know, drove around. Went for a ride."

"Went for a ride on what?"

He looks up from the page. "Motorcycles. I took him on the Million Dollar Highway." His look dares me to be angry with him, and I know that I can't. There's no point. He rode a motorcycle. He lived.

"He must have loved that," I say.

Billy's eyes are glassy. "I did," he says. He closes the calendar. "This doesn't seem that hard of a thing to hand over."

"Shy, I guess."

"Or she had more to say," Billy says.

She must be nervous to come up the stairs, especially with all of

us here. I'd always dread this part of being a guest in the morning—
the tentative yielding into the house's normal traffic. She's not a
guest, I remind myself.

I get up to finish making us breakfast, sort of amused, sort of
charmed by this situation: a girl who was connected to Cully. There's
a comfortable clamor in the room, the smell of bacon and coffee, as
if we are just all normal people doing normal domestic things. I smile
to myself thinking of Cully on a motorcycle, that stretch of road
through mountain passes. He must have laughed out loud.

"Where did she sleep?" Billy asks.

"In his room," I say.

"Really?" He rubs his jawline with his thumb.

"It was empty," I say. "Why?"

He avoids my hard stare.

"No, nothing," he says.

Why did I let her sleep there? he's wondering and now I am too.
Why not on the couch? At the time I didn't even think about it and
wonder if this is good—if it has become what I intended it to
become, a spare room. I place strips of bacon in the simmering pan.
I drank a lot last night but am experiencing a nice energy. My house
is full.

Kit appears at the top of the stairs.

"Hi there," I say. She looks puffy-eyed and pale.

"Morning," she says.

"Hi," Billy says. He holds a hand up in the air.

She mimics his gesture, looking like she's taking an oath. "Hello,"
she says.

"That's Billy," I say. "Cully's father. We're not married. We were
never married."

"That's quite an intro," Billy says.

Kit tucks her hair behind her ear and scratches her nose. "Nice
to meet you," she says, taking him in. I wonder if she's seeing Cully
everywhere like I do.

"Thanks for the calendar," he says.

She makes to answer but then doesn't say anything, embarrassed.

"Come sit," I say. She sits on the same stool as she did last night. "Here we are again."

She smiles and covers a yawn.

"Listen to this," my dad says to the person on the phone. "In half an hour I've found the solution to your little problem. You tell Critter Conservation, Center for Colorado Ecosystems, WILD, whomever—tell them two words: chytrid fungus . . . You don't need to know what it is, I don't even know what it is exactly, but I do know that it's killing them. The toads are going extinct with or without your expansion! With or without your existence! You tell these people this and all the attention will move to Fish and Wildlife, who are going to get their asses sued for not putting froggy on the endangered species list."

"Who is he talking to?" Kit asks, amused.

I look at my dad on the edge of the couch. "Someone from his old job, I assume."

"Oh, right," she says, as if recalling something they had talked about.

"I heard you had a fun night, Kit," Billy says. He walks over to us, joining me on my side of the counter.

"It was something," she says. She is wearing her dirty shirt, though I can't see the bloodstain.

"Do you want to borrow a sweater?" I ask.

"I have mine," she says. "Somewhere."

"It's over here," I say. "I hung it up."

I walk to the closet by the front door and get her sweater. Like her coat it's well made, understated, and elegant.

"And get this," my dad says. He has raised his voice. "Research has shown that golf courses are the ideal habitat for the toad. They'll go crazy over that; probably tell you to go on with the expansion—better than a golf course any day. All the groups will back off, figure they may as well go retro and start fighting for the whales again. Tell Dunbar maybe instead of hiding the toads and skirting the issue, he *advertises* their existence and their demise. The resort could be the savior. Make a promise to the EPA to build artificial hibernacula for the ailing amphibians."

We all look at one another. Kit puts on her sweater.

"Hibernacula," my dad says. "I don't know, google it. Hibernation units. Toad condos. The units could stay on the mountain but down near the base. Prime real estate. Okay . . . okay . . . roger that. Good. You bet. Glad I could help. Hup," he says, then lowers the phone and peers at the buttons. "No one says goodbye anymore," he says. "Hello, Kit."

"Hello, Lyle," Kit says.

He stands and walks over. "Well, all right." He nods, appraising her. "Sarah told me all about your late-night vandalism. You sleep okay?"

"Very well," she says.

"Can I get you some breakfast?" I ask. "Eggs? Or more cereal?"

She doesn't laugh at what I consider to be our inside joke.

"No, thanks," she says.

My dad comes into the kitchen with his mug. "Kids, kids, kids. Crazy, crazy kids. Yesterday I was telling Kit—Billy, this was when she was our hired hand—I was telling her about the old days."

"You were?" I say.

"Old, old days." He brings his fist over his mouth and burps silently. "Criminals would come here to hide, rich guys from the East Coast would come here to slum, fancy women who didn't want to be fancy anymore. They'd all migrate to our town to find their fortunes, begin again." He smiles to himself while filling his mug with coffee. He adds his milk and sugar and I tap in some cinnamon because I read somewhere that it's good for your heart or immune system. I forget which.

"Guess you found an adventure, Kit," he says. "Pretending you're a snow shoveler, delivering a token. Boy."

"I didn't think of it that way," she says.

"And you shouldn't," I say. I may have sounded gruff, but this is hardly some western adventure. Delivering belongings to a heartbroken family. Or I guess it does sound like a plot.

"Why didn't you just tell us you had it?" my dad asks. He shakes his head, as if not needing an answer. He lets her off the hook, and I try to remember what her explanation had been when I asked her last night. I recall it being long-winded.

"Those toads you were talking about?" Kit says.

"Yeah?" my dad says.

"They have red warts."

"Really? Goodness, that's another strike against them." He's next to me, stirring in the cinnamon, and then he pours coffee into another mug. "You take cream? Sugar?"

"Both," Kit says.

"Atta girl. Did you see your truck out there? It's completely buried."

"I can help you dig it out," Billy says.

"But she's the snow shoveler, right?" my dad says.

"I wouldn't say that," she says.

He walks back around the island to her with her coffee. "I wouldn't say that either."

"I was telling Sarah last night that I'm sorry about doing such a stupid thing. I can help clean up or . . . the sheets. I can wash the sheets."

My dad waves her words away.

"One night my grandson, Cully, who you knew of course, he drove right into someone's wooden fence on Harris. He was inebriated, had just gotten his license, and now had to deal with a torn fence and a cut through his eyebrow." He makes a sound as he slices his face. "Instead of driving the one-minute drive home, he drove up to Shock Hill to Sarah's bountiful friend's house—she wasn't as bountiful then, though. He went there for help. He asked Dickie—

he's the husband—he said, "Can you say I was playing football and that I fell and got a concussion, and that you drove my car home and accidentally hit a fence on the way over?" My dad uses a comically whiny voice.

"So, Dickie actually agreed. He comes over here—and I'm here for some reason—and he starts with this story but can't see it through. He starts to crack up. And you know how red Dickie gets when he laughs. Looked like he was going to implode. So he gives up the lie, hits Cully on the back, and says, 'You take it from here, kid. Take it away,' then tells him it's good to be grounded. Gives you an excuse to stay home with your mom."

"And the moral is?" Billy asks.

"I don't know," my dad says. "Kids do stupid shit."

"I'm sorry," Kit says again. Her gaze drifts over to the television behind her, where my program is on. It's an old segment, shot almost six months ago.

"In addition, these residences reside on sixty acres of land, forty of which are a conservation easement," Penny, the property manager says. She had an accent that I couldn't place.

"Now what does that mean?" I ask on TV.

I look at myself, feeling compassion for this past self, afraid for what her life is about to become. At the same time I don't exactly want to be her again.

"Will you guys turn this off?" I ask.

"Well, it means that nothing will ever change," Penny says. "No one will come and build something to obstruct your views and our forest won't be destroyed."

"And no one wants that," Katie says.

"No," Penny says.

Billy and my dad both laugh. I do too. It's as though we're watching a sitcom. I look so interested, so sincere. I understand now the disappointment Holly and Katie must feel in me, but watching this makes me feel that I will never be able to show that interest ever again.

I look like the women on Dad's show, going over the same things with disproportionate enthusiasm, nodding mechanically as the people we interview say over and over again, "We're really excited."

"—really excited about this one in particular, which is designed to capture the timeless quality of quaint and elegant European villas, but the architects have fused it with that rustic Rocky Mountain character we know and love."

"Look at that chandelier!" Katie says. "Are those antlers? Are they real?"

"Are those antlers!" Billy says.

"Are they real!" my dad says.

"I honestly don't know how I'm going to do this again," I say. I walk to the couch, click the TV off.

"Maybe you shouldn't," Billy says. "Begin again. Do the opposite."

I try to think of what the opposite would be: demolition derby? piano tuning?

I go back to the kitchen and lay the bacon out on paper towels and use its grease to scramble the eggs. I will cater to her hangover and make her comfortable to indulge. I look up to see if she's tempted. She's crouched on her chair, as though bracing herself. Her eyes are closed.

"Are you okay?" I ask. "You want some juice?"

She nods yes or no. I can't tell.

"Use your words," Billy says, and smiles.

"I should go," she says. She stands up but doesn't move.

"Whoa there, you all right?" Billy asks.

"I think I might be sick," she says. She looks at me with a pleading sort of look, runs to the kitchen and straight to the sink, where she proceeds to throw up in a way that makes her look possessed. Some splatters on the bacon and eggs. We all watch, our mouths agape. When she's done she stands over the sink and takes deep breaths, then turns on the faucet and splashes her face with water. She stays over the sink, letting the water run, and water drips from her face.

"Wowza!" my dad says from behind. "That was some fine work."

"Stop it," I say. "Hon, are you okay?" I gather her hair and let it fall on her back. I hand her the towel from the hook on the wall.

"Why don't you dry your face off," I say.

We all stand close to each other, huddled.

"This?" she says. The towel is dark blue and has a design of a small cat licking its paw.

"We can get you another one if it offends you," my dad says.

"Stop it, Dad," I say.

"I just don't want to dirty it," she says.

"That's what hand towels are for," he says, and then sincerely, "You all right, sport?"

"No," she says.

Billy takes a glass to the bathroom. I hear him turn on the faucet. He comes back and places the glass of water beside her.

We are all attending to her and I'm sure she is mortified. She drinks the water and my dad pats her back as she drinks. "You're okay." His touch makes her cry, and she has given in, relieved to cry. He pats and rubs circles into her back.

"I'm so embarrassed," she says. She looks at each of us, almost as if forcing herself to do so. Her face and neck are flushed. I'll have to lend her a new shirt and sweater.

"Don't be embarrassed," Billy says.

"This isn't supposed to happen this way." I notice her hands shaking a little. Billy and I exchange glances. What way was it supposed to happen?

"Funny how that emotion, embarrassment, is just deer-in-the-headlights debilitating," my dad says. "You can hurt someone and go around thumping your chest like a baboon. But to be embarrassed, that's tough. Makes people veer quite incredibly from logic."

"Dad," I say. The way he speaks, I swear.

"Just breathe," Billy says.

"I'm trying to help," my dad says.

"I know," I say.

She puts her forehead down on the edge of the sink and takes deep breaths.

"Billy," my dad says. "Get down on your knees and stick your butt in the air. I want to show Kit a technique I learned from my dad, who learned it from his father before him. Billy, get your chest on the ground. Show her this technique to help her relax and breathe. I do it all the time."

Billy hesitates, then makes his way to the floor. Kit, still leaning against the counter, turns to look.

"Now put your forehead on the ground, Billy. And splay your arms. Splay them." Billy situates himself into an exhausted child's pose.

"There you go," my dad says. "You see that, Kit?"

She nods her head on the counter.

"Now really look at Billy," my dad says. "Look at him there. Hell, I don't do that all the time. It may make it harder to breathe for all I know, but nothing you do today will be as embarrassing as what he's doing now."

Billy lifts his head but stays down on his shins.

"You're a little nuts," Kit says.

"I know," my dad says.

"We all know," Billy says, "but he's kind of always right. It's annoying. It actually feels great down here. I'm very relaxed."

Kit turns back to the sink and stands up straight. Tears are really flowing now, like a quiet snowfall.

"Take a deep breath," I say softly. "Ignore the idiot gallery behind you." I gesture for Billy to get up and he does. "I learned something from my father," I say, "and I swear I'm not making this up. He'd always tell me to say something, to talk about something that has no meaning, that won't trigger any emotions. Just get talking, get breathing, you—"

"The toads," she says, and I'm surprised by her steady voice.

It's as though she really is snowing or raining and not crying, the tears just a natural phenomenon. "Lyle. Those boreal toads you were talking about? The way they mate is the male jumps on the female's back and she carries him around for days. This stimulates her to lay the eggs. That's all he does. He sits on her back. When she delivers the eggs—that's when he fertilizes them. I don't know why my dad knows so much about the way creatures mate. He was always interested in it. That and the heart. He loves the heart."

"That's good," my dad says. "That was really good. See, you're fine. You're doing great."

We stand there, surrounding her like coaches.

"Oh God," she says, and does it again, throws up in the sink. We all automatically take a step back.

"I'm pregnant," she says, when she's done.

"Holy shit," Billy says.

Chapter 12

Billy's response, "Holy shit," echoes through my head. I mouth it. I say it out loud. I feel it and hold on to it, not wanting to think or feel anything else right now.

I look out the window of my room, trying to gauge the weather—it looks like holy shit. I put on black jeans and my gray oversized sweater, as if the news demands a new costume. I somehow put on makeup while avoiding the mirror, as if not seeing my reflection saves me from admitting or understanding something. I have nothing else to do in my room. Taking a shower or making my bed would feel ridiculous, like tidying up your house while it was burning down. I have to go downstairs now. I open my bedroom door.

The three of them wait at the bottom of the steps and I walk down, feeling like a debutante. By the looks of them I know they have talked, decided on something, and I will be shuffled because I'm too stunned to think straight. I'll float like flotsam. Drift like driftwood.

"The car is packed," my dad says. "And I lent Kit some things from the laundry room."

At first I don't know what he's talking about, then remember our one-night trip.

"Did you get my bag?" I ask.

"Yes," he says. "Everything's taken care of. We can head out, but first I thought we'd get something to eat—all of us."

Kit is wearing one of my favorite sweaters, the dark gray one with diagonal ridges.

"We need to get Suzanne," I say. "We're late. I hate being late." I guess I won't be shuffled after all.

No one bothers to answer me, making me understand that our lateness is hardly a pressing matter right now.

"We'll get some lunch at the Whale's Tale," my dad says. He looks at his watch. "Brunch."

He has always done this. When we have a conflict or an issue to address, he takes it to a restaurant, to neutral ground. He thinks one behaves better and thinks more clearly, carefully selects words. The meal serves as a timeline. By the end something needs to be determined, accomplished, but it doesn't seem like the right thing to do.

"Not now," I say. "Not for this."

"We are not speaking about anything here," he says, then walks outside.

"This is stupid," I say. "We can talk right here." Kit and I look at each other and I feel like a child who's been wrongfully blamed.

"Save it," my dad says. "No sense repeating yourself, repeating yourself."

We all follow him out the door. Kit puts on her nice coat. I look at her stomach, then look away.

"Careful," I say to her, when she starts to walk down the icy steps.

WE WALK IN to the saloon-like restaurant, a place I'd always go to with my father when I was young. It was our night on the town, just the two of us. It's funny that it was special to me because it was always just the two of us, but I guess the excursions felt like a celebration of our duo. I switched up the tradition and took Cully to Steak and Rib for our night on the town. Just the two of us. As an adult I saw it was as much a favor the child does for you as one you do for them, especially as a single parent. He was my company.

The restaurant is dimly lit and nearly empty. It feels better to be here than back at home, less claustrophobic. My father is always right.

"Four of you?" a hostess asks in a chirpy way. I feel bad. We're going to ruin her day with a lifeless response, but she is steadfast and oblivious.

"Would you like a tour of the kitchen?"

"God no," I mumble, thinking of their greasy food.

"Hey, aren't you Sarah St. John from *Fresh Tracks?*"

"No," I say.

She laughs uncomfortably, then looks frightened, hurt, and lastly, pissed off. We follow her. She throws down four menus on a table in the middle of the restaurant, right next to a table of five, four of whom happen to be licking their fingers. The father at the table presses his finger onto his plate, then puts it into his mouth. The girl looks on disgustedly and I'm assuming she's the girlfriend of the boy whose thigh she's squeezing. He looks at her and smiles with a full mouth. "What?" he asks, but she just shakes her head.

I take a seat and my dad sits next to me and begins to pat my back, something that annoys me at first but then soothes me.

For some reason Kit has placed Cully's day planner in the middle of the table between the two round candles that are creating an oddly romantic light. She moves it so that it's straighter. "Sorry," she says. "I arrange. I'm always feng shuiing . . . "

My dad clears his throat. He fingers the ridge of his jaw, starting from behind his ear and working his way to his chin. I know he's about to say something either mildly intelligent or intensely confounding.

"Sometimes," he says, "I feel my face, making sure it isn't becoming elongated, like a caricature of a sad man."

Billy nods as if this isn't a bizarre thing to say.

"Sometimes," he continues, "I think Sarah expected me to break years ago—"

"What are you talking about?" I ask.

"That my wife's death or my job would either break me or turn me into a fool, yet I've managed to strike a balance. Sheila is gone, but I've made it, and I've been happy, and while I've worked hard all my life, I've played too, and before the horrific present, have felt pretty well armed against the latter-life crisis." He looks at Billy, as if for confirmation.

"I don't get too depressed, I haven't suddenly taken up yoga or groped or eloped with a waitress—"

"Or bought a yellow Boxster," Billy says.

"Or decided to write a memoir," my dad says.

Kit blinks and furrows her brow. She catches me looking at her, but I don't look away.

"Life is my Rubik's Cube," my dad says. "When I can't do it, I put it down."

I'm amused by Kit's efforts to feign comprehension.

"I am not, however, equipped for this," my dad says, his hands including all things present and all things unseen. "I can't even understand what this is."

I put my hand on his thigh. His voice wavered.

"I have been beaten," he continues. He clears his throat in a way that only men can do without being gawked at. "I've been sucker punched by life. My late wife I could do. I was prepared, I had time going in, and I've had lots of time going out. But my grandson's death is something I can't—"

His voice again. My throat. It's like I've swallowed down a jigger of vodka. There aren't many things worse than seeing your dad fight back tears and collapse. Billy too; he looks like he's fighting a sneeze.

"So," my dad says. "Let's talk, once again. A little bit faster now. I'm prepared for both a very simple story or a very complicated one, but let's walk a straight line."

Kit remains still and quiet, with a wilting and pained expression. The sun is bright in the doorway. It ricochets off the snow that's glossed the roofs.

I'm about to pardon my father, explain that he likes speeches, always has, always will, but her silence is bothering me. She has had ample time to spit it out, interrupt and save him.

"Is it his?" I ask her.

Of course it's his.

She nods. My eye twitches and I'm embarrassed and then can't believe I'm able to feel something as small as embarrassment at a time like this, but for some reason my eye jerking and fluttering is important.

"I thought you said you weren't dating?" I laugh, hating the sound of my bitter laughter. I look quickly at my father. He puts his hand on my back again, lower this time, a secret gesture like a ventriloquist's hand. "I thought you said you weren't his girlfriend?"

Billy looks like I've said something naive, and then his eyes light up. "Lux," he says. "Cully told me he liked a girl named Lux."

"My last name," Kit says. She looks heartened though weakened by this. "That's what he'd call me sometimes."

My dad moves his hand off me and I feel a coldness on my back and a deep sadness. *Lux*, I say to myself and keep repeating it, letting it drum in my head.

"So you were or weren't his girlfriend?" I ask. My dad puts his hands on the table.

"Please, Dad, I need to have some kind of control over this."

"I didn't say anything."

"You did in your own silent way," I say.

"How am I supposed to control that? Here—I'm sending you supportive silent thoughts. Here comes one now! But since you've given me the floor, may I offer one suggestion?"

"See!" I say. "I could feel you suggesting! Wanting to suggest!"

Kit shifts her gaze between me and my father, back and forth, back and forth. I feel like I'm in one of those movies where the criminals begin to argue and shoot each other, allowing the victim to back away slowly toward the exit.

"I just think you should be quiet," he says. "That's all."

"I know, I know," I say, and then explain to Kit. "He has always told me to be quiet. After your speech, let the other person ramble on. It puts you in a position of power; it's a more effective way of gathering information, but I can't help it just now. My mouth runneth over or whatever."

"Keep things relevant, darling," my dad says.

"This is relevant! I'm very confused right now. First I find he's a drug dealer."

"Not really," Kit says.

"Who cares if the boy slung some Mary Jane here and there," my dad says.

"I care!" I see our waitress heading toward the table and I quickly say, "And now he's impregnated a waitress!" I look at Kit and she brazenly shakes her head as though I've made a false accusation.

"What can I get for ya?" the waitress asks. "Do you all need more time or . . ."

"Yes, more time," I say.

"No worries," she says.

"Actually I'll take a Bloody Mary," I say.

"That sounds good," Billy says. "I'll have the same."

"Sure thing," our waitress says, then pivots soldier-like to the table beside us.

"I'm not a waitress," Kit says.

"I know," I say. "I didn't mean it that way. Even if you were . . . I just blurted it out, okay? Strike it. God, I hate when people say, 'No worries'!"

"Why don't we get back to the matter at hand," my dad says.

"Just what is the matter at hand?" I ask.

"Kit is pregnant with our son's child," Billy says.

"Our son? You shouldn't even be here. This has nothing to do with you."

Billy gives me a challenging look. "He's my son," he says. "Just

because you wanted me to have as little to do with him as possible
because—"

"Oh, please," I say. I look to my dad for some support. He crosses
his arms and gazes toward a murky side window.

"You act as though I walked out on him," Billy says.

I shake my head to indicate the futility of this conversation, but
really I have no comeback. I know he's right and don't know how to
defend myself.

"Kit?" my dad asks.

"Yes, sir," she says.

"It's Lyle to you. Now, you're okay. Let's ease up. Let's keep it simple. We're all assuming it's his," my dad says. "Thus your . . . lurking
around."

"Yes," she says.

Her answer makes me disoriented, and there's French music
playing in the background, loud and mildly avant-garde, which adds
to the confusion.

"How do we know?" I ask. I look across the table at her stomach
covered with her napkin as if for proof of life.

Kit looks back at me with strength and conviction. "I can give
you more details, but I really wouldn't make something like this up.
I'd rather avoid all of this."

"But how am I supposed to know for sure?" I ask. "Not that you're
pregnant, but that it's his."

"Because I'm telling you," she says. "And it has to be his because"—she lowers her voice—"there was never anyone else."

"What?" I say. I almost blurt, *How lame!* but then she says, "Since
I've lived here."

My father and Billy look away toward the window.

"How can we trust you?" I ask. I bring my fist down hard on my
thigh, a clumsy gesture I hope no one saw. I'm not sure if I'm stricken
or hopeful and the conflict is making my chest hurt, my breath shallow.

"You can trust me," she says. "But I understand if you don't."

"So he didn't know . . . of course." I hold my neck. Of course he didn't know.

Our waitress feigns sneaking up to our table. She puts the Bloody Marys down.

"Are ya'll ready to order or do you still need some more time?"

More time, more time. Tell us the specials. Tell us where you're from originally. Tell me how to react to all this.

"The pancakes are awesome," she says. "Or the crab cakes . . . fish and chips."

We all look at one another, not knowing how to answer, just knowing we've made a bad decision. We can't be here.

"We'll take the fish and chips," Billy says. "We can all share." He shrugs at me, asking me to go along with it.

"No," I say. "I'm sorry, but we won't be eating. We have to go."

"None of you want to order anything, or . . ." The waitress tries to meet one of our gazes.

"No," I say. I pinch the skin between my eyebrows, thinking about the eggs I made, Kit puking on them and in my sink.

"I guess we won't be staying after all," my dad says to the girl.

"Just the check for the bloodies then?" she says through a clenched smile. She takes away our silverware, creating a violent clatter, then turns to the other table, the happy, ravenous one (minus the girlfriend), and says, "I'll be right back with those shakes."

Our table is silent, chastened.

"I hate when people say 'bloodies,'" I say. "So gross."

"Christ, Sarah, you're real particular with language, you know that?" Billy says.

I know. Cully and I both were. We'd have gut reactions to words.

"Do your parents know?" Kit shakes her head. No. She looks surprisingly good now, rested, the sun hitting the left side of her face, showcasing her smooth, golden complexion. She is so young. I touch the small line on my face that runs from the side of my nose down to my chin.

"Where are you from again?" Billy asks.

"New York. Westchester. A town called Bronxville."

He nods as if this information is useful.

"Are you . . ." I can't complete the sentence. "Are you going to keep it?"

She puts her hand on the calendar and moves it, slightly. "I have an appointment tomorrow in Denver," she says.

"Is this a prenatal appointment or something else?" I ask.

"Something else," she says.

Billy and I look at each other across the table, then both take a sip of our drinks.

"I'm still a kid," she says in a way that indeed sounds very childlike.

"Do you have anyone to help you?" Billy asks.

"Help me?" she asks.

"Yes, help you," he says. "Drive you, care for you after—"

"No," she says. "But it's okay."

It's like the thought of her doing this alone has just occurred to her. How horrible, I think. I look at her hand on the table and have a brief urge to cover it with my own. She seems so close to me, yet so far away; someone I want near and someone I never want to see again. Why would she tell us this? I'm surprised by my restraint in not asking this out loud.

"We'll take you," my dad says.

As soon as he says this I know we will. I need to protest, but I can't. I don't see what the alternative could be. The alternative would be letting her go. Letting her leave us. We'd all feel guilty, as if walking by someone who was begging for help. We'd be left forever wondering.

"You don't need to do that," she says. "I'm fine, and . . . it would be hard . . . for you and me."

"We'll take you," my dad says. "We're going to Colorado Springs for the night. I would love if you came with us. We'll get you your own room, of course. Then take you to your appointment tomorrow."

"To her abortion appointment," I say, seeing the other side of things and being okay with the guilt of passing someone by, avoiding eye contact. "Dad, realize what you're offering here."

"I can't imagine you doing this alone," he says to me. "Driving yourself, for God's sake. That's terrible. That's just terrible." There is something in his voice—something horribly fragile and full of sorrow.

I think of her alone in a waiting room. Nurses with scrubs that have My Little Ponies on them. Thin magazines that illustrate the stages of pregnancy with the silhouette of a woman, a fetus like a shrimp inside her womb, the words below saying things like, "Soon her neck will be complete. She'll have fingerprints and will start to urinate." Peanut, cherry, plum, orange, grapefruit: the growth of the fetus in the nine-month span. It's such a short time in the scheme of things.

I remember being on my back, looking at those posters of the evolution, the tadpole fetus in the slim belly, then the belly jutting and harboring a third-trimester male, floating in an amniotic sea. I remember the loneliness, the vulnerability of lying there, waiting. I remember finding it absurd that nurses and doctors knocked, that they come in, then leave to let you undress in private, when soon everything will be exposed.

"Is that okay?" my dad says to Kit.

"You don't have to," she says. "But yes. It's okay."

Kit's look toward him emanates gratefulness. Sometimes it's good to be reprimanded, grounded. You give up responsibility. Let the adults take over. She wipes her mouth with her napkin even though she hasn't eaten anything.

"You should eat something," I say. I must be concerned for the baby, I realize. The baby needs to eat, and I wonder if part of me feels entitled to her body, as though it's housing something of mine. Shouldn't she ask for my approval?

"I don't know if I can do this," I say.

"Yes, you can," my dad says.

"Are you sure you want to do this?" I ask Kit. There. I said it.

"No," she says. "But yes."

I take a sip of my drink. I once had the same dilemma—before Cully. I was sixteen. *No, I'm not sure, but yes, I am.* That's exactly what I felt.

I make brief eye contact with my dad, then say to Kit, "I need to know though, what was your purpose?"

"What do you mean?" she says.

"I know we've been over this before, but especially with the new revelations, why didn't you just knock on our door and tell us? What were your intentions?"

She takes a moment.

"It's just something—once I knew he was rooted to someone—it was something I felt you should have."

I catch my breath before realizing she's talking about the calendar and the backpack, not the baby.

"I guess I was curious too," she says, "to see who you were. To see who he belonged to."

"Why did you tell us you're pregnant?" Billy asks. The question makes me hold my breath.

"I don't know," she says. "I mean, I was never going to tell you. I didn't plan on it, then I . . . I threw up, and then I told you guys. It came out. I felt comfortable with all of you . . . I . . . I don't know why."

Her shoulders sink, and I believe her. I believe the feeling of knowing what you're going to do but not knowing exactly why. The reasons come to you eventually—these things you already know; they arrive. I consider the alternative—her not telling us, leaving us with his calendar, then circling back outside and out of our lives. I am inexplicably grateful.

"We passed the test," Billy says, lightly. At first I take it lightly too, but a few moments later it's something I question. Passed what test?

Was she checking us out, seeing if we'd work in her life, interviewing us for a very permanent position? Sometimes our reasons take a long time to get to us. Maybe she doesn't realize that she's looking for someone to change her mind.

Chapter 13

On Main Street tourists walk in a directionless way, taking scenic inventory. Parents of young children are less at ease, at the ready to reel them in and overcorrect. I hear a mom say, "Your tongue belongs in your body," and remember the desperation I'd feel, sometimes the fury, when Cully misbehaved.

We must look like a family walking together down the street, past the crepe stand, which makes the air smell like buttery ice cream cones.

"Here's this," Kit says, handing me Cully's calendar.

"I don't need that," I say. "Not here." I glance around as though we're doing something illegal.

Billy does something that surprises me: he hooks his arm around mine so that I feel like his square dancing partner. I'm grateful since I'm feeling really sick now: weak, nauseous, and weepy. Crying could be such a good way out of this, but I keep plodding on, leaning into him.

When we reach the car I say, "Get in," to Kit as if she needed that direction. My dad gestures to the front seat. The men take the back. Kit and I both get in and put our sunshades down and this identical move embarrasses both of us.

I look out onto the bright road, the liveliness of the street, the shops full of sweaters with the images of snowflakes falling on prancing creatures. I pull out of my parking spot right when a boy with a snowboard tucked under his arm runs in front of the car.

"Watch out!" Kit says.

I slam on the brakes and throw my arm out in front of her, crossing her body. She looks at my arm in front of her stomach. We lock eyes for a moment. I lower my window, aggressively, yet it goes down slow. "You shouldn't run in front of a car like that!" I shout.

"Fuck off, geezer," the boy says. His eyes are spread far apart, practically on the sides of his head like an herbivore's.

"Whoa!" my dad says. "What a dick!"

I automatically bring my hand to my face, then back to the wheel.

"You don't look old, babe," Billy says. "He must have been talking to me. You're still smokin'."

"It's true," Kit says. "And you look young."

"Please," I say. "Stop."

I check all mirrors this time, pull out, continue, my hands shaky. Everything is reminding me that life can change in an instant.

"What are we doing now? Someone tell me."

"I thought we could take Kit home," my dad says. "She could pack some things. Sound good?"

"Yes," she says.

She holds the strap of her seat belt across her chest.

"Where do you live?" I ask.

"The condos up on Ski Hill."

I turn at the end of Main, pass the Village, not looking in at the valets. I follow a line of cars going slowly even though the strong sun has turned the snow into a safe slush. I turn on Ski Hill with everyone else.

Shouldn't this be harder? I feel there needs to be more friction against this girl. She can't just jump into our car and become a part of our tribe. I wonder what Cully would have done or thought, what I would say when he came to me. Then I think: maybe he wouldn't have come to me. If he were alive this is something I'd probably never know about. A mother of a daughter would possibly know. A mother of a son would not.

Seth, the boy I was with when I was sixteen—his mother didn't know. Then again, neither did he.

My dad went with me to the hospital, though he didn't go in the room. The first appointment was with a doctor who was probably the age my dad is now. I was so uncomfortable at first, but I will never forget his gentleness, his kindness.

The next appointment, the actual D & C, was a week later. The doctor was a youngish woman, crisp and mechanical. She was descriptive: she told me everything she was doing and everything I'd feel in a dispassionate way that in the end was comforting. I looked up at the ceiling and I wondered, inside of me, what did it see? No eyes. What did it hear? No ears. What did it feel? No brain. It didn't feel or see or hear a thing, I guess. I didn't know. There was no language to use to describe it. And I couldn't miss what was never there. No one could. Nothing was feasible. Nothing had changed.

Except everything. Afterward, I had touched my abdomen. I pinched my skin. I thought it was possible that that moment, that particular choice, would hurt me for the rest of my life. Or maybe it wouldn't. I would never know. Everything just becomes a part of you. Gets woven into the tapestry. The next day was an ordinary day.

I drive through what must be at least a foot of snow, but it moves away like dust.

"You don't even need me," Kit says. "If I were really a snow shoveler, I mean."

"It doesn't stay this way," I say. "It hardens. It builds and doesn't budge."

I take a breath of the fresh air and feel something approaching satisfaction because of the snow, the warmth, the thump of music from passing cars, and the idea of Cully, some hint of him beside me.

"Which complex?" I ask.

"Gold Camp Two," she says.

I smile to myself.

"We had a friend who used to live there," Billy says.

"Seger," I say. "Remember? He was always baking some kind of casserole and he had that weird girlfriend. She was always sucking on Rolaids."

"She wore some tight jeans," Billy says.

"I wonder if she needed the Rolaids from the casseroles or the jeans," my dad says.

I was so in love with Billy then, or in love with the idea of him, his cool recklessness, the things it lent me. I wonder what Kit and Cully talked about, what they did with one another, what they felt. *Lux*, he called her. What else did he call her? So many questions I can ask, so many more layers to unearth. It's kind of like the helicopters coming back, a hopeful noise returning.

Something has taken not a turn but a slight shift. Cully is here.

No. No.

No, not true.

It's like rattling a box. It's luggage overhead. Contents may shift, but once you land, everything inside is still the same.

I turn into the lot of her building. The snow is piled thick on the roof like frosting, making the dark-brown complex look like a fabled gingerbread house.

I park behind an old orange truck with three dogs in back. One barks at us, then slumps down, his chin resting on the rim of the tailgate, which says CHE ROLET.

A shaft of light cuts across her building, illuminating the dirty windows.

"I'll be quick," Kit says. She gets out and all I can think is that she shouldn't be quick. She should take her time.

THE THREE OF us sit on the bumper of my car. Both Billy and my dad are quiet on either side of me. How have I ended up here with these bookends? I cup my hands in front of my mouth and blow.

"How's the GTO?" my dad asks.

"Starter's fried," Billy says.

"Have you tried banging on it with a hammer?"

"Yeah, that worked for a while, but the gear's spun. I've got the parts on order."

I look at both of them with disbelief. "Now what?"

"I just have to wait," Billy says.

"I wasn't asking about your stupid car. I'm asking about now. Now what do we do? This isn't right."

"What isn't right?" Billy says.

"I don't know," I say. "This whole thing we have going on. We're driving to a five-star resort with a stranger who's pregnant with Cully's baby. Our grandchild." I emphasize the *our*. "It's like a Lifetime movie. I just hope she's thought about this hard enough."

"I'm sure she has," Billy says. "She's twenty-two. She seems like a smart girl. Having a baby right now? Sorry, but that would mess up her whole life."

"Or enhance it," I say.

"Think if it were Cully," my dad says.

"That comparison doesn't work." I cross my arms over my chest and bounce on the bumper. I look up to the condo that Kit went into.

"I know," my dad says. "But would you want him to have a baby if . . . "

I don't answer. I don't know. Or I do know but don't like my answer. I would be embarrassed if Cully had a baby. I know how wonderful my choice ended up being, yet I also know how much was cut away from me. It was a loss of the very brief time in my life when I was responsible for just myself. Kit could have a baby and it would be a loss of the person she was about to be. Or she'd have a baby and it would be wonderful. There's a way to justify everything you do.

"I don't see them together," I say. "I don't believe it. She seems so reserved, so . . . smart. Sorry, but Cully wasn't very ambitious, obviously."

"Cully was very smart," my dad says. He looks straight ahead.

"I know," I say. "I know."

"And you don't move here to find guys pursuing careers," Billy says. "You come here to play. They sound like us, like how we were."

We all take a moment to contemplate this. The similarities are awful. Here we go again, repeating ourselves, right on time like Old Faithful.

"It was brief," my dad says. "A fling."

"Exactly," I say. "Think of the ratio here. Five guys to every girl. She must have gotten so much attention. She must have, you know, gotten around."

"She said he was the only guy she was with here," Billy says.

"I don't believe it. What young girl comes to live here and only has sex with one person?"

"They can't all be like you," Billy says.

"Oh, shut up, I wish. I should have shopped around."

He laughs and I look down at our shoes in the snow, side by side.

"I'm just saying she didn't make this up," Billy says. "I can tell."

"You can't tell the time! How would you know? You don't know anything. Dad, tell him. Do something."

I look at my father, desperate for him to fix all of this somehow. I push off of the bumper and look at the two of them in this parking lot. A gust of wind blows their hair in a similar direction. I put my hands in my coat pocket. It's cold in the shade, but I like the briskness.

"I think," my dad says, "that you need to get over it. We all know Kit is telling the truth. That's not the issue. That's done. I also think that if Cully were here, he would not want to have a baby, and you'd support that. I'm not even sure what we're talking about. Kit is doing what she's doing. If she were your daughter, you wouldn't want her to raise a baby on her own. I know you always wished you had gone on to grad school—"

"But I had Cully instead! At twenty-one. The same age, pretty much. I don't think you could argue—"

"You wanted to apply for that scholarship," my dad says. "What was it called?"

"Maxwell," I say. "And so what? I'd be some serious reporter and not had Cully? Who knows if I would have made it anyway? I'm an idiot. I never would have done anything anyway."

I remember something insignificant just then from college—leaving an interview and not knowing how to get back on the freeway. It's silly to think that I've forsaken an opportunity, silly to think that I could have been somebody when I couldn't even find the freeway . Diane Sawyer could have done it on mescaline, and there I was in a cul-de-sac asking a girl with a single dread popping out of her head like a cactus where to go.

"I don't regret having him and having time to actually raise him," I say. "I know you laugh at me and my job, but I happen to like my life, or I did."

"No one is saying any of that," my dad says. "We're only saying—"

"We? What's all this 'we' shit! Why are you both so supportive? Do you just go around telling everyone to get abortions?"

They exchange looks as if I'm insane and want to keep that information hidden from me.

"*I* am only saying that Kit is passing through," my dad says. "She wants to move on to other things. This is her experience, one of many. This is her mistake."

I know all of this. I know, but still I feel the need to argue, to defend something or someone I can't name. How has my son repeated my mistake? It would be different for him though than it was for me. Kit would probably move back home, Cully would continue on his trajectory. I wonder if Billy's thinking the same thing. There wasn't as much change for him, as much sacrifice and consequence. I'm surprised by their support, their effortless understanding. I'd think their egos would come into play, or their wanting of Cully. I'd think, I don't know, that they'd be more men-like, whatever that means.

"It's not like we want to do this," Billy says.

"But we are," I say. "We're taking her to do this to your son's baby. Our grandchild. Dad, your great-grandchild."

They don't say anything for a while.

"It's not a baby," my dad says. "You know that."

I look at my father as if he has just hit me. He knows he can win this battle. So does Billy—they have reserves to draw from. They know my past. God, first time I have sex I get pregnant. I was like an after-school special. They know I donate to Planned Parenthood, that I go to their pink ball every year and give a "Let Your Child Be on TV!" package to the silent auction. They know I would be adamant against Cully's having a child at this stage in his life. Maybe they're just being his voice or supporting Kit—noble men, congratulating themselves for being on a woman's side. No, that's not it. Maybe it's because really, they know I'm arguing against myself, not wanting to admit that I understand Kit and that part of me, a big part, supports her. They're being Cully's voice, and my reluctant one. I shake my head, sick with myself, with all of us, with her.

My dad leans back, straightening his back against the trunk and tapping his fingers on his knees. "I love you," he says in a casual way. "I love my grandson. None of that is changing. It never lessens."

It doesn't. That love for a child—it just grows and grows, which makes things both harder and better. My vision blurs. Tears fall or slide or drip—they do whatever down my face. I take my time. I go through some feelings, rifle through them like pages in a catalog, circling what looks good, changing my mind, settling on nothing.

I make my voice even: "So we take her to her appointment and then what?" I imagine us dropping her off, saying *Good luck!* I feel we've been over it already, but I still want to talk and talk until everything feels right, though it probably never will.

"Why do you want to take her anyway? Why do you want to have anything to do with her?" I know this is a false question, the kid in me wanting to show off an ability to be cold.

"I think she could use the company," my dad says. "She's alone. Scared. I'd like to be there for her. She came to us for a reason and took such a roundabout way of telling us because this is difficult stuff. But she did it and I respect her for it."

Billy nods his head beside me and I realize how quiet he has been.

"Will you be able to do this?" my dad asks.

"I don't know," I say.

My son is dead. And now my son's child will be dead and my dad's great-grandchild will be dead, and yet everything will be the same. There is no child and my son is and will always be gone.

My father laughs inexplicably.

"What's so funny?"

He stands and twists from side to side. "I was thinking about this time with Cully. We were in the car and some guy behind us honked his horn. Cully yelled out, 'Make like the wind and blow me!'" He chuckles again, the smile still on his face, remembering. "I don't know why I thought about that just now. He wouldn't have wanted a baby, hon. Not now. You know that."

I think about when he was born—out popped Billy. Well, maybe the total resemblance took a few weeks or months to appear. They both had jovial, wide mouths, grins that took up most of their faces. What if this one were to come out looking exactly like Cully when he was born? What if it's a girl? What if she looked like me?

"In a way he'll be dying all over again," I say.

"You can't think about it that way," Billy says.

"I know," I say, and the truth is, I don't. *But I have nothing left*, I think to myself. "But no one can tell you what to think, you know?"

"I do," Billy says. "I think it too."

"Think what?" I ask, but as soon as I say it I understand what he's talking about. He is thinking and feeling all the things I'm feeling and saying, and my dad probably is too. They are both scared, and they're behaving like men, wanting to be in control of this fear somehow. They know what she wants, but not necessarily what they do.

Billy stands and the car bounces. He wipes his hand over the back windshield to remove the snow that has accumulated, then blows two puffs of air into his fist. My dad looks lost, glassy-eyed, but when we make eye contact his face brightens. I hear a door close above us and see Kit carrying a small bag. She has changed into black jeans but still wears my sweater under her coat. When she walks down the steps we make eye contact for a moment, and in this look I recognize a kinship.

Billy opens the passenger door for her.

"Remind me to put some WD-40 on this hinge," he says to me.

"Okay," I say. "Thanks."

It's time to get Suzanne. I imitate my dad's twisting stretch before I get in. It's a beautiful day, I realize. I live in a beautiful place. The surrounding pines, so impossibly tall, sparkle with snow. I tilt my face up and inhale, willing my surroundings to enter me somehow and to remind me how small I am.

Chapter 14

I drive under the bridge that marks the entrance to the Shock Hill subdivision, though "subdivision" doesn't seem like an apt word for something so grand.

"What is this place?" Billy asks.

"Expensive," I say, passing a home the size of a lodge. "They started building in two thousand, I think."

"Can't imagine what these people's first homes look like," Billy says.

"They have their own gondola," my dad says. "Goes to town and the mountain."

I shake my head at the size and heft of these homes, yet mine is relatively large as well, at least compared to the historic homes in the center of town. You sort of get used to it. Not only that, but like it better, in a way. I think of my childhood home, the Victorian on Ridge Street—I thought of it as large, but now it looks so small, like a quaint inn or a youth hostel. Older models of cars, or little Styrofoam cups of coffee we all used to be content with. Now it's impossible to go back.

I turn into Suzanne's cul-de-sac and idle in her driveway. Maybe mountain homes are so large in order to compete with the mountains. The view from Suzanne's living room looks out upon the ski hills, the town, and the ten-mile range beyond.

"Let's try to keep this to ourselves," I say, but the home seems to have made everyone forget.

"This place is really on the large side," Billy says.

"It ain't shy," I say. "And Kit, the heated driveway makes your fake job obsolete." We all gaze at Suzanne's home and the clean block of pavement. Sometimes I see beauty, sometimes I see maintenance. The many peaked roofs make it look like six homes put together.

"What happened to the bear?" Kit asks.

"Good God," I say.

At the head of the roundabout is a wood-carved cub holding up his paw. Dickie insisted on this ubiquitous decoration to give the home a sense of humor. Apparently someone humorless chopped his head off. I'm not sure why all mountain home owners feel it necessary to have a wood carving of an eagle or a bear in front of the home. Maybe it's the same thing as the fish-faced women—a kind of member's badge.

"I wonder if Suze knows," my dad says. "Could be a vandal. My roofer."

"Or a drunk girl," Kit says.

"Ha," I say, and feel a sense of relief.

Two of the four garage doors open and all the lights in the home shut off. There's an empty spot next to her war-starting SUV. I recall our fight, those old problems, with fondness. Suzanne waves me in.

"Looks like we're switching cars," I say.

"Why?" Billy asks.

"She likes hers better. Actually, it will be way more comfortable with all of us."

"What is that? A GL550?"

"I don't know, Billy, God."

I pull into her garage. Everything is so organized. Wealth seems to buy order. She keeps waving me in, even though I know a red line of light will appear on my windshield, the garage sensor that tells you when to stop. She looks so little in here. How lonely it must be in this house.

I turn off the engine.

"She looks different," Billy says.

"How so?" my dad asks.

"Dad," I warn.

"What? Billy can't put his finger on it. I was going to suggest trying his foot or something larger."

"That doesn't even make sense," I say.

"No, I get it," Billy says. "Because she's bigger, right?"

"Bingo," my dad says.

"Stop it," I say.

"Not *that* much," Billy says.

"I don't get why you have to keep harping on about it," I say.

"It's just for fun," my dad says. "I'm testing my creativity, that's all. Like I did with that guy you used to date with the cross-eyes."

"He was not cross-eyed."

"I know, not really, but same thing with that one. Testing my creativity."

"Hardly," I say. "All you'd ever say is, 'Is he cross about something?' 'What's he so cross about?' It was lame."

"You think he thinks you're a twin?" my dad adds.

"That wasn't funny either," I say.

"Or," my dad says, "you think he's seeing someone on the side?"

Kit and Billy both laugh.

"See?" my dad says.

"I'm about to open the door to this car," I say. "On the count of three we're going to get out, switch cars, and not be creative." I lower my voice. "We're not going to discuss Kit being pregnant or anything about fat and body weight for the rest of this trip."

"What about Fat Boys?" my dad asks. "Can we talk about Fat Boys? They're a kind of bike. Or Fatty's Pizza."

"One, two—"

"Or what about Fat Albert?" Billy says.

"Kung Hee Fat Choy," Kit says.

I look over at her, so confused about how I should be feeling right now, and yet at ease with our clip.

"Sorry," Kit says. "Three."

We make the switch.

I DRIVE OUT of Shock Hill, then wind down toward town and Blue River.

"Camp Gorgeous, booked it," Suzanne says to whomever she's speaking to on her phone. Devon, Ann, Fran, Skinner—one of her many girlfriends whom I'm not genuinely friends with. They all seem to take turns at spa-hab or "Camp Gorgeous," as they call it, and they all speak like gossipy transvestites.

"Yeah, Sarah's here now with her band of brothers—I don't know what the hell is going on."

I roll my eyes at my dad in the back seat, but he's on his cell too.

"They don't even do it," he says to someone. Kit sits next to him and she's actively listening as if part of the conversation. I see then that he turns to her while talking as if fact-checking. "But when the female makes her delivery, he creams 'em like eggs benedict." He looks at Kit and she nods her head and mouths something. "Amplexus," my dad adds. "It's called amplexus."

I'm amused at their collaboration.

"Yeah, great," my dad says. "Just thought it was interesting. Good to know thyself and thy frogs." He shrugs at Kit. She shrugs back.

Billy's in the third-row seat, working on his laptop. He has drive and ambition, smarts. I just wasn't patient enough to wait for it all to surface. I used to envy Rachel early in their marriage, like she got something I was tricked into not wanting.

Suzanne ends her call and sighs.

"What happened to the bear?" I ask.

"You know I never liked that bear."

"You chopped his head off?"

She nods, her hands primly on her lap. "I tried but couldn't. So I had Pablo do it. He had no idea what was going on. He was so worried he wasn't understanding my English. 'Chop off? Head off? No more head?' It was quite comical. Speaking of no more head, I need to get this over with."

She gets on the phone again. She's the kind of person who has no problem carrying on phone conversations in front of strangers in small spaces where everyone is forced to listen. I know by her fake reluctance she's going to call Dickie and that he's not going to answer. What item of his has she managed to dig up? What excuse, need, demand?

"Dickie, hi, it's me." She moves the phone away from her ear and holds it like a walkie-talkie. "I found your cufflinks in the pocket of my coat. I think you asked me to hold them or something at the Maroneys' when you were arm wrestling their nephew. Seems like ages ago. Anyway, I have them. They're very nice. I think I gave them to you for your birthday one year. Forty-fourth. Just wanted to make sure you weren't looking . . . not a biggie. Call if you want. I'm off to see Morgan. I'm sure I'll see you there . . . on your own. You'll come alone, I'm assuming, since we're going to a party your daughter is organizing. Okay. Bu-bye," she sings.

There's a slight tremor in her hand as she ends the call, and inside of me, a sympathy valve twists wide open. She's still very much in love, not just with her husband but with the life she had. She's no longer a couple, and this was her identity for so long, just as my identity was being a mother. It hasn't even hit me yet, their separation. I would always go out with them, a happy third wheel or sometimes with a date. They'd argue with one another in front of me, making me take sides. They'd ask about my dating life, and we'd talk about the new crop of divorcées. They'd set me up on dates, but the men Dickie was friends with didn't find a toddler then later, a teenager, very appealing and most never set up permanent residence here anyway. I liked those outings with just the two of them. It felt like being with parents. They paid, they led the way, expressed concern. They were my adults.

My purse is on Suzanne's side on the floor. I reach down for one of Cully's CDs and put it in. "Bring the motherfucking ruckus," the rapper growls.

"Okay!" my dad says. "Will do."

"So," Suzanne says, "who are you?" She brings her mirror down to look back at Kit.

"This is Kit," I say. "You already know that."

"Yes, but who are you? Why are you here et cetera."

"She's a friend . . . she helps around the house. We're giving her a ride. She's coming with us."

"Can't she speak for herself?"

"I wouldn't if you were talking to me that way," my dad says.

"Something's fishy," Suzanne says.

"What are you talking about?" I say. "Why do you have to turn everything into an episode of *Matlock*? Nothing's fishy."

"Except fish," my dad says.

"I'm Kit," Kit says.

"Yes, I know that. And I'm Sarah's best friend." She turns to Kit, who is looking lost, like a runaway. "We're not, you know, life partners or anything. I bet that's what she thought." She hits me on the shoulder.

"I didn't think that," Kit says.

"Relax, I'm just fucking with you," Suzanne says. "God, we'd look good together though, wouldn't we? You'd be the trophy. I'd be Mrs. Payroll. Or we'd let ourselves go and just be butchy together. Buy matching fleeces. Maybe snowshoe to various huts. Don't they snowshoe? Or curl. I could see lesbians getting into curling. Anyway, whatever, don't ask, don't tell." She moves her hands like she's conducting a symphony. "I'll just sit back and relax. I don't need to understand a thing."

"I've gone over it with you already," I say. "We all want a little getaway. Kit needs a ride. She helps around the house and we're giv-ing her a lift to the eye doctor tomorrow."

Why did I just say that? Eye doctor?

"I was worried there wouldn't be enough room for all of us," my dad says. "Seems to be a lot of junk in the trunk—"

"This car is perfect for all of us," I say.

"It fits seven," Suzanne says, thankfully not getting my dad's joke.

I stop at the light before turning out of town. A man crosses in front of Suzanne's car, moving as if on stilts. The cuffs of his tight jeans are stuffed into his ski boots. He wears an American flag ban-dana on his head, blue sweatbands on his wrists, and a sweatshirt that says Let Freedom Rule.

"Jesus Christ," my dad says. "I think this is what Tocqueville meant by garrulous patriotism."

Kit's the only one who laughs.

When the man reaches the other side, my dad cracks his window and yells, "Excuse me, sir? You ever heard of the Overly Patriotic Act? An act passed by Congress banning excess use of flag fashion." I press the gas, but my dad and Billy continue the little skit as we drive on.

"You're limited to two items of patriotic clothing," my dad says. "Please remove your sweatbands, bandana, or T-shirt."

"I'd recommend the sweatbands," Billy says. "They serve no pur-pose. Your wrists don't appear to be sweating."

"Why aren't you driving, Billy?" Suzanne asks. "You're the big car person."

"I'll drive whenever you want me to," he says. "I'm just finishing something up back here. Dealing with this client—pain in the ass . . . "

"You'll like this car," Suzanne says. "It goes from zero to ohmygawd in five seconds."

"Lyle, what do you think of this?" Billy says. "This guy wants an old-school bobber, but he's telling me he wants a single-sided swing arm. It's just not working for me."

"Oh, like Dad knows," I say.

"I know," he says.

"Dad had this chopper," I explain to Kit. "He had Billy put in a jockey shift and a suicide clutch. Why? So when someone asked if they could go for a spin, he'd say, 'Sure, but it's a suicide shift,' making the person feel inadequate."

"It's a test," my dad says. "Only people in the know can—"

"Except even you couldn't figure it out! He was always stalling it, and whenever I came by and he was in the garage staring at it, he'd say, 'It's fine, just fine. Damn it, Sarah, give it a rest.'"

"Give it a rest," he says.

"That's funny," Kit says.

"If something's funny, one should laugh," my dad says.

I smile to myself, not quite understanding the rhythm to all of us, to all of this, but preferring it over solemnity. I feel slightly free.

I drive through Blue River alongside the lake and in between the fracture line of trees. On the stereo the rapper stops yelling and a slow song comes on, working like a kind of pacifier on everyone. I like the guitar, the soft horns, the male singer's high falsetto. I move my shoulders away from my ears. Suzanne begins to sing, making up her own lyrics to the song.

"Now I'm an old coug, my husband traded me in," she croons.

"Suzanne's getting a divorce," I explain to Kit. "She's having a very hard time and I haven't helped. I've been selfish."

"I guess you can be," Suzanne says. "That's the thing. You have everyone trumped."

"I can't have that attitude forever," I say.

"But you can for now," she says, and I'm grateful that the tension between us has subsided.

"Dickie Fowler," Suzanne sings, "I have your cufflinks."

"I read about him in the paper," Kit says. "He's not in the ski business. He's in the steel, land, and lumber business."

"He said that?" my dad asks.

"No, but in the article an ex-employee said he did," Kit says. "Why are you getting a divorce?"

I'm proud of her for being direct.

"Oh, the usual," Suzanne says. "Fatigue, boredom—on his part, and possibly a wandering penis."

"Well, his name's Dickie," Kit says. "That had to tip you off."

I laugh. She's getting funnier, I've noticed, and the smooth way she delivers the asides makes me think she may normally be this way. She reads the newspaper, she is possibly funny, she touches the bridge of her nose when she's nervous. There's much more to her and I should know better: to not let the one-sentence story always be the thing that walks a few steps ahead. Like my lead-in: The Woman Who Lost Her Son.

"My parents are in the process of getting a divorce," Kit says. "It's hard to see my mom go through it. I'm sorry."

Just like that, Suzanne is on her side. "Why are they divorcing?" she asks.

"My dad evidently met the love of his life," Kit says. "I think she was once an exotic dancer. Now she's a sales rep for Red Bull. I'm serious."

"Last night Sarah and I saw Dickie with another woman," Suzanne says. "She was black, not that that matters or anything. It just took me by surprise. You don't see a lot of the blacks here—"

"Oh my God, Suzanne," I say.

"Wish we did," my dad says. "It's part of the reason the ski business is experiencing losses. The generation today—what are they called? Whoever they are, they're diverse, and skiing is the whitest pastime next to, I don't know, antiquing, so unless we can get Lil Wayne in the half pipe, things aren't looking good."

"How the hell do you know who Lil Wayne is?" Suzanne says.

My dad doesn't answer. I think of him watching shows with Cully downstairs, the clink of pool balls, the murmur of their voices, deep and happy. It's become a memory of perfection.

We wind up Hoosier Pass, the mountains close, touchable.

"Anyway," Suzanne says, "I'm very good friends with an African American couple so . . . "

"Yes," I say. "A senator from DC who names his children after expensive towns. Hampton and what's the other one?"

"I forget," she says. "Nantucket or something."

"Probably not Greenwich," Kit says.

"Look at you go," Suzanne says.

"I'm sorry about your parents," I say. "Your mom."

"Yeah, she's got a lot on her plate," Kit says. "Probably couldn't take much more."

"She probably doesn't have an entire town gawking," Suzanne says.

"My dad's the chief surgeon at the hospital nearby," Kit says. "Small town. My mom forces herself to leave the house. Not that I'm trying to compare. It wouldn't matter if it wasn't high-profile. It's still painful. She's still mortified. The new girlfriend has breasts that look like cannonballs."

"Of course," Suzanne says. "They all do. But I apologize. I didn't mean to compare."

Suzanne is chastened and so am I. You can't compare and rank heartache. Pain is pain is pain. There is no precise measurement. No quarter cup.

"This is beautiful," Kit says, and everyone in the car seems to turn to their own thoughts as we descend from the pass, the mass of towering mountains regal and silent.

I slow down when we reach the dead town of Alma. Cully and I would play our I Spy game here—whoever saw any sign of life would win. The song on the stereo seems to be going on forever, in a luxurious, slow-cooked way. It finally comes to an end and something different comes on, a tune that's folksy and full of catchy energy. I love Cully's mixes—their blend of old and new, things I like and things I don't. I like that there are songs I know and songs like this where he seems to be showing me something new.

"What is this?" I ask. "What are we listening to?"

"I don't know," Kit says, when she realizes I'm talking to her.

"It's one of Cully's CDs," I say. "I thought you may have heard it before."

"You knew Cully?" Suzanne asks, and I realize my mistake, and my mistake in keeping so much a secret in the first place. That seems to be why everything goes wrong, thinking people care about the same things you do. You get yourself stuck in a self-made maze.

I glance at her in the rearview mirror, nod my head.

"Yes," Kit says. "I knew Cully." A long pause and then she says, "He liked the smell of fuel."

"Now that's an odd recollection," Suzanne says, giving me a look.

"I'm into . . . smells," Kit says, and I see her touch her nose. "And I just remembered, that's all. Something he said once."

"What? What did he say?" I ask.

"We were going up Boreas Pass. It was in August, just after I moved here. We were trailing a guy on his dirt bike. He said that he liked the smell of—"

"Two-stroke exhaust," Billy says.

"Yes, that's right," Kit says. "I couldn't remember the name."

I look at Billy in the rearview. He's contemplative and comfortable. He meets my eyes.

"You got here in August, so you'll leave in June?" Suzanne asks. "That's what all you kids seem to do."

"I don't know when I'll go," Kit says.

I watch her gazing out the window and wonder what she's remembering. "What were you doing?" I ask. "When you were with Cully."

"Just going for a drive," Kit says.

As we are now, I think to myself. I turn onto Highway 24. The road is flat, open—rolled out before me, syrupy black pavement and rippling oily air.

"So how did you know him?" Suzanne asks. "From work or . . . "

"Yes, from work," she says. "I was a waitress. He parked the car I borrow sometimes and—"

"Is 'parking your car' a euphemism for something?" She punches the air in front of her. "I'm sorry," she says. "That was—"

"It's okay," I say.

Suzanne turns to face the back. "Did you know him well?" she asks.

"I would have liked to know him more," Kit says.

"Then this will be nice for you tonight. My daughter's putting on a party for Cully."

"Oh," Kit says. "I didn't know."

"They were best friends," Suzanne says. "Grew up together, went to the same college . . . "

When Morgan applied to CC, Cully was irritated, which was rare for him. He told me that when she got there, he sent the message that he had his own life there.

"You go to college to leave stuff behind," he told me over the phone. "For her sake too. She needs her own life."

Now she will always be his best friend, immortalized. I can picture Cully shaking his head, smiling. *Let her have it.* I try to see Kit's reaction. She's contemplative, if not slightly irritated, left out.

"If anyone's hungry, I threw some sandwiches in a cooler," my dad says.

"Can we stop?" Suzanne says. "I don't like eating from a cooler. Makes me feel poor. I like gas station food."

"I do too," Kit says.

"Me too," I say.

"I love Slim Jims," Billy says, and I hold down a smile, feeling strange. I think I might be having fun and can't see how this is at all possible. It's the thrilling illegality. Sometimes I worry that my unhappiness will never end. But what's more terrifying is the thought that it will. If happiness doesn't last, then neither can its opposite.

"We could stop at that gas station next to the antique shop," Suzanne says.

"Okay," I say.

Suzanne's phone makes a noise and she bends over to her purse. "Where is it?" Her voice comes close to trembling.

"It's in the cup holder," Kit says.

The phone stops ringing and she listens to the message. When she's finished, she holds her phone on her lap.

"Just Dickie," she says. "Said I could keep the cufflinks. I can't believe I'll see him tonight. God, I'm depressed."

"We'll be there soon," I say. "You can go right to the spa. Get a massage. Maybe we all should."

I feel guilty for my momentary sense of ease, considering where we're headed. Kit must be so nervous and scared. Or might she be eager? I remember just wanting to get it out.

We drive in silence for a while and I get mesmerized by the road, the fields we pass, and abandoned tractors. I glance at Kit in the rearview, talking to my dad.

" . . . and that's why there's a run called Goodbye Girl," he says. "Twentieth Century Fox used to own the resort—"

"They invested after the success of *Star Wars*," Kit says.

"Yes!" he says. "How did you know that?"

"I took the walking tour," she says.

My father hits her thigh. "Kit," he says, "that's incredible."

Chapter 15

There are two gas stations on either side of the highway. One is a Chevron, which is brightly lit like a grocery store. I'm surprised when Suzanne tells me to go to the less glossy one adjacent to the antique shop.

"They have a great soda fridge," she says.

"When have you been here?" I ask. "And why?"

"Day trips," she says. "Sunday drives."

I imagine Dickie, Suzanne, and Morgan all together in the car. You can know people so well and still make discoveries about them as a family, but you'll never know everything, the mundane day-to-day, the behaviors when the doors are closed. Families are all such elite clubs. I imagine a new woman in the car with Dickie, or on the back of his motorcycle, taking a Sunday drive. It seems worse than picturing her in his bed.

I pull into the gas station. Compared to the robust, shiny pumps across the street, these look skinny, bare, and inoperable. The store would look closed if it weren't for the neon sign in the glass window that says YUM DONUTS©. I turn off the engine.

We all get out of the car. Kit stretches her arms overhead.

"I'll pump," Billy says.

"Yeah you will," Suzanne says. She pats his back, then heads into the store. Their relationship has always been easy. When Billy came to town, mainly for birthdays or around holidays, Suzanne and Dickie always wanted to see him too. Dickie ended up becoming a client. Billy was always so hard to explain to people. With the moms I'd meet I'd find myself defending him—*we just went our own ways, he's a nice guy*—and I'd catch their pitying looks. Suzanne and Dickie always understood that we were all okay without me having to explain or defend him.

"I can't wait to see the facilities in this place," my dad says. "Will you get me some sort of sandwich that doesn't involve egg or tuna?"

"So, what then, turkey?" I say.

"Strike that. I've got the sandwiches. I will take a Tiger's Milk bar, a yogurt, and some beef jerky."

"Billy?" I ask. "Your order."

"I'll have a large bag of Funyuns, a Coke, and a muffin. Oh, and a Slim Jim."

"Kit, do you need money?" my dad asks.

"No," she says. He hands her a twenty anyway. "Go nuts."

He walks toward the bathroom, shaking his right leg as he goes.

The air is dry and windy. Suzanne opens the door for me and a little bell rings. Kit and I wander down the same small aisle. I collect the bar and the chips, then scan the shelf for myself. Every choice is a loss of some other opportunity. I weigh my options, then choose the bag of Flamin' Hot Cheetos. Kit chooses the Sno Balls.

"Is it what you craved?" I ask. "Do you have cravings?"

"I have aversions more than cravings," she says.

"Ha," I say. "So do I."

She looks toward the window at Billy outside, filling up the gas tank. "So you guys never married?" she asks.

"No, we broke up before he knew I was pregnant. He was a fling, but we've remained friends." One of the easiest friendships I've ever had, I think.

"You guys would make a good couple," she says.

I laugh, quickly but maybe with too much effort.

"You doing okay?" I ask. "This must be very strange for you."

"And for you," she says.

Yes, and yet I have to really focus on it, remind myself. I'm almost comfortable in this discomfort. It's like being on an airplane and standing up. A relief. But I'm still on a plane.

"I think I'm okay," I say.

Strange things seem to become normal very quickly, I've noticed. You just adapt. It's like there's some mechanism in us that converts maelstroms and foreign objects into something usable, like yen into dollar bills. Or maybe in my case, it's just my mind, unwilling to fully comprehend that she is pregnant with Cully's child and soon she won't be. What should I be feeling? How should I be behaving?

"I hope this wasn't a mistake for me to come with you guys," she says. "I didn't know about tonight. Seems like a family thing."

"Oh, I think you've earned the right to be there," I say. "To mourn him or celebrate him." I lower my voice. "We're sort of just doing this because we have to. Morgan does these things. Even his birthdays she'd organize. I'd have birthday dinners for him, or graduation dinners, including all of us, and she'd have to do one too. It's how it's always been."

"But it will be nice," Kit says.

"None of his friends even go to school there anymore," I say.

"I probably shouldn't go though," she says. "I don't have anything to wear."

We continue down the aisle, looking at all the packaged goods. I get Dad and Billy's jerky.

"Do you get tired?" I ask, remembering my fatigue with my very first pregnancy and feeling like I didn't deserve it since there wouldn't be an end result.

"Just nauseous," she says, "as you know."

"That could also be from drinking," I say. "Have you been drinking a lot? This whole time?"

"No," she says. "Haven't wanted to, really, until I found out about you. I know it's bad, but I guess I knew it wouldn't matter. That must sound horrible."

"Some people drink throughout the entire pregnancy. I'm sure you're fine. Or you would be. Not that it matters."

We reach the end of the aisle and stand in front of the soda fridge. This is much easier. That line of conversation was too hard for me, but this soda fridge is inconsequential and neat and Suzanne was right: it's a good one. It has the latest drinks as well as vintage cans of Sunkist. I pull on the glass door, which is decorated with a poster of a woman in a silver, one-piece bathing suit riding an energy drink called Galaxy into space. I get Billy's Coke, then choose a root beer for myself, the plastic bottle, because it now has twenty percent more. Kit chooses a Snapple and I'm unreasonably pleased—like this is a good, healthy choice. Something obvious then occurs to me.

"How far along are you?"

"I must have conceived the night before he . . . or a few days before. Or that week before. One of those."

"Oh," I say, realizing what she's recalling. "And it's been confirmed, of course. By a doctor."

"Yes," she says. She looks at me worriedly, like she's explaining death to a small child.

I count back the weeks—all of January, all of February, half of March.

"So it's still just a thing, a speck," I say. "A mung bean."

"I'd have to look up mung bean."

For some reason this makes me snort-laugh, but then I say, "It's not too late?"

"No," she says. She looks me in the eye.

"Sorry," I say. "The mother in me," and then I'm reminded that I'm not one anymore. We walk to the outskirt of the store so I can get Dad's yogurt.

"These are so good," Suzanne says. She's walking down the aisle of Chapstick, miniature packets of pills, gardening gloves, and nuts, and eating from a bag of sour cream pork rinds. "This was all I ate on Atkins." She looks at what Kit's holding.

"Very cool. I had my doubts about you. Thought you'd be one of those almond-and-cheese-stick types. That's what Sarah always gets, but look at you—pink balls tarred in coconut. Think of the fun we can have with those. Enough balls jokes to get us to Wyoming." She sighs as if we've all accomplished something, then walks toward the counter in that slow, open way that suggests you follow. We do. "Only at a gas station are you allowed to buy things like this," she says, nostalgic. "I've had some good times here."

We reach the counter, where there's a pleasant aroma of hot dogs and the interior of a new car. I pick out a single-package banana nut muffin.

"Is this all together?" the clerk asks. He's a lanky boy with hair so stiff from gel you'd think it would make a sound if knocked upon. We put our things on the counter. Kit reaches in her bag for money.

"Don't bother," I say.

"We have a trickle-down friendship," Suzanne says. "This too." She moves four shrink-wrapped brownies toward him and hands over her card. "Hopefully they're laced with something."

He runs the card, with his tongue poking assertively through severely chapped lips. *Chapstick, aisle two.*

"Did you find everything you're looking for?" he asks, belatedly. He bags our things in a way I'd say is overly tender.

"Nope," Suzanne says. She takes her open bag of chips out of the plastic bag.

"Would you like to make a donation to the Eagle County Charter Academy soccer team?" he asks.

"Never heard of 'em," Suzanne says.

She walks out and we follow, the bell sounding its bright chirp.

"Chapstick, aisle two," I say.

"Ha!" Suzanne says. She looks at Kit, still trying to figure her out. "Your balls look so good," she says to her. "I bet you'll eat both of them."

"You're so trippy," Kit says.

"Trippy? Never heard that one before." Suzanne puts her arm around Kit and squeezes her like a fellow frat boy. She holds her other hand out in front of them. "How many fingers am I holding up?"

"Four," Kit says.

"Your eyes are fine," she says, and I remember we told her we're taking her to the eye doctor.

"I'm going to go next door real quick," I say, needing a moment alone.

I walk on the dry gravel to the shop next door and look at the fields with crooked gates and tamped-down golden grass. I think about Cully's fondness for the smell of fuel. Two-stroke exhaust.

A crow caws and I smile to myself. That December morning when I walked away from his body, a crow released a forlorn cry, my shoes against the snow made it sound like I was walking on ice cubes, and I could smell the resin on the trees. I thought, *I can't go outside again because of that fuckin' bird and the sound of my shoes and the smell of sap. Every time I come out here, I'll hear and smell his death.*

But look at me now. I'm walking and the crows can caw their little hearts out.

Chapter 16

The plank flooring in Pete's Antiques is soft; the shop, warm. It smells like ancestors instead of hot dogs. I lean over to look into a huge black bowl mounted on faded, red wooden legs. Dead people once owned everything here. Gave birth on the beds, had sex on the settees, ate from the spoons, banged the gongs.

"A cauldron," someone says, startling me. I turn to see an older man, perhaps Pete. He runs his finger along the bumpy rim of the bowl.

"Some things beg to be touched," he says, and I wonder how other people respond to that because I'm not sure how to. "This came from Manitou Springs." He has an animated voice with a sardonic lilt that infuses his words with air quotes. "Manitou is the witch capital of Colorado."

"Yes," I say, because saying "I know" seems obnoxious.

"Do holler at me if you need my assistance." He walks away, holding his hands in an awkward prayer position behind him. I go to the back of the shop where the larger furniture is displayed. There aren't any customers back here.

I head to the wooden rocking chair but change my direction when I see the bed—a four-poster mahogany. There's a sign that says Please Touch and so I get onto it, letting my legs hang over the edge. I run my hand down one of the posts and look at the smooth board, the eddies in the wood. I had a bed like this when I was a girl and wonder what happened to it. I'd lie back and stargaze at my own arboreal galaxy in the canopy, writing poems and listening to the

Rolling Stones, ruing my life without a mother, but since I couldn't completely remember her, I think I sort of relished the ruing itself. I think of Seth now, the senior to my sophomore. I would lie in my canopy bed and pine for him. Some things beg to be touched.

When I was that age, speakers at assemblies would always talk about all the pressure we'd soon face or were facing—pressure to do drugs, to have sex—but when I turned sixteen and was dying to smoke pot and have sex, I found the search for both to be impossible.

Then there was Seth. Then there was a party. On the top of what's now Peak 7, construction workers had cleared a small amphitheater of space, behind it fragrant trees spaced widely apart, fallen branches serving as benches. We all drove up on the access road, built a bonfire, drank beers and wine coolers. Further down from the clearing was the Igloo, which was really an old wooden shack, a crawl space built for skiers to warm up. It may still be there.

Seth asked if I wanted to go in with him to talk.

"Sure," I said, knowing exactly what was going to happen, or at least knowing what I wanted to happen: I wanted to kiss him. I wanted to crawl out of there with him, with everyone looking at our smug expressions, wondering. He had been flirting with my friend, Amber, but something told me he was drawn to me, something in his flitting, suggestive gaze told me we were going to put our arms around each other, if not that night then the next, or the next, or possibly, hopefully, the next.

I think I was enamored with him just because he paid attention. He'd look at me, almost luridly, which had to be the most flattering thing in the world. I'd feign annoyance, but my heart would race. He was beautiful, and you wanted to be around him because he'd make you beautiful too. He was like Billy in some ways, the way he could make me feel, though Billy was always kind.

That night I would kiss Seth. I would let him feel my breasts. And he did kiss me. For a long time. And he did feel my breasts, for a long time too. At one point he squeezed my nipple and it startled me. "Ouch," I said.

We stopped kissing then, and he drank from his beer. From the Igloo I could see light from the bonfire through the wooden slats. He put his hand on my leg as if to keep me there. I had never met someone so sure of himself. This confidence, I learned, could take a person places, but as far as I was concerned our journey would be ending soon. We had done enough for now. We were on a construction site. I imagined it resuming someplace else.

"I'm good," I said when he offered me a drink, and then I crawled toward the opening of the shack. He slapped my butt, then grabbed me by the hipbones and pulled me onto his lap. It felt territorial and nice. He held me around my waist. "Stay."

"Okay," I said. I could stay a while longer. Outside, the clearing, smallish and asymmetrical like a skating pond; the fat stars, the fragrant trees, the flicker of flames from the bright, illegal bonfire. I was seeing poetry. I wanted poetry.

He moved his hands on my thighs. I could feel myself, my body, wanting. I could feel him hard under me. I moved, slightly, on top of him, and then I turned my head and kissed him, still moving the lower half of my body on his. At another pause I made to leave, but again he pulled me back onto him, as I knew he would.

"We should go," I said, and leaned in for a closing peck, but he kissed me hard and sloppily and I decided to give it a go, give in to total desire, but it didn't work. I was self-conscious about the people outside, about someone coming in and seeing us. I wanted public declaration, I wanted him as a boyfriend. I wanted dinner, a bed, music, sweetness, a mix tape. Love. While kissing, I opened one eye and through my fluttering lid I watched his closed eyes, his moving face. He looked like he was nursing, and I laughed in his mouth, then pulled away. He moved out from under me, then moved his chest against mine, pushing me, his mouth on my mouth, until my back was flat on the ground. My mouth was still in a nervous smile and he licked at my teeth.

"I want to fuck you so bad," he said.

No mixed signals there.

He moved his hand through my hair, then under my jeans and down into my underwear.

"You're so wet," he said, and I didn't know what to say in response. I was soaking but felt anything I said would sound ridiculous. *Indeed, I am so wet? Yes, I'm wet for you?* This was Seth—my object, my focus for so long—I was finally getting his attention, yet his words were making this bright star of a boy fade fast. *Don't fade. Be perfect. Be from a book.* And so I too moved my hand under the buckle of his jeans and the elastic of his boxers. I wasn't really enjoying myself any longer, but holding his penis was somehow less awkward than talking to him, and I hoped it was buying time for him to realize what was happening between us: intimacy. He stopped touching me and undid his jeans. Then he sat up and straddled me.

"I really like you," he said.

"You should," I said, trying to be coy. It was difficult to talk because of his weight, but I thought this made me sound sexy, breathy. I took a chance: "I like you too. I have for a while."

I felt good just looking at him. Us, looking at each other.

"Do a little?" He rose up on his shins, then took his penis out. He poked my chin with it, then brushed part of my jawline with its tip. "Say ah," he said, and laughed.

"Gross," I said. I may have laughed even though for the first time I felt disgust and perhaps fear. I was trapped beneath him and was starting to become aware of the cold. "Let's go back outside by the fire," I said. *Don't fade.*

He moved his hand gently from my hair down to the base of my neck.

"Come on," he whispered. He rubbed my throat. I tucked my chin to catch his hand, and he moved up higher on my chest, then leaned over and placed his hands on the ground above my head. I opened my mouth and took him, my face feeling ugly and contorted. I stopped.

"I can't."

"A little more," he said, a quiver in his voice.

I resumed my task. I was sick with myself for being too embarrassed to say no, but felt I had passed a certain point and that it would be unfair to stop. Finally, I said, "There," and tried to sit up. Did I say, "I'm cold" or "Let's go back"? I don't remember.

He crept down my body and pulled my shirt and sweater up and kissed my stomach, then moved his face down to the zipper of my jeans and he unsnapped and unzipped and pulled both my underwear and pants down at the same time and shoved himself into me.

I said, calmly, "Stop. Stop," and he did, soon after. He shuddered, moved farther in, fast, and then slowly out. The "out," I have to say, was a shameful pleasure. It itched a scratch? I don't know. As opposed to the mean thrusts, it was a gentle sensation, soothing what needed to be soothed. I wanted to cry from the release, from the feeling of having him out of me, almost (though I didn't think this then) like giving birth.

I sat up. I could feel semen slide out of me, down into my buttocks. Seth buckled his jeans. I pulled up my underwear and my pants.

"You good?" he said.

I was not good. I was pregnant. I would find this out one month later. I would be terrified and alone, ashamed and so, so far from good. I no longer felt young. I had aged in seconds.

His voice, its lightness and softness: confusing. I don't think I answered. I was crying, though he didn't know that.

"I'm thirsty," he said. "You're cool, right? You're good?"

He was polite. He said, "After you," and I crawled out, stood up, then walked toward the party above me. I hated everyone there. Really. I walked up the hill, hated everyone. I walked up the hill, looked down at my pants, sure the wetness was visible. The moisture sickened me. It had been easy for him because of it, the residual desire. I thought it was blood because I was in pain, but it wasn't.

I walked toward the fire. I felt my pubic hair freezing onto my skin. Each step, a tug.

He mumbled something and walked quickly in another direction, toward a group of guys by the surveyor line for the new lift. That was how I lost my virginity. It was one of those moments, and there weren't too many of them, when I longed for my mother. I cried for her that night in bed, saying *Mom, Mommy, Mommy* out loud.

Kit walks into the antique shop. She sees me and heads in my direction. For the first time I wonder how my son treated her and if her decision has anything to do with him. I can't imagine knowing something like that about your own child. I'd see Seth's mom at the rec center sometimes, doing her step aerobics class. She always wore a belt around her leotard and would sing along to the music, whereas it seemed like everyone else was out of breath. You could be a good mom and it still didn't matter.

"Nice bed," Kit says.

Something is happening here, something nice, and I partly prefer the way it was before—untrusting and angry.

"You mind?" she says.

Would I mind what? then realize what she wants.

"Hop on in," I say.

She has to jump a little because she's small like me and the frame is high off the ground. I look away as she gets settled because it feels like I'm seeing something private, like watching her dress.

"Are you going to tell Suzanne what's going on?" Kit asks.

"I don't want to," I say. "She's my friend, but I just don't want her to . . . I don't know."

"Know you differently from the way she knows you now," she says.

"Okay," I say. "That sounds right."

"Maybe I'm speaking for myself," she says.

"She's also ridiculously conservative," I say. *I'm protecting you*, I don't say.

We sit together and I look at our legs side by side.

"I had a bed like this," I say.

"What kind is it?" she asks.

"The heavy kind," I say.

She surveys the bed, puts her hand around a post. "Barley twist posters," she says.

"How do you know that?"

"For a writing class in college I wrote a short story about girls who steal their mother's antiques to pay for tickets to a Madonna concert. I researched French antiques with regional chart clues and clarifications."

"Thorough," I say. "Was it based on a true story?"

"It was based on someone else's true story," she says. "I would never do something like that. You are witnessing my wild stage."

"Cully was a result of my wild stage," I say. "My detour."

"Good result," she says, and I want to tell her it was, but at the same time I don't want to sell her anything. Being a mother is so hard. No one tells you how difficult it is and even if they do, language doesn't communicate the varied hues of motherhood.

"You must have done well in school," I say. I eye another rocking chair and wonder how long it's been sitting here and how much longer it will stay. I imagine myself rocking in it, in my empty home.

"I did okay," Kit says. "I liked school, but I wasn't crazy studious or anything. I just know odd things. I remember things you don't need to remember."

"Like what?"

"Like . . . ," she says. We're so close. I try to scoot over a bit without seeming rude. "George Washington had dentures made out of hippopotamus tusk."

"Really," I say.

"Yeah," she says. "Dude had hippo teeth."

"I loved school," I say. "I was that annoying girl who always had her hand in the air." I remember studying the course catalog, strategizing, choosing classes as if packing them for a trip. Each class added a layer to me so that I thought I was building myself. Each year was a chance to start over or to edit what I had built.

"You should go back," she says.

I laugh, then my mind hitches onto the possibility of it, of any and everything. Demolition derby. Grad school. "Yeah," I say, and stop myself from saying, "You should."

"Your dad wants you to go to medical school?" I ask.

"He does," she says. She laughs as if recalling something. "When I was little I'd go to the hospital after school a lot, sit in his office and do homework. Sometimes he'd bring me into the operating room. He'd pick me up so I could see the patient he was working on. He'd point out the liver, the heart, the fat. I loved it."

I imagine her father's forehead wrinkled with surprise by his daughter's ability to look so closely at the insides of a body.

"But I loved that it was his," she says. "His work. I don't think it's what I want to do."

"I have trouble picturing you and Cully together," I say. I see him on the skate ramp. I see him in college, backpacking trails by himself or hiking with his snowboard to untouched terrain. I see him on the Million Dollar Highway, all cool and able.

"I think I was an exception to his rule," she says, and smiles as if remembering something specific. "But he was the same as me. He knew odd things too. I think I let him off the hook a bit. He could be uncool with me. Like, I bet Rocky felt relieved to just be with Adrian and not have to, you know, flex. We watched that movie together. It's a really good movie."

"What do you mean by uncool?" I ask. "How would he be uncool?" I want to lie back, I'm enjoying this so much. It's good to stop for a moment. I feel like we've been moving so fast.

Kit swings her leg off the edge of the bed. "I don't know. We watched a lot of movies, played a lot of pool. Pool was big—we'd take it very seriously. We went for drives and just talked nonsense, like . . . one time he asked me what words made me laugh. I guess he had watched something on the Discovery Channel about the planets and every time they said 'Uranus,' he laughed. It's a word that's always funny."

I remember my dad and Cully laughing about this. I remember them watching this show.

"Titicaca," Kit says. "Balzac. Those were my words. Then we just got into words we liked, based on sound alone. We ran through words for hours."

I close my eyes for a second, warmed by the thought of this commonality he has with me—being so opinionated about words—and also warmed by the thought of him sharing this activity with someone else, and having it be valued and loved. I think he must have loved her and now I do see them together.

"He was sweet," she says. "And super funny. I always felt like I was on an adventure even if we were just sitting there." I watch her thinking of him.

"He was a fling though?" I say.

"Maybe," she says. "I was playing it cool. We were fooling around, I guess, seeing what would happen. Who knows what would have happened?"

She looks at me and by her expression I see that something has changed. She's still remembering him, perhaps, wondering what would have happened. It's taken me so long to realize other people loved him, other people are hurt. My dad, Billy, even Suzanne, yet they must feel they can't compete with me. I give her a moment.

A mother walks to the back section with a toddler on a leash. When the child tries to sit on a hideous needlepoint footstool, the mother gives the leash a tug.

"Your mom should have gotten you one of those," I say.

"One of what?" she says, then understands. A leash.

"Have you talked to her lately?"

"Almost every day," Kit says. "She has phone interventions. She talks about successful people my age. Kelly Caswell got into Harvard Law, Maeve Richy is going to Parsons School of Design, Gigi Strode opened a boutique." She imitates her mother's voice and I envision a posh socialite. "In our last conversation she told me she got me antique earrings from Gigi's boutique—from the late seventeen hundreds. They're little wooden birds and I guess the beaks are gold. She said if she told me what carat they were, I'd absolutely die." She imitates her mother: "'They're marvelous. They're the bomb, as you say.'" Kit looks at me and says, "I have never, ever used that expression."

"She sounds like . . . a mother," I say, thinking how I'd do the same with Cully—constantly bring up the plans and occupations the other kids were doing. Why can't we ever see who our children actually are? Why can't we let them cook?

The toddler on the leash bends over, hanging her head between her legs. "I'm so tired," she says.

"Don't be dramatic," her mother says. "Can't wait until she's her age," she says to me. "Though I suppose that age has its problems too!"

"It goes by very fast," I say, liking her mistake in thinking I'm Kit's mother. Each age did have its problems and yet with each age I remember thinking, *This is my favorite. This is such a fun age.*

She pulls on the leash, and the girl follows her mother toward the front of the store, walking as if up against a strong wind.

"This age has its problems," Kit says to me.

"So does this one," I say.

The clerk walks toward us. We both get down from the bed.

"Isn't she a beauty," he says, then in a delayed gesture, raises his arms to portray his awe. "These are acanthus leaves carved into the posts. It's made of mahogany—"

"Wow, solid?" Kit asks, a question that impresses me and says a lot about the world she must be from.

The man freezes with his mouth open. "Don't insult me," he says, in a teasing voice to hide the fact that he isn't teasing.

I look at her and widen my eyes—an expression she automatically duplicates.

"Please notice the ball-and-claw posts," he says, and waits until we look down at the bed's claw-feet. "They're the size of grapefruits," he says. "Yellow grapefruits."

"Big foot," I say, and hear Kit stifle a laugh.

The man pats the bed, then slides a finger across the birds. "The pine has suffered from woodworm," he says, "but obviously the worms have been long dead and the bed has been treated. The drapes are sold separately, though I assume you'd want to choose your own to coordinate with your decor." He raises his arms: "With this bed you can be lady of the manor." He does a kind of bow, pivots, and walks away.

"Wow," I say. "I should buy it. It could be . . . ceremonious. Or maybe something less heavy."

The clerk walks back, holding a clipboard with sheets of paperwork.

"We're just looking," I say.

He raises his hand. Salespeople must hate when people say they're "just looking." It's like being sprayed with bug repellent. "I wanted to show you this." He hands me a sheet of paper. "Though it's a copy of the original, this, my dear, is a poem that was found with the bed."

Sleep, my sweet. Tomorrow we'll meet.
Then back to bed
where we will show
bliss and love. These stars move slow.

I believe this is meant to touch me. It may be the most horrible poem I've ever read. I hand the paper to Kit. She reads it, then hands it back to the man. He takes it, pivots, and walks away.

We look at one another and stifle laughs.

"That was bizarre," I say. "This is all very bizarre."

"Detours," Kit says. "What an odd dude."

I hear the toddler's mother say, "I've asked you to stop that. One, two, three, okay, that's it. You've lost points. I'm taking points away."

"No!" the little girl yells.

It's always amusing when it's someone else's kid. Kit watches the little girl, and I wonder if this is all confirming things for her, making her relieved that this won't be in store for her just yet.

"Sarah?" she says, her voice breaking. She looks at me with an intense fondness that both warms and scares me.

"Are you feeling okay?" I ask. "We should get going. I can't trust my dad near a store." I begin to walk to the front of the shop.

"Wait," she says.

"What is it?" I ask. "You're not going to be sick, are you?" I glance around and land on the cauldron.

"No," she says. "I wanted to suggest something. Offer something."

"What is it?" I stop by the rocking chair, tempted to sit.

"I'm trying to say—I'll just say it." She takes a deep breath and I smile, thinking she looks like she's about to propose to me.

"I don't want to have a baby," she says. "I'm pretty sure about that, but I would, I'm willing to . . . to give birth to it, or whatever. To have it for you. You and Billy. Or just you. If you want me to. I would do that—"

My smile falls. My grip on the chair tightens. She keeps talking as though explaining something to herself, and her line of thought begins to smooth itself out, making her suggestion, or offer, into what she thinks may be an obvious route and solution. The inevitability of it, her expression reads. The logic. I lean into the rocker. I could break it with my grip.

My body can't seem to register this news. My heart is pounding out joy and remorse and irritation. I think of her growing this child for me, like I've commissioned it. I imagine he or she floating in her womb, kicking her, moving from mung bean to melon, then coming out of her body and into my hands. I open and close my hands.

"What do you mean?" I ask. A clearer explanation will fail to penetrate, I'm afraid. My mind is not taking this. "What are you saying?"

"I'd have the baby for you," she says.

"Oh dear," I say, a ludicrous response. A new life flashes before my eyes like a montage in a rom com. I imagine caring for her, my round Kit surrogate. I'd take her on walks. Through the town, by the lake, the mountains behind us rising in faults and humps, like furniture covered with a white sheet. We could order pizza and watch movies, dipping our crusts into plastic containers of honey. I'd feed her like a goose.

Pop. Montage over. Gone. I look at her, sharply.

"If that's what you want," she says. "It's your choice. You can decide."

But I've already made my choices in life. I've made so many. That's why I'm here by this rocking chair. My choices have somehow led me to this. This isn't my choice to make. What has just happened here? I guess what I thought was going to happen when she first started talking: a proposal.

"You shouldn't have said that," I say. "And Billy? He never wanted the first one, why would you think he'd want the last?" I hurt myself with my own words. "Why did you do that?" I look around to see if anyone is witnessing this. As always, no one. Just the cups and saucers. Just the solid mahogany bed.

"Why did I do what?" she says. She looks frightened as though I'll shoot. I notice her hand on her stomach and I turn and walk away.

"You could at least answer me," she says.

I stop, turn, can't believe she just said that.

"You want an answer right now in Pete's Antiques? Do I want your baby? I'm obviously going to need some time to think about that. Or will we be late for your appointment?"

I walk toward the front of the store, feeling like that toddler, pulled into places I don't want to go, leashed by something I can never escape. I want to throw a fit. I consider calling Morgan to tell her that we won't be coming anymore, that life just got way too difficult, that this is a difficult age, an impossible age. We need to call it off, shut it down. What makes me get into the car? I don't know, but I do it. I see them waiting for me and I sense Kit behind me. I can't think of a better alternative.

Chapter 17

What happens if you cancel an appointment? Does the nurse ask for your reasons? Do they offer advice, question your choices, your future plans, your course of action? Or do they just let you go?

The road begins to elevate slightly. I pass a sign that says View Ahead. Isn't there always going to be a view ahead? There are turns in the road and they keep my mind focused. I drive fast, in an attempt to make everyone nervous. My silent, passive way of letting them know something has shifted, though no one is catching on. Kit, who's up front now, is the only one who knows that everything has changed.

The air is warmer here, the rocks a burnished red; the aromas of the dense pines are strong and a little sour.

I hear the flick of a lighter.

"Oh my God, that's what I smell." I turn to the back and see Suzanne pulling from her little pipe. "Stop it!" I say.

Smoke billows from her mouth like scarves.

"Billy!" I say.

"What? I took a minor inhalation."

"Kit is here and my dad's in the car!"

"I don't care," my dad says.

"I'm fine," Kit says, and I turn to her with a perplexed expression.

"I'm about to eat my snacks," Suzanne says, as if this explains everything. "This is insurance," she says.

"Cully used to sell pot," I say. "Doesn't this bother anyone? Apparently not! You fuckers. You animals."

Everyone laughs, even Kit. I make some kind of noise, a roar, but it comes out as a *roo* so I end up sounding like a spurned cartoon villain. I grip the steering wheel and swerve on purpose, making Suzanne laugh.

"Sarah," she says, "it's okay. Here. I'll stop. All done. Unless, Kit, do you want to insure your balls?"

"No, thanks," she says, then catches my eye and stops smiling.

I hear the crunch of a bag of chips.

I look at Billy in the rearview mirror. He holds a bud right up to his nose and takes a deep inhale. "Where'd you get this?" he asks.

"Yard guy," Suzanne says.

"That's funny," he says. "'Cause he works with grass and weeds."

"Brilliant," I say. "God."

"Sweet," Billy says. "I get sweet. Cherry, but there's a funky undertone."

"Cherry?" Suzanne says. "What are you talking about? More like grape. But yeah, there's a musty bottom."

"High!" I say. "It smells like it will get you high, assholes!"

Everyone laughs again. "I'm not trying to be funny." I try to take slow, calming nasal inhalations, but with Kit next to me I'm conscious of sounding like a mad bull.

"Is it a body or head high?" Billy asks.

"It's like a cannabis convention back here," my dad says.

I make Kit's window go down. I periodically glance at Suzanne and Billy in back, trying to communicate my anger, but they're busy, pensive as if in Napa tasting wine. They mumble to themselves:

"It expands."

"Oaky. Spicy."

"A basic strain."

"But good soil."

"I taste fertilizer. It's not organic."

"I think you're wrong about that. THC is high. Tingly. An up high."

"Citrus lineage?"

"I taste oriental carpets."

Laughter.

"Came from this guy Phil T," Suzanne says. "He is very cool. A pioneer. He took his dinky family business to another level. They were just a marginal mullet operation churning out shwag, but he got into botany, horticulture; toyed around with light, soil, temperature. No one was doing this then, at least not in Colorado. Now everyone's sensitive to the nuances of—"

I see a wide-enough shoulder ahead and pull over. We skid a little on the dirt and I brake hard, then turn to the back.

"You guys are seriously irritating the shit out of me right now," I say. "I am livid. No wonder our son did this, Billy. You sound like a trained professional."

"Cully dealt green marijuana," Suzanne says. "Relax."

"Is there something you're forgetting, Billy? Dad?"

"Come on, Sarah," Billy says. "We're just having a little fun. It won't hurt . . . "

"No one is supposed to have fun and it will hurt . . . you know." I gesture toward Kit but realize they don't know what I know. They don't know what I've been offered, what I need to think about. But if she hadn't made her little offer, would it be okay to make this car into a sweat lodge? Is it okay for her to drink like she did last night? What if she's already ruined the baby's life? Why do I care more now?

"Sorry, sweetie," Suzanne says from the back. "Sorry, Kit. Thought it could help your eyes."

"Sorry," Billy says.

I'm sorry. My anger is curious to me. What or who am I defending? A big rig rolls by, making the car tremble.

· · ·

NO ONE HAS said a word for the past hour. We are almost to the hotel and I feel like I need to tell them it's okay. I'm okay now. They can all leave time-out. I am eager to get to the room and think, though I'm put off that I have to think at all. Half an hour ago, on the road with the curves and trees, I thought, A baby. Yes, a baby. It wouldn't have to end. Cully wouldn't have to end. I can still be a mother.

Now we're in Colorado Springs, on Nevada Avenue, passing frightening motels, EZ Pawn, Bobby Brown Bail Bonds, places to get cash fast! and a baby seems out of the question. My soaring thoughts come down, down, down. Dirty cars speed alongside us. The sidewalks are littered with wrappers and sooty, frothy old snow. I imagine many elderly people have met their ends in these crosswalks. I imagine many young people have met their ends in the Stagecoach or the Chief Motel. We pass a car dealership with red and blue flapping flags and cars that look donated. Above is a billboard advertising the upcoming gun show.

"Look, a hooker," Suzanne says.

I look at the woman walking into a wig shop. Lavender down jacket. Stiletto heels.

"I wonder if business slows when it's cold and prostitutes can't show as much skin," Billy says.

"You think she's buying a wig or doing an a.m. bj?" Suzanne says.

"Maybe both," Kit says.

"A wig helps, I'm sure," my dad says.

Pikes Peak seems embarrassed in the distance, a blush cast down its side.

"You're bound to get shortchanged if you live here, don't you think?" Suzanne says.

"Morgan lives here," I say. "Cully lived here."

"They went to CC. That's not living here," Suzanne says. "That's like a pocket of warmth."

"The hooker's a pocket of . . . never mind," Billy says.

I want so badly to talk to my dad alone and yet don't know what to say. Sometimes I resist his advice, then doubt my own choice in the end. I need to talk to Billy instead. I stop at a light behind a mini-van with a Baby on Board sticker. Are you kidding me, gods?

"'Baby on Board,'" Suzanne says. It seems everyone is trying their best not to react, but maybe it's just me who's imagining this.

"The message offends me," my dad says. "So if there isn't a baby in the car, it's okay to just plow through it?"

"'Dad Farted and I Can't Get Out,'" Suzanne says.

"No way," Kit says.

"Right there," Suzanne says. I see the sticker on the beige mini-van ahead of us in the right lane. When we pass, we all turn to look at the driver, but the windows are darkly tinted.

"I don't think I've seen this many bumper stickers," Kit says.

"This is a bumper sticker town," my dad says. "But these are good ones. Usually here it's all 'God Bless Our Troops Especially the Snipers.'"

The scenery begins to change, as if the town is shedding a layer. We drive up Lake, a peaceful road that leads to the hotel. I haven't been here before. When I'd visit Cully I'd go to the Antlers. I'm glad the party is here and not on campus. I don't want to be there, to see the buildings where he tried to build and edit himself, to see Slocum Dorm where he lived. I don't want to see the life he had right before he didn't have one.

The trees are scraggly, bereft, making me proud of our bare aspens, the elegant shadows they cast. On the side streets I see homes with shade trees and American flags. Homes with Christian values—sons that play soccer and daughters with mild eating disorders.

The road seems like an entry way to something promising, and sure enough I see the hotel ahead, a beige muddy pink, the many flags in front making it seem like something important.

"It's like a gay embassy," Suzanne says.

Designs are carved into the grass in front. Gardeners are hunched in the hedges, all Hispanic men, probably not knowing why the hell rich people always need to carve shapes into their bushes. Pikes Peak now looks proud. There's a unity of color between the mountain, the strokes of light down its face, and the powdered mustard–rose pigment of the hotel.

I drive into the grand roundabout. It feels like we're in the Mediterranean, not Colorado Springs where only a few miles back was a strip club called Le Femmes.

"I'm going to the spa," Suzanne says. "Clear my head. Who's with me?"

"I can sit in the lobby," my dad says. "Close my eyes and clear my head under an elk carcass. For free."

"Are they antlers!" Billy says.

"Are they real!" my dad says.

"Billy, I need to talk to you," I say. "Can you try and get it together?"

"You kids gonna have a nooner?" Suzanne asks.

"Are we?" Billy asks.

"Everyone, please shut up."

"Oh, come on," Suzanne says. "Everyone's trying to have a good time. We love you. Join us."

"Kit is pregnant with Cully's child," I say to Suzanne.

I stop the car.

"Oh my God," Suzanne says, with a voice I rarely hear her use. "Are you all right?"

I'm not sure whom she's talking to. No one does, or at least nobody has an answer. I look at Kit's hands placed on her lap. Long fingers, chipped nails. She needs more calcium. I wonder if she's angry at me for outing her this way.

"What are you going to do?" Suzanne asks, and again, I'm not sure whom she's talking to.

"Kit's going to go live her life," Billy says. I look back at him, wondering what he'll say when I tell him about her offer.

"Oh," Suzanne says.

"Don't," I say. "I shouldn't have said anything."

"Don't what?" Suzanne says.

"Just don't say or think anything. Now you know." I look back. She lowers her sunglasses and turns away from me.

"How far along are you?" she asks Kit.

"It doesn't matter," I say. "Where the fuck are the valets? Isn't this a five-star place?"

"Well," Suzanne says. "You know how I feel about this."

"I told Sarah I'd have the baby for her," Kit says.

I feel like I hear a collective intake of air. I look at Kit and she's pleased, like she's found the way to get me to engage.

"You what?" my dad says.

"I told Sarah that I'll have the baby for her," she says again.

"That is wonderful," Suzanne says. "It's . . . it's truly beautiful is what it is. It's like a new life for him."

"Stop," I say, my voice weak. "Please." I turn back, pleading. Billy's jaw is clenched. I can't tell what he's thinking.

"Sarah," Suzanne says. "This is a gift. Morgan will—"

"Don't tell Morgan anything," I say. "She'll just take it and run with it like you do. Please get out and go. Do what you do—spend gobs of money and eat enough to fill a void as big as . . . as a whatever. Don't you dare pass moral judgments."

"A crevasse," my dad says. "A hat box. I'm not saying that you're—I'm just thinking of big things—"

"Sarah," Suzanne says, softly. "You can't speak to me that way."

A slick-haired valet opens my door with gusto. He has no idea what he has just interrupted but knows from my look that it's something. "Welcome to the Broadmoor?" he says.

We all get out, avoiding one another.

"Chip will bring your luggage to check-in," the valet says.

Chip has black hair and green eyes and is stunning. He makes us all stutter a bit before getting back on track.

"Hi, Chip," my dad says. "We don't really have much luggage."

"Are you sure, sir?"

"Yes, Chip, thank you," he says. "Traveling light."

He and Kit exchange brief smiles. Billy notices too.

I walk to the lobby and feel like I've been riding on a horse. My legs are sore even though I haven't used them, and I'm exhausted and feel sunburned even though I haven't done anything. I walk ahead of everyone else, wanting distance, or given distance. I hear their voices like a clique behind me, judging me.

"I'll get you your own room," I hear Suzanne say.

"Thank you," Kit says.

"This is going to be good, you know that? It will all be okay."

"It's up to Sarah," Kit says.

It's up to me.

Chapter **18**

I have Billy get me a seven-dollar chocolate bar from the gift shop and bring it up to my room. I've ordered a bottle of zin, why not. I open the drapes and walk onto the balcony. I look out at the fake lake and the fuckin' swans. Then I hear the knock from room service and walk back into the room.

Everything is so floral here, everything so clean and chilled. I want to mess things up, then call someone to make up my room. I love hotel rooms—the empty drawers, our lives condensed and un-fettered. Sometimes I think hotel maids have the best perspective on human nature, all the gunk we leave behind. I want to talk about this with Billy—the lives of maids, the decor in hotel rooms. I don't want to talk about the things that make my heart hurt. I open the door to Billy and a room service waiter who's wheeling in my single bottle of wine.

I'm taken aback for a moment at seeing these two men together, one scruffy, one polished as if by machine. *Couldn't you dress better?* I want to ask one. *Do you really need a cart?* I want to ask the other.

"Come on in," I say.

Billy makes an "after you" gesture to the waiter. He rolls in the wine reverentially. "Where would you like this?" he asks.

In my mouth.

"On the balcony," I say. "So I can see the fake lake."

Billy raises his eyebrows and walks in, kisses the top of my head, which feels natural and yet at the same time alarming.

"Take a moment," he says.

We follow our server to the balcony. He picks up the bottle and shows it to me. I nod. He opens. He pours me a sip and then the waiter waits, one arm behind his back.

Billy does the honors. He swirls the wine, sticks his nose in the glass, then takes a hearty swallow. "Naughty," he says. "Fruit forward. Rebellious. Want some?" he asks the waiter.

The waiter laughs, disproportionately relieved. "Nah, thank you, sir. Thanks." His voice is different now, like it's okay to be himself and not a guy who always wears a crisp white shirt, a black vest, and stands with an arm behind his back. I want to ask this man, *What would you do?* Or better yet, *What are your problems? Take me to them.*

I walk back inside to let Billy deal with the waiter and the wine and the pouring and the thank-yous. I can't do any of it right now. I go into the bathroom, which is like a retreat, and shut the door. More floral. A claw-foot tub. There's a sweetness here that doesn't match the topic. I hear them both laugh and I bet Billy got him to have a sip.

When I hear the cart roll by and the door close, I come out. Billy stands by the door of the balcony, holding a full glass of dark red wine.

"He didn't really know about letting it breathe," Billy says, "but I told him."

"Did you get him to take a sip?"

"This glass was even fuller before."

"Thank you," I say. "Cheers."

We clink our glasses together and I take a hearty gulp. Billy looks around the room and I do too, feeling a need to comment on something.

I pick up the apple next to the two plastic bottles of water. "I love it here." Billy smirks, but I didn't mean to sound sarcastic. "Everything I say sounds insincere," I say. "Look at that mountain." I take another swallow. "It's so indifferent. What is happening here?"

"I don't know," he says.

"I can't stop thinking of him, but I'm thinking of him as a baby and . . . it was so wonderful, but it was all so hard and I want to, I want to do the right thing, but I've failed already and what if I can't do it? If I'm not fit to . . . "

He takes my glass, puts it back down on the desk, and gives me a hug that I give in to. "It's all the right thing," he says. "And you didn't fail."

As we separate he kisses the top of my head and I look up. We look at one another, bemused, and then we kiss on the mouth as I knew and I suppose he knew we would. His tongue is warm and sweet. He has eaten a piece of my chocolate. His hand on my back makes its way lower. It's a slow, dizzying kiss. I experience that vertigo I always used to experience while kissing him. It's a feeling from girlhood when you kissed and kissed and that was all, until it wasn't.

But we're not young and kissing doesn't last long. I hook one hand onto the buckle of his jeans and pull him back toward the bed, but he takes charge, switching me so that he sits down first and pulls me to him, in between his legs.

"Wait," I say, when he leans back and tries to bring me up onto his lap.

There's no way I'm going to be on top; I can't imagine it, straddled naked over him, bouncing, his hands thrusting me forward, it's somehow too comical, too exposed. My face flushes. I am shy. He hasn't seen me like this for twenty-two years. My body is good with clothes on, but my skin hangs a little where it hadn't before. My breasts are in need of a refill. My stomach, my thighs, my ass are loosened. But he wouldn't remember me as I was before. I don't remember him. I recall a thin, strong frame like a cage, a natural, musk scent, a rogue patch of hair on his chest. What will he look like now? This emboldens me—instead of imagining your audience naked to bolster confidence, we should imagine their aged bodies. I unbuckle his buckle.

"You're pretty," he says.

We look at one another up close, my gaze drops down to his mouth.

"You want to have sex. Of course I'm pretty." I laugh, but he looks at me as though he knows I'm saying one thing to couch something else, or he just feels sorry for me, like I can't say and do what I mean.

He presses his mouth to mine because I suppose this is the easiest, most genuine thing we can do right now. I pull back, sense and caution seeping in, and shame—this is not a proper reaction to this dilemma—but he presses himself to me harder until my mouth softens and opens up and holds his like it's starved. It's one of those violent and desperate kisses you see in movies where the characters stand in the rain with their hands in each other's hair, kissing as though a war's about to start. I accidentally moan into his mouth and think, *Who am I?*

The sound of my voice pulls me out of the spell a bit. "It's so cold in here," I say, wanting refuge from the light underneath the covers. The room is so prim and Victorian. I feel like we should copulate while speaking in British accents.

When we were a couple we'd hook up in his silver Bronco, or on his mattress at his A-frame house in Blue River. He had three other roommates, and if we had had enough to drink I wouldn't muffle the sounds of my climax—I'd let it tear through the cabin. It was like ringing a bell, announcing we were united. I hadn't had sex like that in college—and possibly haven't since. Sometimes we'd have sex in the parking lot of Steak and Rib before his shift. I'd send him off with a smirk, feeling both dirty and wifely, then go home to wait for him to get off his shift. We'd head out at ten thirty to the bars—Pounders or the Gold Pan—sleep until one thirty or two. It was like a brief glitch in my life, like my bus broke down and I was forced to get off and ended up having a really good time. I got back on that bus, initially thinking I'd take what I learned and enjoyed with me.

And here we are again. I politely disembark and stand up so we can do a brief, sad striptease. The height of the moment seems scaled already, for me at least, but I know we have to do this. We started something and now we have to get it done. Now I feel a need to prove myself, to show myself as I once was. He takes off his shoes, then his pants but leaves on his white socks. One sock has a red line across the toes and one does not. He removes his boxers, then sits down, his strong thighs flayed. His desire is very apparent. Nothing Victorian about it. He is more filled out now, still trim, but no longer a cage. He has muscles, and a welcome sight of a small roll of belly. He's hairier than he was before.

I take my jeans off, grateful I'm wearing underwear that isn't large enough for two of me. I leave it on, as well as my socks and sweater, then try to get into the bed with some dignity. I end up performing a kind of pole-vaulting maneuver, something that started out silly and cute but ended up ungainly because I didn't commit. It's like switching *hi* to *hello* midsentence and coming out with "hilo."

I get under the covers, kicking my legs to loosen the sheets that are forcing me to point my toes. I laugh even though nothing is funny. I could cry.

Billy lies down on top of me, kisses me, takes off my sweater, my tank top, my bra. I wrap a leg around him and he moves his hand down my body, stopping at my breasts. I think of him fondling one of those squishy stress balls and as soon as I think this I know I can't reach between his legs without feeling a little ill. What has happened to my sexuality? It's so strange being beneath this man who used to make me buck and tremble and now I'm forcing myself to arch my back, forcing myself to slurp his tongue, just trying to conjure something back—the Bronco, the A-frame, the proud orgasms like a yodel in the woods.

He keeps his hand going—down, down, in between. He pokes around with his finger, then stops, licks his hand, and resumes, expertly. How many women has he been with, how many dates, what was Rachel like? I realize I'm tensing my thighs and let them fall open, then I take him and put it in as one puts a cord into a socket. It won't go all the way, so I pull at my skin around him and eventually we lather up enough moisture for it to work.

There. It's working. We are working, and sex does its job of making me forget. It's all sensation, focused sensation, so so so good—actually good, I'm good! And then I remember again, bits and pieces of my strange new world—Kit, Cully, even Morgan, the way they were as babies—the way red dots would appear on Cully's forehead when he cried, the way he'd shake his head as he came in toward my breast to nurse.

I climax anyway, right when I'm remembering all the things I'm supposed to forget, and having an orgasm while thinking of pregnancy, babies, and your dead son feels awful and weird, and at the same time unremarkable and true. This is all life is anyway. Throw in some food and sleep.

Billy moves out and off, then lies back with his hands cupping his head. He turns his head to me, a big childish grin on his face, then his smile goes away as if he's just remembered what sparked all this in the first place: desperation, an inability to think or speak, an urgent need to escape.

We stay still, looking at the ceiling.

"I read something interesting in my room," Billy says.

"Oh yeah?" I say.

"I guess in the main mezzanine," Billy says,"on the ceiling mural. There's a male dancer with two right feet."

I turn my head, but he just smiles and keeps looking up.

"Tell me this is weird for you too," I say, watching his expression.

He blinks twice, pulls his earlobe. "This is weird for me too."

"Tell me you don't do this with Rachel."

"Do what?"

"Go back to her after . . . "

He doesn't blink. "No. God, no. Why? Jealous?"

"No. I just don't want to be part of a trend."

"You are not part of a trend," he says, turning his head to look at me. He's just a head with a body of a sheet.

I look back up at the ceiling. I don't know why I asked about Rachel, why I care about trends. Maybe I see this happening again. It's easy. But then I reconsider: there are far easier things we could have done.

"God damn," Billy says, and I smile, thinking he's complimenting my skills, but I look over and he's crying. "Cully," he says, and chokes on his name. I curl into Billy, putting my face on his chest, which is heaving now. His hand on my lower back grips me like a ledge. "I'm sorry," he says, but I don't say anything. I just let him weep. I cry along with him, just when I think I have no more left. There will always be grief, endless reserves to draw from, which is strangely comforting. It doesn't last too long—this lament. It's like a passing shower. After, we don't say anything for a while and the silence is peaceful.

"I guess we should get up," he says. "A lot to talk about."

"Okay," I say, though I'm far from being ready. I don't know what to do, what I'm supposed to do, what I want. I imagine the dancer with his two right feet, waltzing in circles, the most memorable dancer, the painter's mistake.

BILLY AND I sit out on my room's balcony. We wear the provided terrycloth robes.

"Look at us," I say. "In dresses made out of towel."

"Like newlyweds."

I tilt my face to the late afternoon, imitating Billy's angle. We do look like newlyweds, or people in a hotel brochure acting as them.

When I told him I was pregnant, he drove to Denver, found my dorm, and said, "We can do this. We can marry." That's how he said it: "We can marry," which amuses me still. He was five years older than me, and yet right then he seemed like he could be my son. He

was this young child, trying to do the right thing. I knew he was living with another girl then.

"I'm not going to get married," I said then, and he looked so
relieved.

His parents had come up from Durango when I moved back to
my dad's at seven months. His dad was tall, but then I realized he
and Billy were the same height, his father was just more filled out.
He looked like he could chop down trees for a living. His mother
was short, fit yet round, with cropped brown hair and big earrings. I
liked them immediately. They walked into our home, didn't glance
around, didn't watch their step; they just looked at me as if I had accomplished something. They brought me flowers, then later, dinner
plates and sets of silverware and wineglasses that I still own. They
bought me a crib and a stroller, baby clothes and blankets. His mother's voice and vocabulary harkened back to actresses in fifties films,
a ring of wealth and sophistication. She called the brown crib sheets
"russet ginger." I think my dad felt bad. He hadn't thought of doing
any of these things.

"Do your parents have money?" I asked Billy after they had
whirled in, then basically out of my life. I hadn't really seen them
much after that first year, which made me feel inexplicably (or expli-
cably) discarded.

"Enough, sure," Billy answered. We were at my house, my dad's
house. He kept looking at his watch and I imagined the fights he and
his girlfriend (was her name Wanda?) must be having over me. He
looked around at the house. "The same. My mom though, she gives
things a newer touch." I eyed the dark wood walls, the antique furniture, the countertops, brown and grainy like a bran muffin, knowing
exactly what he was talking about. The homes with wives in them,
with mothers—those were the ones with the nice countertops, with
the painted walls and harmonious decor. I wanted a home like that
one day.

I looked at the set of silver, the deep bands on the handle.

"They're usually not so generous," Billy said. He picked up a fork. "Nice. No monograms. I swear my mom monograms everything."

Of course it's not monogrammed, I later realized. I was in a daze of new gifts, greedy and excited over things that I had never cared about before—onesies! blankets!—and I never thought at that moment how odd it was that they'd give me silver and wineglasses, wedding-like gifts. It was like they were arming me with everything I could need so that their son could be on his way. I thought he was the wild one, but in their eyes, it was me. Billy had gotten off the bus in the wilderness, but now he was back, ready to begin.

The sun has begun to sink a bit, giving Pikes Peak a cold blue tint. I look through the information catalog with images of the hotel, feigning interest in its histories and anecdotes, timelines, facts, and ghost stories. Feigned interest turns genuine. I learn that Julie and Spencer Penrose bought the hotel in 1916. Before that it was a casino and a school for girls. I look at Spencer Penrose in the book. *Hey there, Spence.* He loved a place. He built on it—little odes and anchors. I think of my ancestors, those hearty pioneers. My namesake, Sarah Rose Mather, dropping her anchor to run a dance hall. In her diaries it says, "Gambling, prostitution, and drinking are rampant in this town. I should think these people could use a place to dance."

Cully was my anchor to a place. Now, I suppose, it's my father. I imagine Kit's parents flying in from the East Coast, loading me with stemware and baby gear, then waving goodbye. How would that all work out? What if they want the baby? Shouldn't they be the first ones to choose?

"I don't know how I'm going to do this," I say. "I mean, if I do."

I look over at Billy and he's digging deep into his nose with his eyes closed.

"Being a mom of a baby today would be so different," I say. "Actually, I'd be the same age as a lot of moms."

"Yeah, they're having them late now," he says.

"I can't imagine starting all over again."

Billy strokes his chest. He does this unconsciously, pets his chest. I imagine him as a father again, a father with a baby in one of those things—the slings everyone wears now with their little infant strapped to their torsos, the baby looking at the world as if on a slow-moving zip line. I had a wire-framed backpack, the seat made out of a thin canvas. I look back and am proud of the way I got around with Cully—we'd hike in Blue River, we'd cross-country ski, go to the skating rink, the library on Mondays, get ice cream at the Crown. Little routines. I'm sure everything I owned has been recalled or discontinued. I think of strollers, diapers, BPA-free snack containers. Bottles, changing tables, pediatricians, high chairs. All the accoutrements of new life. Most mothers would be in their twenties and thirties—I'd have the exact opposite problem this time around.

"Could you?" I ask. "Do it again?"

"No, Sarah. I couldn't. I wouldn't."

He looks at me to make it clear.

I know this shouldn't disappoint me, but it does. I feel cheated, used. It infuriates me as well, the lack of consequence, the easiness. Babies and children don't necessarily change the course of men's lives, and somehow his not wanting Kit's baby doesn't look bad, but for me, it would. Yet I can't make a choice based on how it would look, how it would seem. I want to be done with those kinds of choices.

"It's like another chance," I say. "Our son never got the chance to be somebody else. Now he can." I think of the adventure park in Frisco, the rec center, the toy store, Spring Fling concerts. Things are better now for children. People like them now. They're allowed to be around.

I think of all the pictures Cully drew, his self-portrait from the back of his head, the school assembly where he played a folk song, "Four Strong Winds," on the guitar and everyone watched, stunned.

"I didn't know he could do that," Suzanne had whispered next to me.

"Neither did I," I said, taking picture after picture.

I also think of watching the clock, longing for his nap time, for his bedtime, for peace. I remember redirecting, scolding, putting in time-out, screaming, pushing him down sometimes. "No! Can't you just be good?" *Is it five yet? Can I have a glass yet? Can I put him to bed yet? Dad, could you watch Cully for a sec while I . . .*

Home videos, photographs—at times those were the only things that made me stop and love absolutely all of it. I smile now, at how crazed he could make me.

"You know?" Billy says. "I think Kit may have got caught up for a moment."

"What do you mean?" I ask, still basking in something.

"I mean, this whole offer. It was obviously a spontaneous idea. We've all gotten along pretty well, she got caught up, it's like getting buzzed and planning trips."

"She wasn't buzzed and she wasn't planning a trip," I say.

"I think this is her way of not making a choice," Billy says. "Or to feel good about herself, like she's giving us something."

"Giving *me* something," I say. "Which she is. Which she would be."

"What made you so angry then?" he asks.

I lift a leg out of the robe and sit up a bit. I was very angry.

"I wasn't angry," I say.

"You were pissed," he says.

"I was overwhelmed." I scratch my chest. "Fine, and a little angry."

"Because?" Billy asks.

"Because it puts the responsibility on me," I say. "Now it's me saying what to do. And her gift, or what have you—it's hard not to accept something like that."

"What are you saying?" Billy says.

"I'm saying, how could I not?" I sit up fully, put my feet on the ground, and hold my robe together. "It's Cully's. It's mine. How could

I not? Maybe that's why I'm mad, because I don't have a choice at all. You have Sophie—you have . . . backup! It's not the same."

This is it, of course. I don't have a choice, and while reminiscing about babyhood is wonderful, a little bile creeps up my throat when I think of changing diapers and being up all night and strolling, and talking to other moms. It would be different, of course. It would be my grandchild! But there'd be no one to return the baby to. It wouldn't be different. It wouldn't be a grandchild. I hear my voice shushing, singing, cooing, but also saying, *No! That's not a good choice, can you find another option, can you share? Can't you just be good? Dad, can you help for a sec while I . . . ?*

I've done it. In some ways I have done enough, and I can see that one day I will be okay with just myself, that I am my own anchor, but isn't a rejection of this child a rejection of him? Am I saying, *I don't want what I had with you all over again?* Because that's not the truth.

"Sophie isn't backup," Billy says. "She doesn't lessen anything."

"I know," I say. "I'm sorry. It just came out that way."

"It's hard," he says. "Seeing her. Not feeling . . . satisfied."

"I'm sorry. I'm really sorry."

"So you're going to keep it?" he asks.

"I don't know," I say.

Even though I think I do know. How could I not let this happen? "A baby." I sigh. "This would be for my dad too. It would give him a purpose."

Now we'd get the "Congratulations!" cards instead of the sympathy cards, those serious sentiments organized in three-part structures: 1. Life can be painful. 2. Love, love, love, and sorry about your life. 3. There's a purpose here, which has yet to be revealed.

"Your dad has a purpose," Billy says. "So do you."

I wave his words away, lean against the chair sideways so that I'm still facing him. "Remember that bookshelf you bought?" I ask.

"What?" Billy says. He begins to call someone on his cell.

"The bookshelf. The really heavy oak one. You bought it when we started dating, or screwing, or whatever. It only fit short books, but you liked the way it looked. You didn't need it. I don't think you owned even one book. You just wanted something nice at the Blue River house, and I bet it surprised you—your desiring it. It's not something you thought you'd ever want, but you grew up."

"Extra olives," he says.

"What?"

"One sec," he says.

"Are you ordering a pizza? I'm trying to have a heart-to-heart and—"

"What room are we in?" he asks.

"Fuck!" I say.

He stands and walks inside, probably to check the room number. He comes back, puts his hands on my shoulders.

"Sorry," he says. "I'm starving. I looked at the room service menu and a hamburger is twenty-four dollars and a coke is six fifty, and I thought we could have a bite and talk this thing out some more. I know you like black olives. I got extra. We'll have tons of olives. Did you want that bookshelf or something?"

NO, I DON'T want the bookshelf. I just thought of it. I also thought of the vacuum I bought when I moved out of my dad's and into my own place in the Silver King Condos on Boreas Pass. A red one. A cheap one. Dinky and in the end useless. When you're young, you always go for the cheapest brand, not realizing it will have to be replaced with something better and that you'll end up spending more in the long run.

I'm thinking about the big moments, the stages in a child's life:

Kindergarten.
Sixteen.
Driver's license.
Eighteen.

Graduation.
College.
Twenty-one.
Marriage.

The big ones. The rites of passage: one of them Cully and I have
never attained. But what about a young girl or a young boy, going
out to buy a vacuum or a bookshelf? Maybe this is when children
really grow up—not when they go to college, but when they make
this purchase, or one similar. Cleaning tools. Domestic things. Cully
didn't get to reach that stage.

I close my eyes and imagine his possibilities, the different hues of
his self, what his face would look like in ten years, the kind of man
he would be. He never had the chance to become himself. He never
had the chance to be anyone else.

"No, I don't want the bookshelf back," I say to Billy. I stand up.
"I was going to tell a story, I had a metaphor about . . . about things.
But never mind. It's ruined. You miss him too. What's wrong with me
wanting to have this baby? What's wrong with *you*?"

Billy walks past me, heading to the door.

I follow him and he stops in the hallway. "I miss *him*," he says.
He holds my shoulders firmly, though his voice is calm. "I loved
him. This isn't a reincarnation. This isn't a redo or a tribute or a
chance—I don't know. That's how I feel."

I avoid his eyes, something Cully would do when I bent down to
tell him not to do something. He'd glance to the right.

Billy shakes his head, takes his hands off me, heads to the door.

I make to speak but can't, overwhelmed by a physical and painful
kind of grief. I am burning with it, afraid of it. *I need you!* I want to
yell. *I need all of you.*

Billy pauses with his hand on the doorknob but doesn't look
back, and then he goes, and I yell at the closed door, realizing it isn't

just grief that's making me burn, but an anger with myself for treating him that way.

He was right to go, and now I'm glad he did, not trusting what would have come out of my mouth. I take some deep breaths, letting his words in, letting him have a voice and, yes, a choice. Without guilt. Something I want myself.

When I have fully calmed down I think of calling his and my dad's room to apologize for having ruined something here that was vulnerable and honest. I'm about to call his cell, since I don't know their room number, when my room phone rings.

I answer and Billy asks, "Did that pizza ever come?" and I smile, one of those big ones you can make when you're alone and talking on the phone. I get that old thrill that came whenever he called, happy and light, and loving it all. Loving him.

Chapter 19

I shower for a long time, my hands against the tile. I watch the water run off me and disappear into the drain. I imagine the other people in rooms alongside, boxes of us showering, lying on beds, eating green apples.

I get dressed for the event tonight. I purposefully picked color over black so I wouldn't look somber. Morgan had better not wear black. I go to gather the group, but I keep thinking that Kit should eat something and that even though she said she didn't want to come, she should. I don't want her to be alone and feel like I'm neglecting her because I know she's waiting for my move. She's the kind of girl who has to be directly invited to something so I walk toward the door, decided, then stop and go back to grab the shopping bag.

I walk down the hall to her room. I knock on 314. I'm nervous, as if embarking on a date.

She opens the door and a feeling comes over me that is strongly maternal. I want to tuck her hair behind her ear. I want to lick my finger and rub off that speck of something below her brow bone. She's wearing black sweatpants and a beige tank top. Her arms are long and thin, shoulders square and strong.

"Wow," she says. "You look nice."

I look down at my tangerine dress, forgetting. "I know," I say. "It's nice. That sounded bad. I meant that it feels good to get done up. Affects your interior somehow."

"I'm sorry about the antique store," she says. "For some reason I thought you'd be happy. Just immediately happy. It's a lot to take in and I'm sorry. I didn't think it through."

"It is a lot," I say. "And I am happy. Or, I'm something. That was just my reaction then. I need to think. I have thought. I am thinking. But right now . . . I'm not going to."

I gauge her reaction: her shoulders, lower. Her face, solemn.

"I'm going to go downstairs," I say. "I need to let things rest."

"Good idea," she says. "I hope it goes well tonight."

"Come with me," I say. "Here." I hand her the shopping bag. She peeks in, pulls away the tissue. "What's this?"

"It's a dress," I say.

"You bought me a dress?"

"I was going to give it to Morgan as a gift," I say. "You should put it on, let things rest with me. They'll have food and we can sit together, okay?"

She takes the dress out of the bag. It's short, emerald green, simple and comfortable and quietly sexy.

"I can't wear this," she says.

"You can't wear what you're wearing."

She looks at the tag. "It's expensive," she says. "I could keep the tags on and not spill, but I guess she'd see me in it."

"She has enough dresses," I say. "Just put it on. And some makeup. Affect your interior."

She holds the dress against her body and I can tell she is pleased. She gets to be a girl tonight.

I WAIT WHILE she goes to the bathroom to get ready. I walk in a slow, directionless way around her small room, thinking about what to do and at the same time not being able to think, to reel in my thoughts. My mind feels like rough seas where I need a still, moonlit lake. I've had sex, wine, and chocolate. Aren't these things supposed to help calm me? I walk back to the other side of the room. Her floral wallpa-

per and her bedspread are different from mine. She doesn't have a balcony, but she has a good view. The mountains are more approachable
here than in Breckenridge. They're low and close, and you can see the
details, the pines, scars, and rock ledges.

"Are you sure I should go down there?" she asks from the bathroom. "It doesn't seem right."

"Oh, it's right," I say. "I have a feeling it will be filled with people
Cully never even knew."

"And will there be speeches or . . . "

"No," I say. "Morgan claims it will be a party, just a celebration."

"So Morgan and Cully were best friends?" she asks.

"Yeah, when they were six," I yell, and feel funny standing by
myself. "Are you decent?" I ask. "Can I—"

"Yeah, yeah, come in."

I stop in the doorway of the bathroom. She has a towel around
her and is putting mascara on her lashes. She glances briefly at me
in the mirror.

"She and Cully did a lot together when they were young," I say.
"And you know—family friends. We did everything together so they
had to too." I think about family friends. You can go a long time
without seeing them but have this link, almost a secret knowledge.
You know how the other started.

"They're very different," I say, "but have a shared history."

"Sure," she says. She applies some pencil to her brows, which
surprises me. In fact, makeup surprises me, and her ability with it.
She's like a girl girl, like a Morgan girl. I laugh.

"What?" she says, her chin tilted up.

"Nothing," I say, but then I think of a story about Morgan.
"When they were around thirteen Morgan took some kind of mining
class. Modern prospectors. She was convinced Cully had gold in his
backyard, the hillside, and she insisted he help her find it since he
may have inherited some sort of gene—my great-great-grandfather
was basically the father of gold dredging—"

"Revett St. John!" she yells, and turns. "I didn't even put that together."

"Yeah, I wouldn't really expect you to put that together, or for anyone to put that together. It's not like he—"

"He introduced Breckenridge to dredge boats," she says, then faces the mirror again to talk to me. "He bought his home through a Sears catalog. Four hundred seventy bucks plus fifty in shipping."

"Right," I say. "The walking tour." *Kit, you are incredible.* "You really absorb information."

"Told you," she says.

I leave my post and walk to the bathroom counter. I pick up a square compact and open it to two swaths of shadow, tempted to try some. I imagine her on the walking tour, taking notes, as someone from the Heritage Society leads her through town.

"What were you saying?" she asks. "About Morgan."

I watch her in the mirror, brushing her hair, seeing her through Cully's eyes. "Our house is built on an old mining drift." I pull my hair to one side, over my shoulder. "After her little mining meetings, which, by the way were filled with people over seventy, she'd come and dig in our backyard for her very own pay dirt."

"Pay dirt," Kit says, as if committing it to memory.

"So I'd sit on the deck sometimes and watch with Suzanne. Cully would heckle her, but she was determined. She has always been determined in this annoying way you can't really articulate or fault her for."

Kit laughs, which makes me want to make her laugh more. I feel like I'm talking with a girlfriend. I'm happy, being with her, and maybe it's because of her link to Cully that I don't feel guilty for this happiness.

"Anyway," I say, "she dug. She found nothing, just her very own gravel. Then one night, Cully and I were at Suzanne's for dinner. Cully went through Suzanne's jewelry drawers, took a ruby ring. He gave it to Morgan and told her to dig in her own backyard."

Kit shakes her head as if I've said something incredible. "That's great," she says. "I love that. That's so him."

We look at each other's reflections. It is so him.

"I'll let you get dressed," I say.

I walk out to the room and sit on her bed. I smooth my dress, adjust my bra. Her interest in my story about Cully made me realize how little of him she knows. We are her portal into all of those unknown spaces.

How will our relationship continue after this? If I keep this baby, will she call to check in? Will she visit? Will she want it back? Or will she slowly back away, as Billy's parents did so that their presence was awkward and, in the end, not wanted.

She walks out of the bathroom, dressed now. The dress fits perfectly across the chest and down her torso. Her skin is smooth, a chestnut tint. A light scattering of freckles on her shoulders.

"I only brought my boots," she says.

"You look stunning," I say.

She touches her nose. "Oh, gosh, thanks."

She walks to the foot of the bed and puts on her black boots. She presents herself, holding her arms up as if there's nothing else she can do. The boots don't go with the dress, but she makes it all look right.

She slides her room card off the desk. "I can't believe you've been here so long," she says.

"In the room?"

"No, I mean in Breckenridge. Revett St. John."

"Oh, yeah, no," I say. I stand, get my purse, make sure her windows are closed. "For a while the town went dead, so I'm not sure what happened to us—my people. I know one of my ancestors ran a dance hall, but then that family went to a neighboring town where there was work."

"Was Lyle born in Breck?"

"No," I say, "Denver, but then he and his parents moved to Vail, when it was just getting started as a resort town. My dad worked as a ski instructor, but also for a lumber company."

She is focused on me, as if I have a better point to make or what

I'm saying is actually interesting, and so I continue. "The lumber company came to Breckenridge for a job and saw the potential. They were inspired by the area, by Vail's success." I laugh. "My dad will tell you he gave them the idea to build lifts on Peak Eight, thereby starting it all." I open my arms, displaying it all. "My dad—"

"Trygve Berge and Sigurd Rockne," Kit says, pronouncing their names correctly. Whenever she speaks, I feel a surge of pride in Cully, for his taste.

"Right," I say, "the Norwegians who got the credit, as they should. Though my dad did help plan out those initial trails and runs—and eventually ran the first ski school, or helped run it. But the sons of Norway were in charge."

She shrugs as if this is of no importance. She'll take Lyle's myth.

I walk toward the door. "You sure paid attention on that walking tour." *You should go and be somebody*, I almost say. I feel it. *Look at you in those boots, look at that polished skin, go and walk around some more. Go and take more tours. Go find that valet, Chip.* Thinking all this feels like a betrayal, but only somewhat. I imagine Cully rooting her on.

I want to tell her how much she reminds me of myself before I got pregnant, but I don't, either because I don't want it to come off as self-congratulatory or I don't want her to think it an insult. But she does remind me of myself back then—that greedy yearning for knowledge and off-the-map experience, that good-girl responsibility edged with a thirst for detours, all for the sake of collection. I remember the feeling of being in Billy's GTO, the pride I felt, the coolness he leant me, something I felt to be latent within me. I also remember being in that car, noting his expressions to save for later, to make them my own when I was away from the source. I was both living and noting. I see her doing it too, living and noting, collecting things before going back on track.

"We should probably be talking about other things," I say.

"But this all matters," Kit says. "It's all so interesting." She takes one more look at herself in the mirror above the desk. "How things come about. How things set."

"Yeah," I say, believing it. "It is." *How did you come about?* I wonder.

"Plus you wanted to let things rest," she says. As does she, I bet, probably terrified to hear my answer.

I look at her stomach, then at her face. Her lashes are long, her eyes large, slanted slightly and dark green like swamp lilies. I think of the combining genes exercise from high school, something I loved to do in my head, using boys I liked to figure out the traits our children would have. I can't remember everything. Punnett square and Mendel, the monk with the peas.

She walks toward me, standing by the door.

"I didn't notice you had dimples before," I say.

"Just one," she says. She touches the dimple. "Right side."

I look down at her boots.

"Are they awful?" she asks.

"No, I was just . . . Are you flat-footed or do you have high arches?"

"Arches."

"How tall are you?"

"Five five."

"Your eyes are green. Cully's were blue."

"Blue genes," she says. "Ha, get it? Blue jeans. Oh, and I can roll my tongue."

"You knew what I was doing?" I automatically roll my tongue. "Of course you did."

What happens to the recessive gene? I wonder. *Where does it go? Does it get masked by the dominant gene but still travel unchanged?* I'd like to think that everything surfaces eventually, everything gets its due.

I'm thinking of Seth for some reason. I wonder where he is now. I'd like to think that he's a good man; that moment shouldn't define him.

"Was he good to you?" I ask.

She looks back at me with a secret sort of smile. "He was."

"But you didn't love him," I say. "It didn't get to that."

"Oh, I don't know," she says. "I felt like I did, but you know—endorphins, oxytocin."

"Sure," I say, not knowing exactly what she's talking about but getting it. She's talking about being caught in the moment, that web of chemicals, drugging you into thinking that what you have is cosmic. I flew with Billy, absolutely flew.

"But now you'll always love him," I say.

She looks confused, then seems to understand. He is frozen in time now. He can do no wrong. He will always be easy to love.

"I will," she says, and I wonder if it's for my benefit. After my mom died, my dad would check in with me, always assuming I was quiet because I was thinking about her. Most of the time I wasn't, but for his benefit I'd pretend my thoughts were on her. I wanted him to stop checking in with me, stop assuming I was unhappy. It made me feel guilty that I wasn't.

A surprise spring of tears floods my vision. My mom, Cully—this loss of life, this beautiful hotel, this beautiful girl. None of it makes sense. Part of me wants to jump off the balcony. Part of me wants to sing from it. I love and hate this life.

"You don't want to do this." I place my hand in the middle of my chest. "Offer me this. I was such a bad mother. I didn't keep him safe. That's all I had to do. I didn't do anything right." I fan my face, shake it off.

"That's not true," she says, and her voice is loud in the narrow hallway before the door. We are standing so close to each other.

"You don't know. You don't know how I'd be. Plus I'm old and—"

"You're not old, but if you don't want it—"

"I'm not saying that, I'm thinking out loud, I'm—"

Someone knocks on the door. "Who's that?" I ask, stupidly suspicious.

"I don't know," she says. She looks through the peephole. "Billy and Lyle."

I adjust my strapless bra, then quickly turn to Kit and grin. "Do I have anything in my teeth?"

"No," she says. "Do I?"

She bares her teeth. "No," I say.

I open the door and Billy looks surprised to see me.

"Oh, hi," he says. He looks back at my father. "We didn't know you'd be here."

I'm confused but figure they assumed Kit would come along tonight.

"Ladies, you look beautiful," Billy says.

"Thank you," we both mumble.

I wonder if Cully had the same effect on Kit that Billy once had, or maybe still has, on me.

"Well?" he asks. "What about me? Don't I clean up nice?"

"Very nice," Kit says. "You too, Lyle."

My dad, in black jeans and a checkered collared shirt, looks so dapper I feel proud. I grin at the idea of him and Billy sharing their frilly room, and I long for Cully right then, to complete it all: my boys in their Little Women–like quarters. I see the faces he'll never attain. Cully and my dad both have that exaggerated, almost malleable face. They both could do so much with their faces—they could make the goofiest expressions.

They walk down the hall, both patting their pockets. We trail behind them, then my dad stops in front of the door that must be Suzanne's.

I knock and she comes out as if she has been waiting right behind the door this whole time. One of her best qualities is punctuality.

"Hi," she says, and seems almost ashamed of something.

"What's wrong?" I ask.

"Nothing, just a little nervous for tonight."

Her uneasiness makes me feel like I should be anxious too, but all I feel is self-conscious, like I'm about to perform.

Billy and my dad walk ahead. Billy's gait is somewhat pigeon-toed and broken, like that of a retired football player. He looks back at me and winks and I flap my eyes in attempted response. I know him too well to flirt.

We reach the elevators and wait. We all look at ourselves in the reflection of the doors, and when one opens and we all step in, we do it again—look at this grouping, first in the gold-framed mirror on the wall, then, after turning, in the reflection in the doors. The walls are padded in a satiny material that makes me think we're in a high-class sanatorium.

I look up at the mirror on the ceiling, the cluster of us, and go over the sequence of events that brought us here—my returning to work, Kit's happening upon the show, linking me to Cully. Has it only been two days that I've known her? My dad rocks on his heels. I see him elbow Kit.

"How you doing, sport?" he says. "Give me a factoid."

"When squirrels mate, the males will chase each other through the trees," she says. "They jump from branch to branch, showing off for just one female. She'll choose the one she thinks is the strongest."

My dad and Kit have a rhythm too, a closeness brought to us all courtesy of Cully, courtesy of his death. I'm nervous about what the next step in the sequence will be. Before I look down, I see my dad look over Kit's head at Billy and swear I see him nod, as if giving Billy a kind of go-ahead.

"I was listening to NPR the other day," Billy says.

"You were?" I say.

"A story about an actor who feels he needs nine months to get into a role. 'My character needs to gestate,' the actor said. 'I need to live with him for a while before he can be brought to life. Before he can be born.' He said it just like that."

I wait to see where he's going with this. The elevator door opens, but it's not our floor and no one gets in.

"So nine months," he says. "That's a long time." Billy looks around at all of us.

"Great segue, Bill," I say. Kit looks embarrassed, as she should. "God, is this why you came to her room? You thought you'd give her a little lecture without me there?"

"Would you stay here the whole time?" Billy asks Kit, ignoring me. "Or would you want to be near home?"

"I haven't really thought about it," she says.

"But you're going to tell your parents," Billy says. "You can't really hide something like this."

She looks to my dad, maybe because he has been so quiet. He's letting her speak, of course. I feel trapped and conned. And we're in an elevator.

"We're in an elevator," I say, right when the doors open.

"And now we're out," Suzanne says. She has been so quiet too, for Suzanne. "These are good questions."

"Sarah hasn't told me what she wants to do yet," Kit says, leading the way.

I catch a flicker of amusement on Billy's face. It's annoying how good-looking he is. Back when we were together I always felt honored to be with him but also unsure, like it was a big joke on me.

"Sport," my dad says, but that's all he says. He knows me. So does Billy. They know I can't let him go again.

We walk out into the grand room with its high ceilings and endless details. Every inch of space seems labored upon.

"I'm hardly one to give advice or, you know, provide any kind of counsel." Billy waves a hand, indicating his inadequacies. "You are doing a very noble thing," he says. "But before you decided to do this, before you met Sarah, you weren't going to have the baby, right?"

She nods. We continue to walk together with purpose and I get an image of us strutting like a gang, *Reservoir Dogs*–style, but on the *Titanic*.

"And you're okay delivering your baby, giving your baby away, and having your child exist in the world," my dad says. "Your child."

"What are you asking?" Kit says, quite forcibly. "What do you want to know?"

My dad hits his thigh with the palm of his hand as if Kit has finally said something right. We all stop walking and pause before the glass doors that lead outside. "We just thought you could talk this one out a little more," he says. "Everything is happening very quickly. We thought we could slow down."

"We?" I say. "What is all this 'we' shit again?"

"And how is this helpful for me to talk about this kind of stuff with strangers? With strange men? It's my body!" Kit adds, ridiculously. We all give her outburst a moment of silence.

"We didn't concoct some sort of scheme," Billy says. "We're just on the same page."

"Billy and I have always been on the same page," my dad says. "He's the son I've never had." He reaches behind me and hits Billy on the head.

"Ow," Billy says.

"You're a champion, Billy," my dad says.

"You are," Billy says.

"You guys are total morons," I say. "You can't bring up this traumatic stuff, then goof off like . . ."

"Total featherbrains!" Kit says, and I almost laugh because I've never heard her yell so much—and what kind of an insult is "featherbrains"?—but she's completely serious.

"Sorry," Billy says. "I know this is an absurd situation, that it's very personal, and we're here in this lovely . . . place." We all look around at the well-dressed people in the room. A faint throb of music comes from one of the surrounding rooms. Everything harkens back to a time when people had the same problems yet used a different language. I imagine Kit in a gown, dwarfed by one of these long-backed chairs, the menfolk counseling her.

"We thought you could use strangers," my dad says, "even though I think we're past that now, aren't we? We're friends, we're like family." I cringe at the word even though it's the very one I was thinking of.

"We want to help," my dad says.

"You're all strangers," she says, looking around at each of us.

"I don't mean to upset you," Billy says. "We don't. We just wanted you to be able to talk freely, to think this through."

She looks straight ahead. Suzanne edges up to her. "Maybe she has thought this through."

"I'm not telling you to do one thing or the other," Billy says. "No one is. I just wanted to make you feel good about the other scenario too. Women do it. Girls who aren't ready. Girls have abortions."

"Jesus, Billy," I say, looking around at what I take to be college students, many of whom are uncomfortably striking, heading into the room with the music. Are kids prettier and taller these days?

"Let *me* tell you something," Suzanne says. "You know who almost got scraped?"

It takes me a second to figure out what she means. "Good God," I say.

"Cher," she says. Her eyes widen and she tugs her pants up. "Her mother came this close to getting rid of her." She holds her thumb and pointer finger together like she's holding a joint. "I think it was Cher, but that boy—I know that for sure. That football player who won the Heisman? His mother came forward and said she considered an abortion and now look. Look what he's done, what these people have done. Frances Bean. That's another one."

"Who?" we all ask.

"Frances Bean Cobain. Courtney Love's daughter."

I look around in disbelief.

"I guess we know what you would do then," Billy says. "You would want Morgan to have a child right now."

"Right after her senior year," I say.

"It wouldn't be my preference," Suzanne says, "but of course I would. Billy? Your daughter?"

"Hell no," he says. "She's fourteen! If she was Kit's age, I still wouldn't want her to."

"Well, Morgan is the last Birckhead," Suzanne says. "The last of my bloodline. My brother has a kid, but he's adopted. I mean, I love him and he's family, but not blood. We are the last Birckheads. That's it! The end of the line." She looks at me wide-eyed like I need to raise my arms up against this, the extinction of the Birckheads!

"I'm pretty sure the adopted kid counts," Billy says, but Suzanne runs over this comment.

"This child could be the last of your line," she says, moving her gaze around to include all of us. I feel this is the closing statement and that it should have more impact on me than it does. Do I not care enough about my line? Might I when the clouds clear and I can see and feel again? I think of my roots going back to those hollow-eyed men with long, white goatees, the dance hall owners, the school-teachers, Revett and his dredge boat. They'll all still be dead no matter what happens to us, and at this moment I feel no allegiance.

My dad looks hooked on a looping thought. "Who the hell is Frances Bean?" he asks.

Billy mumbles to me, "And who cares if Cher had never been born? Or the football player. The last Birckhead? Fuckin' A."

Kit catches the last of this and doesn't react. She looks focused, as though she's about to run across a mat and do a triple backflip before a room full of judges.

"Listen," Billy says. "Yeah it's hard and it sucks and there could be regret and it's a tough decision and some people do have the babies and it all works out and great, we have Cher, blah blah, and so on."

"Fuckin' A," Kit says, with no emotion. It makes me feel like we're all completely unraveling, and yet the annihilation of composure is almost relaxing.

"This is a ridiculous place to have this conversation," Suzanne says.

"Every place is," I say.

"Girls have abortions," Billy says.

"Oh my God, stop it." I look around at passersby. The statement out there alone is laughably absurd, and yet none of us can laugh, right? Our eyes wander carefully over to one another.

"So they make a mistake, but then they move on," Billy says. "They go back to high school or college or whatever. The path of their lives stays relatively the same. They just go on, go forward. Get degrees, go to keg parties or grad school, get married, have kids . . . later."

"Is that what I'd do?" Kit says, her voice hard, mocking, which is good, I realize. We are like stand-ins for her parents, challenging her.

"I don't know," Billy says, the fire in him dwindling. "I don't know what I'm talking about."

"Cully wasn't a mistake," Suzanne says. "You don't regret him."

"Of course not," Billy says.

My dad leans forward and we all move closer, as if in a huddle. "But this isn't their story, Suze." Billy nods vigorously, as if reminded where he was going.

"Kit," my dad says, "you need to know what *you* want. That's the point of all this. Don't leave it up to my daughter. It's generous, what you're doing and all, but at the same time, it isn't. It isn't fair."

I look at my father and feel young, protected. I briefly look at Billy and understand now their method. Both Billy and my father are trying to rescue me.

"I guess that's all we're getting at," Billy says.

"You don't need to speak for me," I say to my dad. *You don't need to rescue me*. He looks at me with surprise and what seems like worry, and then the expression hardens.

"Very well," he says. "Now, would there be some sort of contract or plan?" he asks. "There are legal matters. The child would have to be adopted."

When he says this, a wave of fatigue hits me. There is so much involved in this, so much to do.

"Guys?" Suzanne says. She keeps looking over at the nearest ball-room. "We should go in now. To the . . . thing."

She looks strange, near tears and truly apologetic.

"Well, let's go then," I say.

"I'm . . . I'm so sorry," Suzanne says again.

"It's fine," I say. "We'll talk later. Or not."

"No, it's just that tonight—I don't think it's going to be what it was supposed to be."

We walk with Suzanne toward the ballroom. "I was helping Morgan earlier with setting up and didn't quite understand the theme of this party. I guess to get funding, her sewing club has to put on their normal fashion show, which happens here this time of year. Every year. And Morgan's directing this year, so she thought she'd . . . I don't know what she thought. I kind of said something, in my way, and Morgan snapped my head off. I'm just so sorry. All these Saab hippies—"

"Do you know when they mate," my dad says, "they jump from branch to branch."

We all pause at the doorway of the ballroom.

"Whoa," Kit says.

"You weren't kidding," my dad says.

I take in the dimly lit room. Chairs have been set up on both sides to face a cleared space down the center. Club-like music is playing.

"This is Cully's memorial?" I ask.

"I think we're about to watch a fashion show," my dad says.

I watch a man across the room slip a shrimp into his mouth.

"She says it will be dedicated to him," Suzanne says.

"Just what he would have wanted," Billy says.

"I am so sorry," Suzanne says. "I don't know why she had to hide it this whole time. Why tell me there's going to be a celebration for Cully? Why make you guys come all this way?"

My dad puts his arm around her. "It's fine. Whatever this is."

"There's food," she says. "And wine."

Part of me feels comforted that her child is disappointing her. Both pride and displeasure in one's children seem to make mothers bond.

"Cully was going to come," I say. "It's perfect that we're here."

"What do you mean?" Suzanne says.

"It was in his calendar," I say. "To come to the Springs today. Probably to be right here, to see Morgan's show."

"That's nice," Suzanne says. "That's so nice."

"So we're here seeing what he would have come to see," Billy says.

We stand at the edge of the room, as if we're about to jump into an icy pool.

"Should we get something to drink and eat?" my dad asks.

"Yes," I say, but no one moves. Kids are in clusters talking and moving to the music, making pouty faces. Why does everyone make that same face when they dance? More shrimps are put into mouths. A girl near us issues a frustrated sound. "Damn it," she says, looking at her pink dress, a splotch of spilled liquid above her hip.

One of the guys in her party lifts his shirt, exposing a muscled stomach. "Would you like to borrow my washboard?" he says. "I'll get it clean in no time."

The girl doesn't laugh, but Kit does, quickly. I bet this boy has been waiting all night to use this line, perhaps his whole life. He happens to see all of us witnessing this and narrows in on Kit. If I'm not mistaken he gives her a look of complicity, as if to admit his cheesiness, or to distinguish Kit from the girl in pink.

Without looking at us, Kit walks in.

· · ·

THE SETTING HAS rendered us speechless on the prior topic. Where it was ridiculous to have the conversation out there, it's even more so in here. My dad, Kit, myself, and Billy are clustered together, wallflowers at the dance.

"Zero-entry infinity," my dad says, looking through the glass doors to the pool below. "Makes people feel like they're at the beach. You never see beach pools making people feel they're in the mountains. Places need to dress as themselves."

"Dad," I say, in a loving voice. There's nothing else I feel capable of saying. I put my hand on his back, turn his attention to the room. I point out persons of interest—the boy by the speaker who has dyed his dreadlocks gold and black, the school colors; Morgan herself, with her headset and clipboard, who seems too busy to bother. She is by the microphone, set to the side of the runway. She's wearing a black dress.

I imagine Cully here tonight, how if I came, we'd be eyeing each other right now, making secret expressions. Morgan's catching up to him. Soon she'll be older than him. If she has children, they'll probably never know she had a friend who died, or they will because it will be one of her narratives, but it won't mean anything to them.

"There's Suzanne," Kit says. She's across the room by the drinks table, standing with Dickie. They look like a fitting couple. Their outfits even match. Dickie has his hand on her shoulder, making her seem like a familiar resting place. I gaze at this peaceful view.

Dickie sees us and nods in our direction and waves, but stays back when Suzanne makes her way toward us with two glasses of wine. I see Dickie talking to a waiter and know he's sending more our way. Both he and Suzanne become anxious when people around them don't have a drink. After a dinner party at the Fowlers', where glasses are never empty, guests wake up the next day using the expression "Fowlered again."

Suzanne hands me my wine. "Everyone okay?" I turn to face the growing crowd in the darkening room.

"We're fine," I say.

"It's time to sit down now," she says. She's been shamed, I think, by this whole night, and yet I am completely at ease. I think everyone feels this way, maybe a bit guiltily, like we've gotten out of something. We won't have to feel after all. I follow, go where I'm told, sit down in between my dad and Kit. The crowd—about fifty college students and some adults—settles when Morgan stands in front of the curtain. My dad looks at me, raises his eyebrows. Billy looks around, amused, maybe eager for a good show. Dickie looks the same as always, as though someone's whispering jokes into his ear.

"Hello, everyone," Morgan says into a microphone. "Thank you so much for coming tonight." The voices quiet down. My thoughts do too, as if something has been extracted, letting things fall into place.

"This is such a special night for me." Morgan looks out into the crowd. "It's my last year here at CC, my third time chairing our annual fashion show, and my first time directing it."

Some students clap and cheer aggressively and we follow along.

"I want to thank the Broadmoor for allowing the Back Row to be here tonight. Sorry, but this is much cooler than Armstrong!"

Everyone laughs and I do too, relieved and surprised by Morgan, standing at the helm, commanding this room with such grace.

"I also want to thank the Colorado Springs chapter of Dress for Success, the CC Sewing Club and Arts and Crafts, and the Student Government Association." She pauses and looks toward our row. "I want to thank my parents for their support and friendship. This has been hard to put together. It's been a difficult time—" Morgan waves her hand in front of her face and I look at Suzanne doing the same thing. I tear up too, and laugh. I turn to Kit and her eyes are watery.

"So sweet," Kit says, looking at Suzanne.

"In December I lost a friend who was like a brother to me," Morgan says, her voice back under control. "I want to thank his mother, Sarah, for being here tonight."

People clap weakly. They turn to see whom Morgan's addressing and smile sympathetically when they see me.

"Cully's father, Billy, is here, and his grandfather, Lyle St. John. Thank you guys for coming tonight." There is more applause and then Morgan clears her throat. She takes a big breath, sucks in her lips, then exhales. I'm edgy, like she's about to sing.

"This isn't totally what I had planned," she says. "I wanted to have a celebration of Cully, but then I realized something." She pauses.

What did you realize?

"I realized that he would have wanted the show to go on."

I feel my company communicating something, and holding something back. It's funny how feelings are always more urgent when you're supposed to be quiet.

"So instead, tonight will be dedicated to my friend, Cully St. John!" Morgan takes another dramatic pause. She looks up at the ceiling. "Cully," she says, "this one's for you."

My son. I see him shaking his head, rolling his eyes, but he's okay. He's happy. The surrounding blank gazes—none of these people knew him—they are here for the show that will go on. Billy looks over at me and I laugh softly at our preparation for this. It is perfect.

"Okay, let's get this started!" Morgan says. Music begins to play and it fills my chest. "You are in for a visual and musical treat. Welcome to *Andiamo ex Machina, To Fall in Love with a Machine!*"

The volume turns up higher, music pumping into the space. Kit and I make eye contact during the loud applause, letting ourselves laugh. "To fall in love with a machine?" she asks.

"I have no idea."

Billy is moving his head to the beat. The row of us all look happy, relieved that this isn't about Cully. Our emotions won't have to be on stage.

The first student model appears in an armor-like bodice and a skirt made of feathers. She waltzes down the runway and I move a bit in place, filled up with something that the music helps usher in, a little merriment, a little hope.

I watch the show, lost in it at times, proud of Morgan. I've known her all her life. Suzanne is enthralled, and I recall all those assemblies we attended together, the plays and races, recitals and matches. Your own children are so fascinating.

I let tears fall. I don't want to reach up to wipe them away, partly not to draw attention, and partly because it feels good to unexpectedly mourn him. At our service I was too preoccupied with ordering food and feeling like I was being watched and appraised—my every movement interpreted. And the ashes ceremony failed to do much of anything.

The day after the service just my dad and I spread some of his ashes at the pass. Maybe some of them are still in the same place, weighed down with snow. After I tossed them into the air, most fell in a clump. My dad and I looked down at them.

"Do we just leave them like that?" I asked.

"We could cover them," he said.

"Maybe we should have thrown them over the railing," I said. "Or hiked a bit more." I kicked some snow over them, then stopped, not feeling right about doing that.

"I'm going to save the rest," I say. "I don't like it here."

"I know," my dad says. "It's cold."

We stood there for a while, looking at the ashes in the white snow.

"Do you want to say anything?" my dad asked.

I tried to think of something to say. I tried to remember an old prayer. We had hiked a bit from the road, but I could see a car pull over, a family get out to take pictures. A young girl carried a red sled.

"Let's just go," I said.

"We can't just leave him," he said. It was a ridiculous comment, but I agreed.

"Get him then," I said. "Let's put him back."

My dad scooped up the snow with the fallen ashes. "Do I put them with the dry ones?"

"I don't know. I guess so?" He put the wet ashes in with the dry ones. He did this as I kept on the lookout, like we were stealing something or doing something wrong. We got him back. For the first time I think that I'm ready to try again and Billy should be there. Maybe Billy knows a better place for him. We will do this. I can do anything right now. Something is breaking in me, but instead of feeling broken, I feel as if something better is building in its place. I keep wanting to get to the other side, but what if I'm already there? What if this is what it looks like?

Two girls walk together down the catwalk, mock serious in stiff skirts that look like they're made out of tent stakes, and so are most likely tent stakes, and I feel close to soaring. This has nothing to do with Cully and everything to do with him. Suzanne's marriage was a failure, Morgan's intentions for a celebration: failure. Cully's drugs, his death, this pregnant girl beside me. My mom's death, a failure to beat a disease. My dad's inability to let his work go, Billy and me. All failures. And ones that I want to worship, renegotiate their labels. If these are failures, then I'll take them all.

I make eye contact with Kit, communicating something. She looks wistful, thoughtful.

Morgan announces the next batch of students and Kit says something to me that I can't hear.

"What?" I ask.

"I didn't think I'd want a baby," she says. I lean in toward her. Her voice, calm and low. "I don't want to be pregnant. It's selfish of me, but I didn't want a baby out there in the world. I didn't want to be a girl with a baby. I just want a clean slate. I wanted this part of my life to end."

The people around us applaud and the music's volume rises.

"Kit," I say, after taking in her words, "you're mixing tenses. 'Didn't, don't, wanted, want.'"

"I don't know what I want. I see you guys and I . . . I like what you have. I like what you and Cully had, or must have had. I'm confused. Maybe I can do it. Maybe this is what's supposed to happen to me."

Everything inside me seems to screech to a halt. The music is suddenly deafening. I take a moment. I'm about to speak, but my mouth is frozen into a little *o*.

She looks scared, like she jumped into that icy pool and can't get out, and her fearfulness gives me sudden clarity. I take her hand for a moment, squeeze it with a quick pulse like Morse code. Whatever is happening is about to begin.

"Come outside with me," I say.

I tell my dad we'll be right back. We walk toward the exit of the ballroom. Soon it will be just the two of us. No other voices in our heads. No other opinions. Two people. And now I know that what I need to do is whittle it down to one.

Chapter 20

We walk out to the path around the lake. Jupiter and Venus are both clear in the sky and the surrounding lanterns are lit. The cool air is rich with pine and a trace of what I think may be goose shit. Pikes Peak is moonlit, unamused. It doesn't care about us, no matter what we choose.

"I don't know what I mean," she says.

"Let's just put one foot in front of the other," I say.

I gather my thoughts as we walk past the willows, the spa, past a sign that says Only Golfers Allowed Beyond This Point. We are walking in time with one another and I purposefully try to change my clip.

"When I was about six years younger than you are now, I went through the same thing."

She looks at me, unsure.

"I got pregnant," I say. "I eventually went to my father for help. My mother wasn't alive."

"You were seventeen?" she asks.

"Sixteen," I say. "When I think about it now, I'm pretty amazed at how great my dad was. For all his two cents he let me be an adult. He helped me without telling me what to do, without making me feel bad."

She nods beside me.

"Then again when I was twenty-one, I went through it again. I got pregnant again and I went to my dad. Watch out."

She hops over the tendril of goose poop. "Thanks," she says.

In the grass a goose sleeps, an orange anklet tucked under his wings. We continue toward the bridge.

"Sometimes I feel like I've known you for a long time," I say.

"I know," she says. "So the second time you were pregnant with Cully."

"Yes," I say.

"Do you regret the first time?" she asks.

I take a breath. "No."

We walk slower as we get closer to where we started.

"I guess my point is that you need to go home."

"I didn't think that was going to be your point," she says.

"I know," I say. "I'm not as good as my dad at this."

We both look straight ahead. I can't see her response.

"I'm revising my point," I say.

"Okay," she says.

"I had help. That's my point. I went to my father. You need to go and be without me, without my dad, Billy, Suzanne, this place."

She looks around at this place.

"Breckenridge," I say. "You need to be in your place, talk to your mom, your dad—yes, sorry, more talking, but you need your family and your turf. You need to do whatever you're going to do back at home. Do you understand? Does this make sense?"

As I say this, I get a feeling of déjà vu. It's not the situation I've lived before but the process of prescription, the family meetings in the living room where I assigned tasks to Cully, telling him how to be. This wasn't just to help him but to help myself, to apply order to our lives when I felt there was none.

We walk up the hill of the bridge and stop at the apex, above the murky water where I can see the thick bodies of fish moving.

She looks at me in a way that makes me think she sees through me, that my prescription, return home, is something to bring *me* back to health, to help me move, perhaps not on, but along properly, in the way the books endorse.

"You're kicking me out of Breckenridge?" she asks.

"No," I say. "Well, yes." I cross my arms in front of my chest as if for reinforcement. "Yes, I am."

I keep quiet, letting her mull this over. I never considered her disagreeing with me.

"Can you do that?" she asks.

"I think you know it's a good idea."

She doesn't say anything. She's much better at silence than I am.

"I can't imagine a daughter going through this without me," I say. "As a parent, it's the worst thing to consider—you kids not letting us help you."

I wonder if Cully went to Billy sometimes, not because he was a man, but because he thought I was too busy, or too stressed out with the business of raising Cully. I'd make such a big deal about schedules—and they mattered, I know it all mattered—but did he know that he could always, always come to me? Did he feel, as Kit feels about her mom, that I had too much on my plate? Not coming to me. Not using me. Because I had a big interview with a nail salon or I had to cheer up tourists if they weren't sold on the cold. Considering this gives me a sinking feeling, a dark despair. What was the point of me if he didn't use me? The purpose of me as a parent? What's the point of everything parents do if the kids aren't going to employ us?

"You need to go to them," I say.

"I thought you could help me," Kit says. "I went to you."

I try not to get lost in her helpless look, try not to hug her or see her as mine. Nothing about her belongs to me.

"I'm going to help you with a plane ticket home," I say. "I'll give you a number, and a girl named Nicole will arrange everything. Just tell her the time you'd like to leave on Monday."

She furrows her brow in a way that is cutely petulant. "That's the day after tomorrow."

"It is," I say. "You don't have a lot of time."

"I'm like White Fang," she says. "You're releasing me into the wild. The wilds of Westchester."

Her joke is reassuring. It tells me she understands. Maybe relieved to be grounded.

"Let's go back," I say. To the show that must go on. We walk down the bridge toward the ballroom, to the light and the music. I feel steady and accomplished, nearer to somewhere I should be.

"We need to cancel your appointment," I say.

She walks a few steps before saying, "I already did."

I stop walking and she stops too. I automatically look at her stomach, shaking off the idea of fingerprints.

"When?" I ask.

"When you dropped me off at my condo to get clothes."

I make to speak but can't. She has said so much. She came along anyway, knowing the whole time not what was going to happen but what wasn't.

I'm about to ask why she did this, but I don't need to know. I feel that this whole side trip has been a kind of test drive for her, seeing how this foreign vehicle runs: its capabilities, deficiencies. How does it feel in the seat? Is it practical? Or does the gut reaction of love override sense? It all comes together. It all matters.

"I just wanted to be with you guys," she says.

I look at all of her—her face and arms, her beat-up boots, this girl on the brink of something. I glimpse a tag under her arm. "You left your tags on," I say. "Turn around."

"Oh yeah," she says, looking under her arm. "I tucked them in. I'll give this back to you."

"Don't be silly," I say. "I'm not going to return it."

"Please," she says. "I feel bad. The room too. You've done enough. I shouldn't be taking her dress. It's her gift. Or you could wear it after. We're the same size, I bet. I might get bigger anyway."

A flash of fear crosses her face, as if she's seeing a version of her life appear, then disappear.

"Here," I say. I try to turn her around, but she resists and falls a step toward me. "I want you to have it," I say. "Unless you don't like it."

"No, I like it," she says. "I love it, but—"

"Then let me give it to you. I want to give something to you. I want you to have something from me. Just let me take off the tags." I bring her to me, hold her still in a forceful embrace, and rip off the tags, hurting my hand and jostling her body.

"Sorry," I say. I stay there with my hand on her cool back, then close my embrace. Her arms are down by her sides and then she raises them and puts her hands on my back. I am holding my breath. I let it go.

"I don't know how to do this," she says.

Her cheek is warm against my neck. I savor this sensation of a child holding me, needing me.

"It's good not to know everything," I say.

We face one another, locking our gaze, which is a hard and rare thing to do with someone. We memorize one another and then, through a silent consensus, we continue toward the glow of the hotel.

"I haven't looked this decent since . . . since I had sex with your son," she says, and laughs but chokes a bit on the laugh. A cry. There really should be a word for laughing and crying at the same time. There is one. When Cully was around eight we'd do Mad Libs at night, plotting the nouns, verbs, adjectives. Then we'd read our concoction and laugh so hard he would cry. *Claughing*, we'd call it. I would laugh at him laughing, wanting more. It was addictive.

"Will you go back then?" I ask.

"Yes," she says, and I try to picture what she's going back to, her roots and sources, the climate and landscapes, all of which will guide her to tomorrow. I picture curvy roads and gray skies, red leaves and barbecues, Scrabble and sports coats.

She will see her father and maybe she will understand him, his call to go, his right to make mistakes, and discover how difficult it is to see your father, and maybe one day your son, as men, with needs and base desires.

I try to picture her mother's face, but Billy's mother comes to mind. I almost laugh at imagining Billy telling his mom he got some girl pregnant. I see her jaw not dropping but doing just the opposite. She'd emit a sharp yelp, the sound a dog would make if you stepped on its tail. What will Kit's mother do? How will she respond? Not just her family, but the entourage of a family. They'll have to adjust, relearn her, discover the reservoirs, complexities, and back alleys that will lead them to someone they always knew.

We walk up to the deck. "Why did you wear a dress?" I ask. "With Cully."

"I don't know. I just felt like it. I put on makeup. Wore a dress." She looks down. "And these boots."

"Where did you go?" I ask.

"Steak and Rib," she says.

Perfect. Just perfect. I smile even though my heart hurts. At this moment I love this life.

I almost ask her for more, but this is something a mother shouldn't know. This is something she can keep and return to. It's her memory and so I let her have it.

She walks ahead of me to open the gold-rimmed doors. I hear the music and am struck by the desire to dance and move. I watch her walk, a slight bounce in her step. I'm giving this girl back, she'll be okay no matter what, and for some reason I know and deeply care that my mother would be proud of me.

Chapter 21

My father, Billy, Suzanne, and I sit in the mezzanine, waiting for Kit while people-watching and sharing a bag of Funyuns.

"Morgan was wonderful last night," I say to Suzanne. "So poised." She's looking at a magazine about what stars wore at awards shows.

"Wasn't she?" Suzanne says. "We had breakfast this morning. She wanted me to say goodbye. She didn't have a chance to see you after, so . . . "

I sense a bit of irritation and quickly try to run over it. "I'm sure everyone wanted to talk to her," I say. "When she gets to town, I want to take her out and talk about it. It really was perfect, Suzanne. Just the way it was." She looks up and curls her lips in, something she does when she's shyly proud.

"What do they do with the clothes now?" my dad asks.

"What do you mean?" she asks.

My dad has chip dust on his lower lip. "I mean you can't really wear those clothes to the supermarket—"

"I'd wear the clothes to a supermarket," she says.

"You'd wear anything to a supermarket," my dad says.

"You have shit all over your face," Suzanne says, and my dad wipes his forehead.

I look up at the ceiling to see if I see the dancer, but there's a painting of a water nymph on a horse-drawn clamshell. Opposite me is a portrait of a blond-haired man in a red smoking jacket, cross-legged and holding a cigarette holder. He looks a bit like Billy's father.

I look across the way at a young woman. The woman's husband holds one of their kids while the other one reams his calf with a plastic truck.

"Kit canceled the appointment," I say.

"Oh my God," Suzanne says. "Are you—"

"No," I say. "We are just going to go straight home."

Billy and my dad take in the news but don't say anything. Everyone seems to be creating their own scenarios.

"Look who's here," Billy says.

We all watch Dickie and Kit walk toward us, laughing about something. Maybe they happened to be in the same elevator. I'm betting in a short amount of time he has offered her a job or use of his cars or homes, just because she made him laugh. Their laughter makes all of us grin a bit, knowing how it feels to be talking to him: thrilled, privileged, with a touch of stage fright. I notice a new energy about her, a possession.

We all stand as they near and Dickie has words for each of us.

"Lyle, I miss you already," he says to my dad. "Billy, when are we going to ride? Sarah, my friend." He pulls me to him and kisses the top of my head, and then to Suzanne: "Sue-bee, who is this Kit? Where have you been hiding her?"

Suzanne, Sue-bee, places her arm around Kit. "She was Cully's girlfriend," she says in a way that moves me.

Dickie looks at Kit, head to toe, and flattens his palm against his chest. "Of course," he says. His eyes water. "What a morning. What an a.m.!"

I catch Suzanne looking at him with unabashed love. I walk to her side. "You okay?" I ask.

"I'm good," she says.

"Come on, Sue-bee," Dickie says. "I'll give you a lift home."

"That all right?" she asks.

"Is it?" I ask.

"It's fine," she says. "I can't stay mad at this fucker."

"Yes, you can," I say. "But I'm glad you're talking."

"The girl he was with," she says, "she's the girlfriend of the new general manager who was there as well."

She says this casually, though I know she's relishing her mistake. I am too, relieved to be able to like him. "I'll bring your car back tomorrow."

"Okay," she says.

"We're off like a herd of turtles," my dad says. "Did you take all the shampoos?" he asks Kit as they walk toward the escalator.

Suzanne and I let them all walk in front of us. I have everything in my large purse and Suzanne rolls a small suitcase behind her. We get on the escalator behind our group to descend.

"Thank you," I say. "Thanks for being tough with me. I appreciate it."

"Anytime," she says. "Let me know if you need anything. I'm a good listener when I drink."

I want to tell her that I love her, but that's not how we work. We understand this.

"Are you going to be okay? With Dickie. With everything."

"I will," she says. "You?"

I don't answer at first, but then I say, "Yes," because I'm beginning to believe it.

I GO THE other way to get back to Breckenridge. A little variation and some new scenery. Also, I want to drive by his college. I take Cascade toward the school, looking down the side streets we pass, the small homes with porches, chipped paint, and weeds, then later, small homes with nice paint and prim front yards.

When we reach the campus, cars slow for the student pedestrians and we inch our way to the crosswalks. There's Rastall on the left where he ate, and to the right, Slocum where he slept. There's the gray looming chapel where we went to baccalaureate. I almost point these things out like a campus docent. Skateboarders jump off the steps by Rastall, and I imagine that Cully would have done the same when he was here. It's suspenseful, each attempt they make down the set of stairs. I notice we are all watching as we inch toward the crosswalk. It reminds me of watching the valets, observing these boys, these very alive boys, going through motions Cully himself had made and should still be making, but it feels different right now than it did not so long ago. I guess the difference is that I'm not angry at them, and I'm not ashamed to be watching. I'm happy when they land, and the sound of the wheels cracking against the pavement is satisfying.

I move up and now I'm the first car. "So polite," Billy says.

"I noticed that," I say. Each kid who crosses in front of us waves or nods their appreciation of our stopping. They all look at one another too when they cross, meeting each other's gaze in a silent greeting. At an opening I move to the next crosswalk. I picture Cully crossing this street over and over again, nodding at the cars, at the other kids passing by. A group in the quad kicks around a hacky sack. Another group is playing rugby, then further on, in front of his old dorm, are kids in a square of sand playing beach volleyball.

I remember settling him into his Slocum dorm, my sad attempts at finding reasons to stay in the room. Do you need a microwave? A brighter lamp? I couldn't believe how his roommate slept through my entire stay and departure. I mouthed, *Is he okay?* pointing at the large boy from Maine, his mouth agape like a hippo's, long legs hanging off the edge of the bed, his palm pressed against his chest as if pledging allegiance.

I couldn't get myself to go, wanting to make absolutely sure he had everything. Cully assured me he was fine, he didn't need anything else, but he looked so forlorn and small, like my father sometimes does in the back seat of a car. *How would Cully get on here?* I thought. The boys in his wing all wore things ironically, and the girls seemed to be either Texan beauty pageant contestants or hideous statements against those contestants. Long skirts over jeans, armpit hair, heads wrapped up in cone-like contraptions. It was like being in Africa or India. I smile at the memory. He got along just fine. He loved it here.

Further down the street through the intersection I see the beginning of the large homes, Victorians with robust mailboxes that have legible numbers. They're the academic residences; the kind with *New Yorker* magazines not staged on a console but used and read. Herb gardens and bread makers, teenagers that blog.

"Cache La Poudre," Kit says.

"What about it?" my dad says.

"I saw a street sign back there," she says.

"Hide the powder," Billy says. "*Cache La Poudre* means 'hide the powder.' I looked it up after sending him a care package. But I bet you wouldn't have to look it up, right, Kit? Am I right?" Billy scoots up a bit from the back seat to Kit in the front.

"I would have," she says. "I took Chinese."

MY FAVORITE PART of the drive from Denver to Breckenridge is the section of huge, isolated homes on precarious cliffs, then Lookout Mountain, the site of Buffalo Bill's grave. I love his grave, especially because of the nearby herd of buffalo. I always try to make eye contact with the beasts, sure they're seeing me too, commiserating. They seem to be presiding over Buffalo Bill, standing in for him, mourning him eternally. Wide, open spaces, stoic beasts, hooves trumpeting their affirming sounds, as if to declare, *Buffalo Bill was here! He existed!* and then less emphatically, *He was important to us and we loved him*.

Grainy ashes. We live. We disappear. Sometimes I feel so sorry for all of us.

I pass the herd of bison. Goodbye, Buffalo Bill.

Kit has missed it. She's asleep. Everyone is. I feel comfortingly alone, trusted, guiding my craft filled with loved ones. I meditate on these full days, knowing I need to keep working out the kinks. I don't think I can go back to my job, and the thought of this inability fills me with hope and energy, like the sky has opened up. It's not that I'm too good for it, it's just that I've changed. I no longer fit it. As my dad said, this life has so many lifetimes, and I'm ready for the next one.

I look beside me at Kit and then in the mirror at the other sleepers. It comes to me that I am dreading something my dad and Billy will have to do too. Let this all go. Let her be on her way without knowing what will happen.

The flat, lazy land rolls by, or we roll by it. I look for bumper stickers. I look at lives inside of cars, station wagons, and SUVs, kids in a back seat watching videos on the back of the front seats.

I Love Loveland.

Denver Broncos.

There's No Excuse for Animal Abuse.

Four out of Three People Can't Do Fractions.

When we're almost to the Silverthorne exit, Kit stirs and opens her eyes to outlets and fast food. I am so scared for her, so excited for her, for whatever will be.

"Hey," I say.

"Hey," she says.

"They're asleep," I say, and she looks back.

I turn up the stereo, change the station, landing on some sultry, wordless jazz.

"My dad used to come home saying he sat on jazz all day," I say. "He had a massage chair that would poke and prod from all directions."

"He sat on Max Roach," Kit says. She stretches her arms, touching the ceiling, and says through a yawn, "In college I tried to like jazz."

"We're already in Frisco?" Billy says from the back.

"Who did what to who?" my dad says.

It's as if they smell the onset of home or feel the change in the weather. My eyes can feel it. It's dry and brisk. We curve around the iced lake. The mountains are so much bigger here—a lame observation—but after being in the Springs, I notice it more. They're a part of the background there, whereas here the mountains are the foreground. They dominate, intrude, and they give me the inelegant thought of *Fuck yeah. This is my house*.

"That was quick," my dad says.

"So says the passenger," I say.

"I'm going to miss this," Kit says.

"You going somewhere?" he asks, which makes me hold my breath. I don't dare meet his gaze. I didn't tell Suzanne either. I want Kit to be able to slide out just as she slid in.

"Will you come back to the house?" my dad asks. "Have some dinner?" She looks at me, as if for approval. *Do I need to go yet?* she seems to ask. *No,* I want to answer. *Don't go.*

"You should," I say.

"I could eat," Kit says.

"I'm starvin'," Billy says.

"Like Marvin," my dad says.

"I walked across this lake with Cully," Kit says.

"Oh yeah?" my dad says. He sounds like a little boy listening to a story. "Why?"

"To get to the other side," she says. "No, it's kind of a funny story."

I take glances at Kit while she tells the story. She takes her time. She has changed since we were in the car yesterday, driving out of town. She was quieter then, shy, stingy with her humor. She tells us about the lake, how it was covered in snow, and on the edges there were small gray hutches. They walked along the edge at first, and then Cully ran toward the middle where the snow was thick. He hurtled through the snow and she followed, exhilarated. He stopped and waited, but then had a look of alarm.

"I looked behind me," she says, "and I saw this *thing*, this beaver."

Billy laughs.

"He was waddling toward us, flapping his tail."

She describes his crusty-looking tail, his old-man mouth and yel-

low canines, his marble eyes gleaming with rage. "Cully told me to
run, so I ran, you know, kind of laughing, but kind of scared, right? I
mean, I knew they could be vicious and—"

"They have scent glands in their anal region," my dad says.

"Jeez, Dad."

"Now, that's just cruel," Billy says.

"Oh my God," Kit says. "Lyle, you kill me. Anyway, so when we
got to the other side, I almost expected to see the beaver with his
arm in the air shaking his claw at us. He was so humanlike. He was
really . . . pissed."

"You got chased by beaver," my dad says.

"That's exactly what Cully said," she says. "Time with him was
never dull. I always felt like I was on some huge adventure."

I make eye contact with Billy. I picture our son and Kit reaching
the other side of the lake, catching their breaths by this road. Perhaps a car slows, a family inside staring out, as if spying a pair of deer.
I think of someone looking into our vehicle now. We look like everyone else. We are everyone else. I picture Cully tromping through
that high, deep snow. That's how I feel physically from all of this.
Moving through grief like it's a thick drift, exhausting but enlivening. It makes your muscles ache. It makes you feel you've inhabited
your body completely.

Everyone seems to be thinking about something nice. It's hard
not to on this part of the drive, surrounded by mountains. There's
this sense of pleasant expectation, that something great is imminent.
I like the way it looks going the other way too, upon exiting, the ten-
mile range in the rearview mirror. Snow falls upon the windshield,
then dissolves, leaving foggy marks that look like tiny paw prints. I
imagine us as a scene in a snow globe: snow falling peacefully, our
miniature world vivid and contained.

On the ridge, homes flicker through the snow, wrapped around
them like shawls. There are the aspens, their white bark glowing like

distant lanterns, and there's the mountain face ahead, bathed in a muted light, cutting a perfect silhouette into the deep-sea-blue sky.

Even though we haven't been gone for very long, I feel the comfort of being here. Here are the trees I know, the turns in the road. I slip back easily, entitled. It was important that we left.

"My life is based on a true story," I say. "Bumper sticker." I point to the car ahead, with a license plate from Kansas. *What's in Kansas?* I wonder. *Dorothy and her red shoes.*

"That's a good one," Kit says.

I increase the speed of the wipers.

"Spring isn't ready yet," my dad says.

I see the lights of town, then we come upon Main Street. People, cars, signs of life, all of it now endearing, invigorating, lasting. For the first time in a very long time I am happy and grateful that this is my home. I have an affection for the residents. We've made it work. We've stuck it out. We'll watch the others go.

The headlights accent a small space of road in front of us, the wiper wands sounding like a fast heartbeat.

Chapter **22**

I place everything on the table. Everything and everyone has rested. It's time to eat.

"I'll just toss the salad," I say, regretting it immediately.

"Can Billy help you out with that?" my dad says, and nudges Kit.

We all sit down. No one knows that this is our last supper.

The chicken is spicy and so is the wine. My father has a dangle of spinach hanging between his two front teeth.

"You sure whipped this up," he says. "I don't know how you found the time to do everything so well."

"Thank you," I say.

"Doing it badly would take just as much time," Billy says.

"In Cully's calendar," Kit says, when she's finished chewing, "what did he mean by 'hunting'?"

"I don't know," I say.

"Treasure hunting," Billy says. "When the snow melts they all go under the lifts and find things people have dropped. It's a tradition, I'm told."

"Must be a new one," I say.

"You guys seemed close," Kit says.

Billy nods, finishing his bite. "We were. Took a while though. When he was around sixteen—driving age—he'd visit. I mean, we had always seen each other before then, set up visits, but he just started instigating them on his own accord. It was nice."

He watches me carefully, over the centerpiece that my dad must have put out—a wooden monkey wearing wire-framed glasses, I assume from channel two. I keep my gaze steady, warm, the little clues forming a picture. I wonder why they kept it a secret. Secrets are bonding, I guess. Maybe it was a way to avoid confusion and hurt feelings, or maybe secrets just make room for a little mystery, a little incongruity and magic in life. Cully's secrets: some I now know, some I never will.

We continue to eat, the conversation easy and flowing. I listen to everything everyone says, an urgency to pay attention, to not miss these moments you don't know are moments until they're gone. I narrow in, trying to hold it all in place, even though I think that if you document life this way, the moments will never set. We don't need to remember. Everything just becomes a part of you. And then it's over.

My dad excuses himself and his absence shifts the air. Billy and I look at one another, and I bet the same thing crosses his mind—that this is a different version of us, sitting at the dinner table with a kid. This could have worked. If it had, who would Cully have been, who would we have been?

My dad comes back up the stairs holding something. When he gets closer I see that it's the Home Haircut, a device that looks like a hand-held vacuum.

"Check this out," he says, holding it in front of Billy. "You adjust the clipper to your preferred length and you can give yourself a haircut."

Kit and I silently communicate that my dad is so strange and yet somehow his actions always improve or make the occasion.

"Come on," he says to Billy. "Let me show you. I'll give you a haircut."

Billy takes a sip of his beer and runs a hand through his hair. "Why?"

"I don't know," my dad says. "Why not? You're starting to look like you belong here."

Billy runs his hand through his hair again. "Yeah, okay," he says.
Kit and I look at one another as if to say, *So this is how it will end.*

Billy stands and walks toward the kitchen, sits on the stool. He
claps his hands together. Kit and I walk over to watch.

"Do you have some sort of cape or towel?" Billy asks me.

"What if I happened to have a cape?" I say.

"You don't need it," my dad says. "It has a suction. There's no
mess. You just empty the hairs out after." He poises the clipper above
Billy's head. "Where we're going, you don't need a towel. All right!"
he says, flipping the switch. The trimmer vibrates. He places it on
Billy's head and moves the tiny machine up and down his skull.

"Feels kind of nice," Billy says.

"Won't it all be one length all around?" I ask.

"Would it work on dogs?" Kit asks.

"I bet small ones," my dad says. A sense of power seems to come
over him, a calm. He is sharing his ridiculous self, his ridiculous toy,
and he's being received. I watch him trim Billy's hair and I remember
the small red scissors I used to use on Cully, the *snip snip* of the silver
blades, his smooth brown hair falling to the floor. He was so quiet
during this process, as Billy is now. I remember the bunched wisps
of hair on the kitchen tile. There are no wisps on the floor tonight.

My dad looks over Billy's head at me and we hold each other this
way for a moment. Maybe he's remembering the same thing—my
childhood haircuts, small red scissors—but then I remember that he
wouldn't have those kinds of memories. He never cut my hair. I cut
it myself.

I notice Kit has her coat hung over her arm. She's probably ready
though unsure how to go. Goodbyes can ruin everything. The repe-
tition of sentiment, the staged lines. And what is there to say? What
would I say to him?

My eyes water—tiny pools of feeling—and then my dad turns
the trimmer off, and my emotions follow: they turn off as if by switch.

"Finished," my dad says.

Billy brushes away nonexistent hairs from his jeans. He looks younger, refreshed. It kind of worked.

"Looks good," my dad says. "Right?"

My dad moves to the front of Billy, admiring his work, feeling a bit triumphant as if he has accomplished something, which, I suppose, he has.

"Yeah," I say. "It's good." I look at Billy and tilt my head toward Kit.

"You're off then?" he says.

"Yeah, I should get going," she says.

"You sure you're okay driving home?" my dad asks, holding the device and scratching his forehead with it.

"Of course," she says.

She takes a step toward him. "Thank you for everything." She puts her arms around him. My eyes water and Billy sees this and he gives the impression of understanding not everything but something.

"You call us tomorrow, okay?" my dad says, softly so it's directed just to her. He kisses her on the top of the head. I am working so hard at keeping myself quiet and I think Kit is too.

Billy stands, and widens his arms, welcoming her in. They give each other a hug. I have the odd sensation of watching a graduation.

"Lyle, let's play some pool?" Billy says.

"I'll be right down," I say.

Billy takes my dad downstairs. Kit looks away and gathers her few things.

"Ready," she says, her strong voice trying to cover a weakness.

"This seems so quick, so rushed," I say.

"May as well stay the course," she says.

"I don't want you to leave angry with me. I want you to understand."

She crosses her arms and looks outside.

"I understand," she says. "I do. I'm just scared. I'm scared, Sarah."

"Come sit down for a second," I say, leading her to the couch. Her shoulders shudder. I realize I have never seen her really break down. She is holding so much up. She sits down next to me in her elegant East Coast coat. Her tears are slow.

I think of the shame I felt when telling my father, the relief of his arms around me, then back to the shame (which never really goes away) of having your dad know you've had sex.

"My poor mom," she says. "First the stripper, now a pregnant daughter."

Kit laughs, stops, then resumes, almost hysterically, and I don't know if I should join her or calm her down. "I'm so embarrassed," she says. "I'm seeing the future. My mom . . . God."

I recognize her tone—one of intimacy, of knowing someone so well and having the privilege to be annoyed by them.

"Don't be embarrassed," I say. "Just think of Billy on the floor if you get embarrassed. Or think of yourself throwing up in front of strangers."

This makes her smile. "I actually can't predict her reaction," she says, and the thought seems to calm her. "I don't know what to do."

"You will," I say.

"I guess this is it then," she says.

I add something else to her pile of things: Cully's money. It has found its purpose.

"From Cully," I say.

"Thank you," she says, and I'm glad she doesn't resist.

"Are you warm enough?" I ask. "Are you sure you can drive in all this snow? It's coming down now."

She looks out toward the street. "If I were in New York, they'd call in the National Guard."

"If you want to wait it out . . ." I force myself to not say another word, to not offer her food, water, shelter, more money or warmth.

"Sarah," Kit says, "do you want to say goodbye? Or you know, safe travels?"

"Oh," I say, when I understand what she's talking about. I look at her stomach. "Okay."

She straightens her posture in preparation. She looks up at the ceiling. I turn on the couch to face her.

"This isn't weird?" I ask.

"It's kind of weird," she says.

I put my hand on her stomach. It feels like any other stomach. A hardness, a softness, a digestive grumbling. She places her hand over mine and something awkward becomes okay, becomes both private and shared.

I close my eyes, saying safe travels to something, to cells, to DNA, to potential and possibility. Then it turns into a goodbye, a farewell to something else—to my son, to my anger and my yearning to pin him down. I say goodbye to this that is not my son. I know that. Cully has lived his life. The acknowledgment weakens me, forcing out a whimper. I didn't want to fall apart in front of her. She doesn't say anything, though she must feel me shaking. She must hear me. I cry out quickly and draw my hand back, but she presses her hand harder upon mine, keeping me there, forcing me to go on, to stay the course, to say goodbye and to let myself feel both good and bad, weakened though quenched and revealed.

Goodbye, Cully. I love you so much.

Yet if given the chance, I wouldn't have said goodbye that way. I probably wouldn't say anything. I'd just look at him, knowing that the deepest, truest feelings are best expressed in silence.

Silently, I say goodbye to this time in my life and I say goodbye to this girl, this version of her. She will leave and no matter what she does, what she chooses, whatever happens, a new person will emerge, one that I might never know but I'm certain I will. I wouldn't have chosen these things to take place, but now that they have, I can't stop looking, fascinated by my life, his life, just plain life. I can't wait to see what else happens.

I open my eyes.

I take my hand off of her stomach.

I let her go.

Acknowledgments

I've used my fiction license to adapt a real place. The real Brecken-ridge, Colorado, is perfect as is. It's where I met my husband, Andy Lautenbach, in 1998. With my writing (and other things) he has always been generous with his praise and honest with his criticisms, despite the hazards of doing so.

Thank you Yaddo and The Brown Foundation Fellows Program at the Dora Maar house.

And finally, thank you to my super agents, Kim Witherspoon and David Forrer, for your love and support of this ol' thing and for leading me to Marysue Rucci and Emily Graff at Simon & Schuster. Marysue, thank you for helping me see with fresh eyes and for making it all such a pleasure.

About the Author

Kaui Hart Hemmings is the author of the story collection *House of Thieves* and the novel *The Descendants*, a *New York Times* bestseller that has been published in twenty-one countries and made into an Academy Award–winning film. She has degrees from Colorado College and Sarah Lawrence College, and was a Wallace Stegner Fellow at Stanford University. She lives in Hawaii with her husband and two children.

www.facebook.com/KauiHartHemmings

www.instagram.com/kauiharthemmings